LOCKED DOORS

ANDREW THOMAS NOVELS BY
BLAKE CROUCH

Desert Places

LOCKED DOORS

A THRILLER

BLAKE CROUCH

THOMAS DUNNE BOOKS
St. Martin's Minotaur
New York ⋈

FIC
Crouch

THOMAS DUNNE BOOKS.
An imprint of St. Martin's Press.

www.minotaurbooks.com

Design and photograph by Kathryn Parise

ISBN 0-312-31799-9
EAN 978-0-312-31799-7

First Edition: July 2005

10 9 8 7 6 5 4 3 2 1

For Rebecca, LOMFL

ACKNOWLEDGMENTS

Before we get started, I need to thank some wonderful people. My wife, Rebecca, has been there for me in every way possible—much love to the Becca. Linda Allen, Marcia Markland, Anna Cottle, and Mary Alice Kier are some of the savviest readers and kindest people I've ever known. Diana Szu has been amazing. My writers' group—Shannon Richardson, Dinah Leavitt, Suzanne Tyrpak, Doug Walker, and Richard Koch—provided me with invaluable feedback and helped make this book readable for those who have encountered *Desert Places*. Goddess of Web site design, Beth Tendall, conjured my Internet presence with elegance and humor. Sandi Greene (how many mother-in-laws show up in the acknowledgments?) should be my North Carolina publicist. Andy Smith and Anne Walker gave me terrific feedback. Bill Smith was kind enough to explain hypnosis to me, and in the process damn near put me under. A double nod for the gifted writer and inventor-extraordinaire, Doug Walker, who showed me how to use a generator and several feet of copper wire to lethal effect (it was just for the book—you'll understand in a couple hundred pages). My climbing buddy and master photographer, Paul Pennington, took some killer author photos. A standing ovation for the brilliant detective, Art Holland, who walked me through the realities of crime-scene investigation and inadvertently helped to unravel a crucial plot point. My brother, Jordan, inspired me immensely, particularly through the last hundred pages. And finally, a grateful bow to everyone at the incomparable Maria's Bookshop in Durango, Colorado.

LUTHER

For the angels who inhabit this town,
although their shape constantly changes,
each night we leave some cold potatoes
and a bowl of milk on the windowsill.
Usually they inhabit heaven where,
by the way, no tears are allowed.
They push the moon around like
a boiled yam.
The Milky Way is their hen
with her many children.
When it is night the cows lie down
but the moon, that big bull,
stands up.
—ANNE SEXTON, "LOCKED DOORS"

CHAPTER 1

The headline on the Arts and Leisure page read: PUBLISHER TO REISSUE FIVE THRILLERS BY ALLEGED MURDERER ANDREW Z. THOMAS.

All it took was seeing his name.

Karen Prescott dropped *The New York Times* and walked over to the window.

Morning light streamed across the clutter of her cramped office—query letters and sample chapters stacked in two piles on the floor beside the desk, a box of galleys shoved under the credenza. She peered out the window and saw the fog dissolving, the microscopic crawl of traffic now materializing on Broadway through the cloud below.

Leaning against a bookcase that housed many of the hardcovers she'd guided to publication, Karen shivered. The mention of Andrew's name always unglued her.

For two years she'd been romantically involved with the

suspense novelist and had even lived with him during the writing of *Blue Murder* at the same lake house in North Carolina where many of his victims were found.

She considered it a latent character defect that she'd failed to notice anything sinister in Andy beyond a slight reclusive tendency.

My God, I almost married him.

She pictured Andy reading to the crowd in that Boston bookshop the first time they met. In a bathrobe writing in his office as she brought him fresh coffee (French roast, of course). Andy making love to her in a flimsy rowboat in the middle of Lake Norman.

She thought of his dead mother.

The exhumed bodies from his lakefront property.

His face on the FBI website.

They'd used his most recent jacket photo, a black-and-white of Andy in a sports jacket sitting broodingly at the end of his pier.

During the last few years she'd stopped thinking of him as Andy. He was Andrew Thomas now and embodied all the horrible images the cadence of those four syllables invoked.

There was a knock.

Scott Boylin, publisher of Ice Blink Press's literary imprint, stood in the doorway dressed in his best bib and tucker. Karen suspected he was gussied up for the Doubleday party.

He smiled, waved with his fingers.

She crossed her arms, leveled her gaze.

God, he looked streamlined today—very tall, fit, crowned by thick black hair with dignified intimations of silver.

He made her feel little. In a good way. Because Karen stood nearly six feet tall, few men towered over her. She loved having to look up at Scott.

They'd been dating clandestinely for the last four months.

She'd even given him a key to her apartment, where they spent countless Sundays in bed reading manuscripts, the coffee-stained pages scattered across the sheets.

But last night she'd seen him at a bar in SoHo with one of the cute interns. Their rendezvous did not look work-related.

"Come to the party with me," he said. "Then we'll go to Il Piazza. Talk this out. It's not what you—"

"I've got tons of reading to catch up—"

"Don't be like that, Karen. Come on."

"I don't think it's appropriate to have this conversation here, so . . ."

He exhaled sharply through his nose and the door closed hard behind him.

Joe Mack was stuffing his pink round face with a gyro when his cell phone started ringing to the tune of "Staying Alive."

He answered, cheeks exploding with food, "This Joe."

"Hi, yes, um, I've got a bit of an interesting problem."

"Whath?"

"Well, I'm in my apartment, but I can't get the deadbolt to turn from the inside."

Joe Mack choked down a huge mouthful, said, "So you're locked in."

"Exactly."

"Which apartment?" He didn't even try to mask the annoyance in his voice.

"Twenty-two eleven."

"Name?"

"Um . . . I'm not the tenant. I'm Karen Prescott's friend. She's the—"

"Yeah, I get it. You need to leave anytime soon?"

"Well, yeah, I don't want to—"

Joe Mack sighed, closed the cell phone, and devoured the last of the gyro.

Wiping his hands on his shirt, he heaved himself from a debilitated swivel chair and lumbered out of the office, locking the door behind him.

The lobby was quiet for midday and the elevator doors spread as soon as he pressed the button. He rode up wishing he'd bought three gyros for lunch instead of two.

The doors opened again and he walked onto the twenty-second floor, fishing the key ring containing the master from the pocket of his enormous overalls.

He belched.

It echoed down the empty corridor.

Man, was he hungry.

He stopped at 2211, knocked, yelled through the door, "It's the super!"

No one answered.

Joe Mack inserted the master into the deadbolt. It turned easily enough.

He pushed the door open.

"Hello?" he said, standing in the threshold, admiring the apartment—roomy, flat-screen television, lush deep blue carpet, an antique desk, great view of SoHo, probably loads of food in the fridge.

"Anybody home?"

He turned the deadbolt four times. It worked perfectly.

Another door opened somewhere in the hallway and approaching footsteps reverberated off the hardwood floor. Joe Mack glanced down the corridor at the tall man with black hair in a black overcoat strolling toward him from the stairwell.

"Hey, pal, were you the one who just called me?" Joe Mack asked.

The man with black hair stopped at the open doorway of 2211.

He smelled strange, of Windex and lemons.

"Yes, I was the one."

"Oh. You get the lock to work?"

"I've never been in this apartment."

"What the fuck did you call me for—"

Glint of a blade. The man held an ivory-hilted bowie. He swept its shimmering point across Joe Mack's swollen belly, cleaving denim, cotton, several layers of skin.

"No, wait just a second—"

The man raised his right leg and booted Joe Mack through the threshold.

The super toppled backward as the man followed him into the apartment, slammed the door, and shot the deadbolt home.

Karen left Ice Blink Press at 6:30 P.M. and emerged into a manic Manhattan evening, the sliver of sky between the buildings smoldering with dying sunlight, gilding glass and steel. It was the fourth Friday of October, the terminal brilliance of autumn full blown upon the city, and as she walked the fifteen blocks to her apartment in SoHo, Karen decided that she wouldn't start the manuscript in her leather satchel tonight.

Instead she'd slip into satin pajamas, have a glass of that organic chardonnay she'd purchased at Whole Foods Market, and watch wonderful mindless television.

It had been a bad week.

Pampering was in order.

At 7:55 she walked out of her bedroom in black satin pajamas that rubbed coolly against her skin. Her chaotic blond hair was twisted into a bun and held up by chopsticks from the Chinese food she'd ordered. Two unopened food cartons and a bottle of wine sat on the glass coffee table between the couch and the flat-screen television. Her apartment smelled of spicy-sweet sesame beef.

She plopped down and uncorked the wine.

Ashley Chambliss's CD *Nakedsongs* had ended and in the perfect stillness of her apartment Karen conceded how alone she was.

Thirty-seven.

Single again.

Childless.

But I'm not lonely, she thought, turning on the television and pouring a healthy glass of chardonnay.

I'm just alone.

There is a difference.

After watching *Dirty Dancing*, Karen treated herself to a soak. She'd closed the bathroom door and a Yankee candle that smelled of cookie dough sat burning in a glass jar on the sink, the projection of its restless flame flickering on the sweaty plaster walls.

Karen rubbed her long muscular legs together, slippery with bath oil. Imagining another pair of legs sliding between her own, she shut her eyes, moved her hands over her breasts, nipples swelling, then up and down her thighs.

The phone was ringing in the living room.

She wondered if Scott Boylin was calling to apologize. Wine encouraged irrational forgiveness in Karen. She even wished Scott were in the bathtub with her. She could feel the memory of his water-softened feet gliding up her smooth shinbones. Maybe she'd call and invite him over. Give him that chance to explain. He'd be back from the Doubleday party.

Now someone was knocking at the front door.

Karen sat up, blew back the bubbles that had amassed around her head.

Lifting her wineglass by the stem, she finished it off. Then she rose out of the water, took her white terrycloth bathrobe that lay draped across the toilet seat, and stepped unsteadily from the tub onto the mosaic tile. She'd nearly polished off the entire bottle of chardonnay and a warm and pleasant gale was raging in her head.

Karen crossed the living room, heading toward the front door.

She failed to notice that the cartons of steamed rice and sesame beef were gone, or that a large gray trashcan now stood between the television and the antique desk she'd inherited from her grandmother.

She peeked through the peephole.

A young man stood in the hallway holding an enormous bouquet of ruby red roses.

She smiled, turned the deadbolt, opened the door.

"I have a delivery for Karen Prescott."

"That's me."

The delivery man handed over the gigantic vase.

"Wait here. I'll get you your tip." She slurred her words a little.

"No ma'am, it's been taken care of." He gave her a small salute and left.

She relocked the door and carried the roses over to the kitchen counter. They were magnificent and they burgeoned from the cut-glass vase. She plucked the small card taped to the glass and opened it. The note read simply:

Look in the coat closet

Karen giggled. Scott was one hundred percent forgiven. Maybe she'd even do that thing he always asked for tonight.

She buried her nose in a rose, inhaled the damp sweet perfume. Then she cinched the belt of her bathrobe and walked over to the closet behind the couch, pulling open the door with a big smile that instantly died.

A naked man with black hair and a pale face peered down at her. He wiped his mouth with the back of his hand and swallowed.

The cartons of leftover Chinese food stood between his feet.

She stared into his black eyes, a coldness spreading through her.

"What do you think you're doing?" she said.

The man grinned, his member rising.

Karen bolted for the front door, but as she reached to unhook the chain he snatched a handful of her wet hair and swung her back into a mirror that shattered on the adjacent wall.

"Please," she whimpered.

He punched her in the face.

Karen sank down onto the floor in bits of glass, anesthetized by wine and fear. Watching his bare feet, she wondered where her body would be found and by whom and in what condition.

He grabbed her hair into a ball with one hand and lifted her face out of the glass, the tiniest shards having already embedded themselves in her cheek.

He swung down.

She felt the dull thud of his knuckles crack her jaw, decided to feign unconsciousness.

He hit her again.

She didn't have to.

CHAPTER 2

On the same Friday evening, Elizabeth Lancing lay in the grass at her home in Davidson, North Carolina, watching her children roughhouse in the autumn-cooled waters of Lake Norman.

Her husband Walter was on her mind.

Tomorrow would have been their seventeenth anniversary.

Pushing against her thighs, she rose and strolled barefoot down to the shore.

Jenna had wrangled John David in a headlock and was trying to dunk her younger stronger brother as their mother walked the length of the pier.

Beth sat down at the end where steps descended into the water.

She moved her fingers through wavy carbon black hair just long enough to graze her shoulders. Her fingertips traced the lines these last brutal years had channeled into her face.

Beth knew she was plain. That was fine. She'd been plain her whole life.

What wasn't fine was having the hard countenance of a fifty-year-old when she'd just turned thirty-eight. Lately she'd noticed how lived-in she looked. If Walter were still here maybe what few looks she had wouldn't be deserting her.

She rolled her jeans up to her knees.

A rogue Jet Ski skimmed across the middle of the lake, invisible save for its brief intersection with a streak of moonlit water.

Beth's feet slid into the liquid steel, touching the algae-slimed wood of the first submerged step.

It was a chilly night and she rubbed her bare arms, thinking, *October is the cruelest month. Darling, has it been seven years?*

In one week Beth would have to contend with another anniversary—this coming Halloween night would mark seven years since Walter's disappearance.

The writer and murderer Andrew Thomas had been a close friend of her husband. Andrew's old house still stood in the trees on the opposite side of the cove. Someone had taken up residence there in the last year and it was unsettling to see those lights across the lake again.

The circumstances attending Walter's disappearance had grown no less bizarre or mystifying through the passage of seven years.

On a cold and wet Halloween night in 1996, he'd sat Beth down at the kitchen table and informed her that their family was in terrible danger.

He'd told her to take the kids away.

Refused to explain what was wrong.

Said all that mattered was getting Jenna and John David out of the house immediately.

She could still remember her husband's eyes that night, carrying a component she'd not seen in them before—real fear.

Out beyond the steps, bubbles broke the surface and the water-slicked head of Jenna blossomed out of the lake.

My last image of my love—I see Walter in the rearview mirror as I drive away with our children into the rainy Halloween darkness. He is standing on the front porch signing "I love you," his hands held high in the orange porchlight.

She never saw Walter again.

His white Cadillac was found two weeks later in Woodside, Vermont, parked near a Dumpster, the driver seat slathered in his blood.

Beth knew in her heart that Andrew Thomas had killed her husband.

She could not begin to fathom why.

"Come in, Mom!"

Beth descended two more steps, the water now at her knees.

"It's too cold, sweetie."

"You're such a wimp," Jenna taunted, treading toward the steps. "I might just pull you in."

"Oh no you won't."

Jenna's head disappeared and Beth climbed back up onto the pier, smiling as she scanned the water.

"I see you!" she yelled though she couldn't. "I see—"

Wet arms wrapped around her own and Beth screamed.

"Got you," John David said. "You're going in."

"No, J.D.," Beth pleaded as he muscled her toward the edge. Though only a prepubescent boy of eleven, he was strong and quick. "I'm your mother and I am telling you that if you push me into that water I'll ground you forever. Is it worth it?"

John David sighed and let go.

Beth stepped away from the edge and faced her son, thinking, *You'll be taller than me in two years.*

Beads of water glistened on his hairless little-boy chest.

"Now I want to tell you something," she said with convincing parental sternness. "You listening to me?"

"Yes ma'am."

His voice was still high, at least a year from turning.

"I want to tell you . . . this!"

Beth shoved him off the pier and he screamed as he hit the water. She laughed, raised her hands in victory, and shouted, "Never underestimate the Mom!"

As John David bemoaned the injustice Jenna jerked him underwater by his ankles. The ripples made by the Jet Ski had begun to lap against the beams of the pier.

"I'm going in!" Beth yelled. "Don't stay out long!"

"Come on, Mom. It's Friday night!"

Walking back up the pier, she acknowledged this interval of peace—her children had touched her; what else mattered?

When she reached the cool grass she glanced back at her kids, then on across the lake at the quarter mile of shoreline where the monster used to live.

She'd received a letter from Andrew Thomas after Walter's car turned up in Vermont.

As she walked into the house to fix herself a drink and look through her wedding album, the words of that *thing* echoed in her head:

Dear Beth,

Before I begin, please know that I did not murder my mother. And don't believe what you read in the papers. I say this only to qualify what I have to tell you about your husband. Walter is dead, Beth, and it's my fault, and I am so, so sorry. I want you to know that he died protecting you and Jenna and John David, and he did not suffer. Also know that because of his efforts, you and the children are safe. He's buried in a secluded grove of pines in the

Vermont countryside. I wish I could personally deliver this news to you but I have to disappear now. I hope you understand. I'm not an evil person, Beth. I tried to make the right choices. I'm going to keep on trying to make the right choices. But evil is alive and well in the world. And sometimes all we can do is not enough.

Andy

CHAPTER 3

My name is Andrew Thomas and I live in a world that believes I am a monster.

Once upon a time I was a suspense novelist. I had money. I lived in a beautiful house on a lake in North Carolina. I had friends. Lovers. I knew what respect and a mite of celebrity felt like.

Then someone came along and destroyed all of it.

His name was Orson Thomas and he was my fraternal twin.

Under threat of blackmail he took me to a remote cabin in the high desert of Wyoming.

He was a psychopath.

He showed me a side of myself I will spend the rest of my life annulling.

But the horror of what happened in that desert is another story.

In the end I escaped.

My brother was killed. His accomplice—a soulless individual named Luther Kite—I shot and left for dead, tied to a chair on the front porch of Orson's cabin in the vast and snowswept desert.

That was November 1996 and I faced returning to a world that feared and hated me.

Bodies had been unearthed at my home on Lake Norman.

I was suspected in my mother's death.

I was suspected in Walter Lancing's disappearance.

I was the writer turned serial killer.

Orson and Luther had framed me in every way imaginable.

I couldn't go home.

I was wanted.

And though I'd done questionable things in the name of self-preservation, I was by no means a murderer.

So I ran.

The village of Haines Junction, Yukon, saved my life.

I'd been running two years when I found it—through desert villages in northern Mexico, the Baja Peninsula, the towns and cities of America.

I worked a summer in a lumber yard in Macon, Georgia.

I was a busboy for one week in Baltimore.

A ranch hand for a west Texas winter.

I slept in tents.

Homeless shelters.

Bunkhouses.

Fields beneath stars on cool clear nights.

I grew my hair out.

I didn't shave.

I didn't bathe.

I left places.

Arrived at new places.

I stopped reading.

Stopped writing.

I fulfilled my alcoholic tendencies.

I traveled by bus.

Hitchhiked.

Jumped a train once through South Dakota.

I never talked to anyone.

Because my name had become synonymous with murder and matricide I lived in constant fear, suspected everyone.

At a construction site in London, Kentucky, the foreman asked if I liked to read thrillers. Maybe he was just being friendly. I wasn't there the next day to find out.

My face appeared on FBI posters.

I was the subject of television specials.

Books were written about me.

My novels sold like crazy.

People wanted to know how a serial murderer writes.

They said my stories were windows into an evil soul.

I became notorious.

A darkly comic figure of pop culture.

My name instilled fear.

My name was a punch line.

My name meant murder.

Having never been married, I was accustomed to living alone, but I'd not experienced this grade of utter abandonment.

I was homeless, hunted, and lonely.

It was no way to live.

In December, two nomadic years after my escape from the snowbound Wyoming desert, I took a bus to Vancouver, bought a plane ticket, and flew to Whitehorse, Yukon, a thousand miles north.

I rented a car and drove the Alaska Highway a hundred fifty kilometers west to the village of Haines Junction at the foot of the St. Elias Mountains. I'd researched the village for a book I never wrote. It seemed like a quiet isolated place to die.

I pulled off the highway outside of town, a vast coniferous forest extending in every direction, great white mountains looming in the west. The temperature held at minus thirty. The sky was gray, dusky, the subarctic sun a halfhearted presence over the peaks. The dashboard clock read 1:47 P.M. I would simply walk into the woods, sit down against a tree, and freeze to death. A peaceful way to go. Vaguely romantic. I thought of Jack London's "To Build a Fire." I looked forward to that warm euphoric stillness that would come near the end.

Wearing only a T-shirt, I opened the door and stepped out of the car into crusty snow. The cold was beyond comprehension. My eyes burned.

I walked a ways into the woods, chose a leafless aspen, and sat down with my back against the silver bark. I waited. I began to shiver. My stomach rumbled. I thought, *Why die hungry?* I got up, walked back to the car, and drove into the village, home to eight hundred residents though far fewer in these bleak winter months. I parked downtown in front of a diner called Bill's, the street decorated for Christmas. I reached to open the car door but stopped.

I put my head on the steering wheel.

Wept.

But those dark times rarely haunted me. I'd lived in the woods outside of Haines Junction now for five years and it was sweet and essential to be this other man.

To the community my name was Vincent Carmichael and I'd become a full-fledged resident. The townsfolk might've described me as quiet but friendly. I was the American with long brown hair and an untamed beard. Everyone's acquaintance. No one's friend. But that was okay here. People came to this remote northwest corner of Canada to escape things. Haines Junction was a lodestone for damaged people.

During the tourist season, I worked as a chef in the kitchen of The Lantern, one of two fine-dining establishments in the village. There I earned enough money to live through the winter months, October to April, when there was no work and little to do but stay indoors near a fire.

I spent half my savings on a cabin. Six miles west of town in a valley called the Shakwak Trench, it stood in a grove of spruce, lost in the endless forest. From the window above my kitchen sink, a small meadow could be seen forty yards through the firs—a patch of green light when the sun was strong. Lying in its grass, you could see into the Kluane Reserve and the front wall of the ice-laden St. Elias Mountains that rose from this forest just a few miles to the west. There was even a pond a quarter mile south. I swam in it during the fleeting warmth of summer.

I'd always cherished my solitude but never more than now, sitting alone in a rocking chair on my front porch this cold Friday evening.

Stars shone through the crowns of the trees.

The constellations were sharp.

There are no cities in the Yukon to muddy the sky with manmade light.

As I rocked, my hands shoved deep into the pockets of my down vest, I closed my eyes, resisting one of those twinges of surreal nostalgia that make you acutely aware of all the living you've done and how the choices you've made have led to this moment of introspection. I was forty-one years old, and I couldn't begin to stomach the totality of my life—too checkered, too sprawling. So I tried to live safely and habitually, moment to moment.

It passed, those lethal thoughts of Walter, my mother, and the things I did in Orson's desert now receding back into the prisons I'd built for them.

Though I had supper to make and words to write, I opted for

an evening stroll. Rising, I pulled my hair into a ponytail and stepped down off the porch. I followed a deer run through the spruce grove, the air glutted with the spicy scent of sap, branches brushing against my vest, twigs snapping under my boots.

It was late October—ice rimmed the pond and autumn waned, the arc of the sun diminishing noticeably each day. Even the aspens had shed the last of their heartshaped leaves. Only the spruce held color, an ashy bluegreen, some stunted and withered from the harsh winters, others full and majestic despite existing a mere four hundred miles south of the Arctic Circle.

I reached the meadow. Above the trees on the far side, the first peaks of the St. Elias Range towered in the west, hulking and austere, their snowpack blue beneath the stars. These mountains stretched on for a hundred fifty miles through the southeast leg of Alaska, west to the Pacific. They contained Canada's highest mountain and the largest nonpolar icefield in the world, a hundred-mile river of ice that crept down from the slopes of the Icefield Ranges into the sea.

But the mountains are nothing but cold boring piles of shattered rock when the sky is blazing with the aurora borealis. I gazed up into the cosmos and felt it move me. It always moved me.

As a southerner who'd only glimpsed the northern lights in photographs, I'd thought of this lucent phenomenon as a still life fixture in the sky. But tonight it was a flickering ribbon that appeared to spring from a point of origin just beyond the mountains. It rose and curved sharply, a green mane running parallel to the horizon—a shock of glowing ions forty miles above the earth. It seemed an ethereal symphony should accompany this skyfire, but the night maintained its massive silence.

Breathing deeply and contentedly, I lay down in the grass and, staring into that burning sky, filled once more with the rapture of knowing I was home.

CHAPTER 4

Horace Boone left his trailer in the village of Haines Junction after dark and followed the one-lane dirt road that passed by Andrew Thomas's mailbox en route to the trailheads of the St. Elias Range. He pulled off the road a quarter mile from Andrew's long winding driveway and parked his old Land Cruiser out of sight in the woods.

It was a ten-minute jog through evergreens to the cabin.

The scrawny young man ran it easily in the dark, slowing to a careful walk when he glimpsed the glowing windows in the distance.

Stealing up to a window on the side of the cabin, he peered in, heart beating wildly. This was only the second time he'd come and by far the most exhilarating thing he'd ever done on a Friday night.

The monster stood at the sink washing his supper dishes, the walls of the cabin flushed with firelight. He wore black fleece pants, chili pepper–print fleece socks, and a long johns top. His hair fell in a matted tangle halfway down his back.

A book lay open on the small table behind Andrew. He'd apparently eaten his supper while reading by lantern light.

When he'd dried and put away the last of the dishes, Andrew added wood to the fire, stoked it into a steady blaze, and climbed the ladder up into a loft.

From his cold perspective the voyeur could just make out the furnishings of Andrew's writing nook—a desk, bookshelves, a typewriter, and little notes (perhaps two dozen of them) affixed to the rafters overhead. A poster of Edgar Allan Poe was also tacked to one of the beams. It fluttered in updrafts from the hearth.

Andrew sat down at the desk and then faintly through the glass came the patter of his fingers on the keys.

The master was writing.

Horace grinned, mind racing to process every detail. They would be so important.

This time a year ago he'd just quit the University of Alaska's MFA creative writing program. The meltdown had occurred during a meeting with his faculty advisor, the thirty-something Professor Byron, just a cocky toddler for the academic world. Horace had decided that his thesis was going to be a collection of short stories, all horror, and when he told this to Byron, the professor laughed out loud.

"What?" Horace said.

"Nothing, it's just . . . I mean if you think you're going to make a name for—"

"I'm sick of writing whiny, my-life-sucks fiction set in suburban kitchens."

"You think that's what we teach here?"

"I mean, God forbid a story actually have a fucking plot."

"Mr. Boone—"

"You know I tried to read *your* book, um, what was it called, *Fighting the Senses.*"

Byron stiffened, straightened his glasses.

"Booooooooring. That isn't what I want to write."

The professor smiled, pure acid, said, "You know who *didn't* think it was boring?" and pointed to a cutout of his glowing *Times* review taped prominently to the wall beside a bookshelf. "Now here's the deal, Mr. Boone. I do not accept your thesis proposal. Come back in a week with a real idea or I'll bounce your ass. You won't return for spring semester. Good day." And with that Byron had turned around in his swivel chair and begun typing an email.

So as instructed Horace returned the following week with a new thesis proposal: a comic book. The villain was a pretentious fucking ass named Byron and his superpower was the keen ability to eradicate the joy of writing from starry-eyed students. Horace was the hero, his superpower was quitting, and he stormed out of the office brimming with self-righteous indignation.

He found a job after Thanksgiving as a bookseller at Murder One Books near the campus, spent days helping customers find the perfect mystery, nights trying to produce his own collection of short horror fiction. After two weeks he'd started twenty stories and abandoned them all. By January he'd quit writing altogether, lost the energy and excitement of creation. Those winter months in Anchorage, he sank through frustration, depression, and settled comfortably into apathy. Fuck writing, reading. He lived for the small pockets of pleasure—a case of Rolling Rock, reality TV, and sleeping. His dream of becoming a writer bowed out with hardly a whimper and he never missed it until one life-changing day.

Shivering, watching the shadows play on Andrew Thomas's back, he thought of the cold and sunny April afternoon six months prior, when the most infamous suspense novelist in the world had strolled into his Anchorage bookstore and given direction to his life.

Having watched the customer browse the bookshelves for the last forty minutes, I know irrefutably that this is the writer and murderer, Andrew Thomas, regardless of his thick beard and long shaggy hair. It's the piercing eyes and soft mouth that give him away.

At last he approaches the counter. He looks as I would expect—wary, cold, a man who has seen and done things that most people could not contemplate. My palms sweat, mouth so dry my sandpaper tongue feels leathery and feline.

He sets five hardbacks on the counter. We are alone in this tiny bookstore of new and old mysteries, only marginally larger than a dorm room. It is dim inside the store. The floor and shelves consist of dark knotty wood. There are no windows, but this is no shortcoming. Every book is a window.

"Is this all, sir?" I manage.

He nods and my hands tremble as I begin to scan his selections: a used collection of Poe's short stories, Kafka, three mysteries from one of his contemporaries.

I listen to the rhythm of his breathing—deep comfortable inhalations. I smell the tannin of his leather jacket. His eyes roam over my head to the shelf behind the counter that displays the ten bestsellers of Murder One Books.

"One-oh-three ninety-eight," I say.

He points to the credit card that he's already placed on the counter. I lift it, almost too urgently, and glance at the name welted upon the plastic: Vincent Carmichael.

I look up from the credit card into his eyes.

He's staring at me.

I swipe the card, hand it back to him.

Tearing the receipt from the scanner, I lay it down on the counter with a pen and watch him sign *Vincent Carmichael* in wispy characters that scarcely resemble his true autograph.

Part of me wants to speak to him, to tell him I've read everything he's ever written. But I hold my tongue, reminding myself that the rumors surrounding this man are legendary—if he knew that I knew he would end me.

So I put his five books into a plastic bag, hand him the receipt, and he walks out the open door into the cold Alaskan afternoon.

He crosses Campus Drive and sits down in bright grass in the shade of a juniper, the tangy gin-scented berries of which I can smell even from inside the store. U of A students recline all around him in the weak sun and shade of saplings scattered through the green—reading, napping, smoking between classes.

And as I stare at Andrew Thomas, a surge of adrenaline fills me and the thrill of inspiration rears its lovely head.

I've found my story.

CHAPTER 5

I woke Saturday in the Yukon dawn, donned a fleece pullover, and stepped into a pair of cold Vasque Sundowners to save my socked feet from the frozen floorboards. The Nalgene water bottle on my bedside table was capped with ice. I looked over at the hearth, saw that the fire had reduced itself to a pile of warm fine ash.

I walked out to the woodpile I'd chopped in September. It was stacked seven feet high and stretched for twenty feet between two rampike poplars that had been cooked by lightning last spring. The cold stung. My fingers tingled even through the leather gloves.

I gathered an armload of wood as the sun angled through the spruce branches and thawed the forest floor. The thermometer on the front porch read eight above.

As I reached for the door, something snapped behind me. I froze, turned slowly around, scanned the trees. Twenty yards away an enormous bull moose emerged from the spruce thicket, the branches catching in his giant rack. He walked leisurely behind the woodpile, probably headed for the pond.

Inside I placed a handful of kindling on the metal grate and stacked the logs on end around the twigs in a teepee arrangement. Then I balled up several sheets of the *St. Elias Echo* and stuffed these beneath the grate. There was a hot coal or two left. These ignited the newspaper which in turn lit the kindling and soon the young flames were tonguing the logs, steaming off the latent moisture, boiling the fragrant resin within.

As the quiet pandemonium of the fire filled the cabin, I walked into the kitchen and rinsed the old coffee grounds from the French press. Then I started a pot of water on the gas stove and ground a handful of French roasted coffee beans in the burr mill. While my coffee steeped, filling the cabin with the smoky-rich perfume of the beans, I sat down on the hearth and read over the ten pages I'd revised last night. The new book was coming along nicely. It was the first autobiographical piece I'd ever attempted, a work of confession and catharsis, the true story of my fall from successful writer to suspected murderer. Just last night I'd found the perfect title. If I continued working at this pace I'd have this second draft completed by Thanksgiving. And though it'd be a gangly mess, I had all winter—those days of frozen darkness—to shine it up. I wasn't holding on to much hope beyond that this might be the first step toward clearing my name.

It felt good and strange to be writing again, like many many lives ago.

After breakfast I drove my CJ-5 into Haines Junction, a fifteen-minute trip down the primitive Borealis Road. On the outskirts of the village I passed through a stand of aspens. They'd shed their leaves a month ago and I wondered if this stretch of forest had then resembled a flake of gold from the air when the saffron leaves were peaked and still hanging from the boughs.

I didn't need anything from Madley's Store this week, so I parked at the Raven Hotel and started down the empty sidewalk of Kluane Boulevard.

In the summer months the village bustled with tourists. They came for the mountains that swept up out of the forest just five miles west. Ecotourism was the end result of the three inns, five restaurants, two outfitters, art gallery, and numerous First Nations craft stores. But by October, when the days had begun to shorten and fresh snow overspread the high country, the tourists were gone, the inns and most of the restaurants correspondingly closed, and a hundred people, including me, had lost their day jobs for the long winter.

I stopped under the awning of The Lantern. A thin cloudbank had moved in during the last hour, now a vaporous film diluting the flare of the sun. The air smelled like snow and though I hadn't even seen a forecast I'd have wagered the paycheck I was about to collect that a storm was blowing in from the Pacific.

I entered The Lantern. Julie, the diminutive Aishihik woman who'd opened the restaurant six years ago, was vacuuming the small dining room. This place had the look and feel of the best restaurant in a remote Yukon outpost: the dim lighting, white paper tablecloths, plastic flowers, and opulent wine list—red *and* white. To work here with a good heart I'd been forced to smother the snob in me.

When Julie saw me standing by the hostess podium she turned off the vacuum cleaner and said, "Your paycheck's in the back. I'll get it for you."

She walked through the swinging doors into the kitchen and returned a moment later with my last paycheck of the season.

"What's going on here tonight?" I asked.

"Lions Club is having a banquet. Could've used you, Vince,

but since you don't have a phone it's a lot easier to call Doug than drive six miles out to your place." She handed me the envelope. "Come see me next spring if you want the job again. You know it's yours."

"I appreciate that, Julie. I'll probably see you around this winter."

I went outside and crossed the street. Since it was only 10:30, Bill's was empty. But the hair and tanning salons (Curl Up & Dye and Tan Your Hide) that sandwiched the diner had customers aplenty.

I stepped into Bill's and ordered one of his homemade bearclaws and a tall cup of black coffee. Bill was a Floridian who'd moved up to Haines Junction more than twenty-five years ago. I'd heard somewhere that he was a Vietnam vet, but he never mentioned the war so I never mentioned it to him. And even though he was an American, he didn't do the predictable patriotic things most expats did such as flying Old Glory and exploding fireworks on the Fourth of July. In fact the only time I even heard him reference his native country occurred last winter. Something scandalous had happened in Washington and even the locals up here were intrigued. The Champagne man who owned the ATV and snowmobile dealership just down the street had asked Bill what he thought of the state of affairs in his country.

Bill had been wiping down the counter, but he stopped and stared at the man sitting on the stool before him. With his wooly white beard and scarred face, Bill bore the likeness of a jaded Santa Claus.

"I didn't move into heaven to keep tabs on hell," he said. Then Bill slammed his fists on the counter and grabbed everyone's attention. I'd been sitting alone in a booth, working on a bowl of black bear chili. "Listen up!" Bill hollered. "If you want to discuss current events in the United States, do it elsewhere.

I'll be goddamned if I'm going to listen to it in my diner."

But on this quiet morning Bill was friendly and sedate. Bach filled his diner and I noticed that he'd been writing in a journal.

He handed over my change and asked me whether I reckoned it was going to snow. I told him I hoped so and he smiled, said he did, too.

I sometimes wondered if Bill suspected me. There was this kindred energy whenever we locked eyes. But I didn't worry about Bill. Different circumstances might have guided us to Haines Junction, but we both desired the same thing. And we were getting it, too. I think we sensed the repose in each other.

Gathering my cup of coffee and pastry, I left Bill's and headed toward the last building on this side of the street, a two-story structure that looked more like a ski lodge than a public library. But it was appropriate architecture for this bucolic community.

As I walked, the clouds continued to thicken.

It grew cold and still.

I wanted to be home before the snow began to fall.

The first floor of the library comprised a book collection that was almost endearing in its degree of deficiency. But I hadn't come to check out books.

I passed by the front desk and climbed the spiral staircase to the second floor which consisted of a study room, the periodical archives, and a computer lab that provided the only dial-up internet access in all of Haines Junction.

I entered the lab and sat down at one of the three unoccupied workstations.

The connection was laggard.

I unwrapped my warm bearclaw and pried the plastic top from my cup of coffee, praying the mean librarian wouldn't see me with my contraband.

First I checked my email. I had several messages from my

Live Journal friends, so I spent the next hour reading the new mail and responding.

Years ago I'd have done myself in for even considering making online friends. I thought it to be the telltale sign of a lonely pathetic existence. But I embraced it now as my only channel for meaningful interaction with real human beings.

Because I was in hiding I was forced to keep a distance from my neighbors. No matter how well I liked someone in the village, if I were to form a bond of any sort I'd be jeopardizing my freedom. So in the five years I'd resided in Haines Junction, no one had ever been invited to my cabin for dinner and I'd never accepted an invitation to anyone else's home. I would've loved to have spent Christmas or Thanksgiving with some of the interesting people I'd met while living here, but it was too risky. Loneliness was the price of my freedom.

But to my Live Journal community I could bare my heart—albeit cryptically—and they could lay open their souls before me. Their companionship brought me tremendous comfort. I was no longer ashamed of myself and it disheartened me that I ever was.

When I'd sent my last email of the day, I glanced through the window at my back. Though I couldn't distinguish them from the buildings across the street, the haze of snowflakes was apparent against the backdrop of evergreens.

I smiled.

The first snowfall of the season still excited that southern boy in me who'd spent most of his winters in North Carolina where snowstorms are a rarity.

Before leaving I visited the webpage of a local news station in Charlotte, North Carolina. I browsed the Web site each time I came to this computer lab. It was my only method of checking in on Elizabeth, John David, and Jenna Lancing, the family I'd deprived of a husband and father.

Even if something were to happen to them I'd probably never know or have the chance to prevent it. But it eased my mind to peruse the news of Charlotte and its suburbs, if only for the symbolic gesture of me watching after my best friend's wife and children.

Once I'd seen that the headlines didn't reference the Lancings (and they never did) I entered Beth and Jenna and John David's names into a search engine. Nothing came up. The only successful search I ever conducted concerned Jenna who had turned thirteen in August.

Last winter she'd won the hundred-meter freestyle in a middle school swim meet and I stumbled upon the results which had been posted on her school's webpage. I'd been tempted to send her a congratulatory card. The Lancings still lived in the same house on Lake Norman. But for all I knew, Beth believed that I'd murdered her husband. So I'd settled for merely printing out the swim meet results and highlighting Jenna's name.

A dogsled magnet still held that page to my refrigerator door.

When I stepped out of the library it was midday and the snowfall had frosted Kluane Boulevard, parked cars, the woods, and rooftops in a delicate inch of powder. I buttoned my vest, pulled a black toboggan down over my ears, and strolled back up the sidewalk toward my Jeep.

The village was so quiet.

I could almost hear the snow collecting like a subconscious whisper.

I anticipated being home and the fire I would build and the peaceful hours I'd spend in its warmth, writing while the forest filled with snow.

God, I loved my life.

CHAPTER 6

Karen Prescott woke, the darkness unchanged.

She sat up, banged her head into a panel of soundproofing foam.

Consciousness recoiled in full.

She felt around in the dark for those familiar invisible objects of her small black universe: the two empty water bottles at her bare feet, the huge coil of rope, the gascan, the blanket.

Her head throbbed with thirst; her jaw was broken, her fingertips shredded from picking glass shards out of her hair. The car was motionless, its engine silent for the first time in hours. Karen wondered if it was night or day and for how long she'd lain in her bathrobe on this abrasive stinking carpet, still damp with her urine.

How far was she from her Manhattan apartment?

Where had the man with long black hair gone?

Perhaps the car was parked in front of a convenience store

and he was inside using the restroom or filling a cup at the soda fountain or signing a credit card receipt. Maybe the car sat in the parking lot of a Quality Inn. He could be lying in bed in a motel room watching porn.

What if he had a heart attack?

What if he never came back?

Was the trunk airtight?

Was she whittling away with each breath at a finite supply of air?

He'll let me out eventually. He promised. I'll keep calm until—

She heard something.

Children's laughter.

Their high voices reached her, muffled but audible.

Karen wanted to rip away the soundproofing and scream her brains out for help.

But her captor had warned that if she yelled or beat on the trunk even once, he would kill her slowly.

And she believed him.

The driver side door opened and slammed.

He'd been in the car the whole time. Was he testing her? Seeing if she would scream?

As his footsteps trailed away, she thought, *Spending a Friday night by myself in my apartment isn't lonely. This is lonely.*

CHAPTER 7

Me and Josh and Mikey were playing with a slug and a magnifying glass I took from my big brother's room. My brother's name is Hank and he's eleven. I'm only seven and I hate it.

Mikey found the slug on his driveway before he left for church. He isn't afraid of slugs, so he picked it up and put it in a glass jar in his garage. I'm not afraid of them either. I just don't like the way they feel when you touch them.

We were playing at the end of my street where no houses are. Mom says if I want to play in the road this is where I have to do it since no cars ever come down here. She doesn't want me to get run over.

Mikey had pulled the slug out of the jar and put it on the road. It was crawling very slowly. It left a silver slime trail behind it. Josh made me give him the magnifying glass. He's very bossy sometimes, but he's bigger than me so I have to do what he says.

"Get out of the light, shrimp," Josh said to Mikey.

Mikey moved. He's more afraid of Josh than I am. Josh is nine. He has his own BB gun. When Josh held the magnifying glass over the slug the sun went through it and made a bright dot on the slug's back.

"What are you doing?" Mikey asked.

"Just watch."

"What are you doing?" Mikey asked again.

"Shut up! I'm trying to concentrate! Billy showed me how to do this."

I wanted to know what he was doing, too. It was sort of boring just watching Josh hold the glass. After a long time the slug started smoking. Josh laughed and got real excited.

"Do you see that?" he yelled.

"What are you doing?" Mikey asked.

"I'm burning him, Mikey." Mikey got up and went home crying. He's only six years old and my mom says he has a very tender heart. Josh asked if I wanted to do it, but I told him no. The slug wasn't crawling anymore. Or maybe it was and I just couldn't tell.

I heard a loud whistle. Josh looked up. "Oh no, my mom," he said. Josh dropped the magnifying glass and took off running down the street. I watched him go. He could run very fast. He was scared of his mom. She turned mean after his dad went away.

I stood up and stomped on the slug in case it was hurting. It stuck to the bottom of my shoe like nasty gum. I was getting ready to go home when a man got out of a gray car that was parked at the end of the street near the woods. He was very tall and had long black girl hair. He came toward me. I was afraid, but he didn't even look at me. He just walked right past me up the street.

Something fell out of his pocket onto the road, but he didn't notice. I went over and picked it up. It was shiny and expensive-looking.

"Mister!" I yelled. The man turned around. "You dropped this."

The long-haired man came back. He looked down at me. He didn't smile. Most grownups smile at little kids. "You dropped this," I said. He opened his hand and I put the shiny thing in it. "What is it?" I asked. It looked very neat.

"A laser pointer. It makes a laser beam."

His teeth were scary—brown and jagged like he didn't brush them ever.

"How?" I asked.

"Open your hand. I'll show you. Come on. It won't hurt." I opened my hand and a red dot appeared. It was the neatest thing I ever saw. "You should see it at night," he said. "If it were dark I could shoot this beam across Lake Norman and it would light up an entire house. But you have to be very careful. If you shine it in your eye it'll blind you. You want to try it?"

"Yessir." He handed me the laser pointer.

"Push the gray button," he said. "Shine it on my hand."

I pushed the button and shined it on his hand.

The long-haired man sat down in the road and took his laser pointer back. Then he took a piece of yellow candy from his pocket and ate it. I wanted one, too, but I didn't ask.

"What's your name?" he said. He was smiling now.

"Ben Worthington."

"Ben, that was awfully nice of you to tell me I dropped this. You could've kept it. You're an honest boy. If I give this to you will you be careful not to shine it in your eye?"

"I would be very careful."

"I can't give it to you right now. I have to use it this afternoon but—"

"Why?"

"I lost something in a tunnel and I have to find it with this."

It made me sad that I couldn't have it right now.

"But maybe . . . No, I shouldn't. Your parents probably wouldn't let you have—"

"Yes they would."

"No I don't think—"

"They would too."

"Ben, if I give this to you you can't show it to your parents. Or your brother. He would steal it and play with it. Your parents would take it and throw it away."

"I won't tell them."

"You promise?"

"Yessir, I promise."

"You can't tell them about me either."

"I won't." He got up and looked down at me.

"Later tonight I'm going to come knock on your window. You have to go to your back door and open it so I can give this to you. Can you do that, Ben?"

"Yessir."

"You have to do it very quietly. If anyone wakes up and sees me I'll have to leave and you won't be able to have the laser pointer. Do you want to have it?"

"Yessir."

"Say that you want to have it."

"I want to have it."

"Say it again."

"I want to have it."

"You're obedient. That's a good boy. I have to go now. I'll see you tonight."

"Can I do the laser again?" The long-haired man sighed.

I didn't think he was going to let me, but then he said, "All right, once more."

CHAPTER 8

Luther Kite straddles the thickest limb of the pine fifteen feet off the ground. It is suppertime on Shortleaf Drive, quiet now that the children have been called home, each house warm with lamplight and lively with the domestic happenings of a Sunday night.

His stomach rumbles. He has not eaten. He will eat afterward because this is North Carolina, land of Waffle Houses that never close. He'll consume a stack of pancakes and scrambled eggs and sausage links and torched bacon and grits and he'll drown it all in maple syrup. Especially the bacon.

A breeze stirs the branches and the dying leaves sweep down in slow motion upon the street. The sky has darkened so that he can no longer see the silhouette of the water tower that moments ago loomed above the rampart of loblollies across the lake. Only the red light atop the bowl signals its presence.

The October night cools quickly.

It will be warm inside the house he has chosen.

He smiles, closes his eyes, rests his head against the bark.

Just four hours.

The moon will have advanced high above the horizon of calligraphic pines, burnishing the empty street into blue silver. He sleeps perfectly still upon the limb, the smell of sap engulfing him, sweet and pungent like bourbon.

CHAPTER 9

Horace Boone had used credit card information to track Andrew Thomas to a postal outlet in Haines Junction, Yukon.

But he didn't leave right away.

He continued working in Anchorage from April to August, saving everything he earned. In September he quit his job at Murder One Books, put what few possessions he owned into storage, and embarked in his stalwart Land Cruiser for the Yukon with four thousand dollars, a suitcase of clothing, and blind faith that he would find Andrew Thomas.

Upon arriving in Haines Junction, Horace staked out the downtown, studying the village's sparse foot traffic for his man.

On the fifth morning, while wondering if he'd made a giant mistake, he watched the same long-haired man who'd graced Murder One Books several months back enter Madley's Store to retrieve his mail.

Horace was elated.

The next day, his twenty-fourth birthday, Horace rented a rundown trailer on the outskirts of the village and began taking copious notes for the book he wholeheartedly believed was going to make him a rich and famous and oft-laid writer.

His second week in the Yukon he ventured onto Andrew Thomas's property late one night and spied on the cabin from a distance with binoculars.

The following week he'd crept all the way up to a side window, watched the man wash his supper dishes and write in his loft late into the night.

Now, more than halfway through October, his fourth week in Haines Junction, Horace had decided to take his first real chance.

It was Monday morning and the snow from two days ago still dallied in the shadows of the forest. A full but feeble moon remained visible in the iris-blue morning—a clouded cataractous eye.

Horace sat behind the wheel of his Land Cruiser in that worn space between the trees where he always parked. Andrew Thomas's Jeep passed by right on schedule, village-bound, a dirt cloud rising in its wake. On this calm morning it would be almost an hour before the dust of its passage had settled.

Horace closed his purple wire-bound notebook and set it in the passenger seat.

He'd already finished outlining the second chapter of his memoir, tentatively titled *Hunting Evil: My Search for Andrew Thomas*. He was so excited about the book he was having trouble sleeping. It was a concept that couldn't miss because he might be the only person in the world who knew the whereabouts of the most notorious murderer of the last decade.

Horace had grown up poor.

He wasn't handsome.

Never been popular in school.

Writing was all he had.

He believed that after twenty-four years of having to see his stupid reflection in the mirror he was entitled to wild success.

Horace climbed out of the Land Cruiser and started down the faintly tread path to Andrew's cabin, making sure he didn't track through the patches of snow and leave evidence of his presence here.

He soon glimpsed the cabin through the trees.

He reached the front porch.

Turned the doorknob.

His hypothesis was correct: people who live in the wilderness aren't compelled to lock their doors.

He stepped inside, his heart convulsing epileptically, brain teetering between exhilaration and outright terror. Unbuttoning his down jacket, he slung it over the railing of a daybed and commanded himself to settle down. He would hear Andrew's Jeep coming down the driveway long before it reached the cabin.

Stepping forward, he glanced once through the monster's home, committing to memory every detail—the sinkful of dishes in the kitchen, the halfeaten pie on the breakfast table, ashes steaming in the doused fireplace, the bearskin rug at his feet. The place smelled of woodsmoke, baked raspberries, venison jerky, and spruce. The floorboards creaked beneath him. He couldn't believe that he was actually here.

He unlaced his boots, walked in socked feet to the ladder, and climbed into the writing loft. His eyes gravitated first to the poster of Edgar Allan Poe and those stormy melancholic eyes. Then he read one of the numerous Post-it notes stuck to the rafters:

describe the woman in Rock Springs in the puffy pink jacket who heard Orson yelling in the trunk

Stepping carefully over an unfolded roadmap of Wyoming, Horace found himself standing before Andrew Thomas's writing desk, bookended by bookshelves, cluttered with a typewriter, dictionary, Bible, thesaurus, and *The National Audubon Society Field Guide to North American Trees: Eastern Region.*

He found what he'd come for in the middle drawer—unbound pages stacked neatly between boxes of red felt-tip pens. Taking a seat in Andrew's chair, Horace lifted out the manuscript with trembling hands. *What in the world has this man been writing?*

The title page:

"DESERT PLACES"
a true story by
Andrew Z. Thomas

Horace heard something outside, stopped breathing to listen. He decided it was only wind moving through firs. He turned the title page over on the desk and read the short preface:

The events described hereafter
took place over seven months,
from May 16 to November 13, 1996.
* * *
"And I alone have escaped to tell you."
—JOB 1:17

Horace flipped the page to Chapter One and began to read.

On a lovely May evening, I sat on my deck, watching the sun descend upon Lake Norman. So far, it had been a perfect day. I'd risen at 5:00 A.M. as

I always do, put on a pot of French roast, and prepared my usual break-fast of scrambled eggs and a bowl of fresh pineapple. By six o'clock, I was writing, and I didn't stop until noon.

CHAPTER 10

In the North Carolina night Luther shins down the pine. On the ground he checks the time and dusts the bark off his jeans. He shoulders the Gregory daypack that holds the tools of his trade: duct tape, latex gloves, .357, small tape recorder, hairnet, two pairs of handcuffs, four Ziploc bags, sharpening stone, and one very special bowie, constructed of a five-and-a-half-inch battle-proven blade and ivory hilt. He appropriated the knife seven years ago from Orson Thomas's desert cabin. He treasures it and is thinking of giving it a name.

Shortleaf Drive runs for a quarter mile along the shore of the moonlit lake, a cul-de-sac at each end, the houses built on roomy wooded lots, draped in sweet suburban silence.

As Luther walks down the road he registers all sounds: the handful of chirping crickets which will be silenced by month's end, a jet cruising in the darkness above, the horn of a distant train carrying across the water.

The Worthingtons live in the brick ranch with long eaves, second from the cul-de-sac, surrounded and shaded by tall broad oaks. The house is dark. Because the blinds aren't drawn he is tempted to sit in the driveway and stare through those windows into rooms he will soon inhabit. But that isn't how one carries oneself on a residential street at 1:30 in the morning. So he moves on down the driveway past a Volvo and minivan, each adorned with the obligatory bumper stickers boasting of terrific Honor Roll children.

He creeps along the side of the house into the backyard. The grass runs down to the water where a pier is rotting into the lake. A monster oak stands in the center of the lawn, an elaborate tree house built twenty feet up upon its staunchest limbs. A rope swing hangs from a branch overhead and on this calm October night is absolutely still, like the minute hand of a watch that no longer keeps time.

Luther kneels down in the grass below the boy's window, thankful that the old oak shades him from the brilliant harvest moon. He unzips his backpack and removes the latex gloves. After pulling his hair into a ponytail he slips on a hairnet and rises.

The window comes to his waist.

He peers inside.

The boy lies asleep in bed. A nightlight spreads soft orange illumination upon the wall beside the open doorway.

Caricatures of stars shine weakly from the ceiling.

Luther aims the laser pointer and a red dot appears on the boy's pillow. The laser moves onto his face and holds against the eyelid. The boy jerks his head, rubs his eyes, and is still again. The pinpoint of bloodlight finds the eyelid once more. The boy sits up suddenly in bed.

With his middle knuckle Luther raps twice against the glass.

Seven-year-old Ben Worthington regards the dark shape of the man at the window.

The laser shines on Ben's pajama top.

In the blue darkness the boy looks down at the glowing dot on his chest, then back at Luther, smiling now, remembering.

Luther smiles, too.

Ben waves to Luther and climbs down out of bed. He walks in pajama feet through scattered Legos to the window. Sleeplines texture the left side of his face.

"Hey!" he says at full volume.

Luther touches his index finger to his lips, dangling the laser pointer between his thumb and forefinger.

And boy and man whisper plans to make their rendezvous at the back door.

CHAPTER 11

Four hours later Horace returned the manuscript to the drawer. He sat for a moment in Andrew's chair in sheer shock. If he were to believe the preface, that this manuscript was true, then Andrew Thomas was one damned unlucky human being.

He climbed down from the loft, laced his boots, buttoned his jacket, and stepped out into the premature darkness of the afternoon.

On the way back to his Land Cruiser, he couldn't stop thinking about Orson Thomas and Luther Kite, how they'd destroyed Andrew Thomas's life.

A splinter of pity worked its way in.

Since he had grown up with all those terrible stories about Andrew Thomas, that manuscript was hard to believe. Maybe it was full of lies. But why would a man living in the middle of nowhere in assumed anonymity have any reason to lie? What if the monsters were really Orson and Luther?

He was running through the woods now, eyes watering from the cold.

When the idea hit him, Horace laughed.

But by the time he'd reached the Land Cruiser, he knew what he would have to do for his book.

Next time he came out here, he would drive right up to Andrew Thomas's cabin, knock on the door, and politely ask the alleged serial killer for an interview.

CHAPTER 12

Ben Worthington turns the deadbolt as Luther grins at him through a pane of glass. When the boy has opened the back door, Luther extends an arm from behind his back and unfurls his long slender fingers to reveal the coveted laser pointer.

"All yours," Luther whispers.

The boy steps through the doorway onto the deck, bigeyed as his little fingers grasp what has been foremost on his mind since midafternoon.

Luther gently places his right hand against the back of the boy's skull and his left palm flat against his forehead.

"You're a bad boy, Ben," Luther says, and twists his little head around 180 degrees.

The warmth of the house envelops him as he closes and relocks the back door. He stands in the kitchen holding the dead boy in his arms, the linoleum Kool-Aid-sticky beneath his feet.

The sink blooms with dishes.

The odor of burnt popcorn permeates the air.

Two greasy Tupperware bowls sit on the Formica table beside him, the unexploded kernels still pooled in the bottom.

The liquid crystal display on the stove turns to 1:39.

He hesitates, listening: the muted breath of warm air murmurs up through vents in the floor. A water droplet falls every fifteen seconds from the faucet into a slowly filling wineglass and in another room the second hand of a clock ticks just on the edge of audible. The refrigerator hums soothingly. As the icemaker releases new cubes into the bin, the sound is like a great glacier shelf calving into the sea.

Luther kneels down, stows the boy beneath the table. Then he moves on into the dining room, turns right, and passes through a wide archway into the den.

Plushy cushioned furniture has been arranged in a semicircle around the undeniable focal point of the room: a gargantuan television with satellite speakers positioned strategically in every corner for a maximum auditory experience. A third Tupperware bowl has been abandoned between two pillows on the floor. Bending down, he scoops out a handful of popcorn and crams it into his mouth.

He walks to the edge of the hallway, eyes still adjusting to the navy darkness. The electronic snoring of the kitchen cannot be heard from this corridor of the house. But there are other sounds: the toilet runs; a showerhead drips onto ceramic; three human beings breathe heavily in oblivious comfort. Beneath this soundtrack of suburban sleep the central heating whispers on and on, safe as his mother's heartbeat.

Luther stands in the hallway scraping chunks of popcorn from his molars, thinking, *They need this noise. They would go mad without it. They think this is silence . . . they have never known silence.*

He steps through the first doorway on the right, a bathroom. Opening the medicine cabinet above the sink, he takes out a box of grape-flavored dental floss. When his teeth are clean to his satisfaction he returns the floss to its shelf and closes the cabinet. Stepping back into the hall, he tiptoes across the carpet into the first room on the left.

A black and orange sticker on the door reads "Private—Keep Out!" and below it in stenciled characters: "Hank's Hideout."

The room is tidy—no toys on the floor; beanbags pushed into the corners.

A dozen model airplanes and helicopters hang by wires from the ceiling.

A B-25 sits near completion on a desk. Only the wings and the ball turret remain to be affixed.

He smells the glue.

A bevy of Little League trophies lines the top of a dresser, each golden plastic boy facing the bed, frozen in midswing. Luther reads the engraving on the base of one of the trophies.

Hank's team is called The Lean, Mean, Fighting Machine.

He won the sportsmanship award last year.

Removing his backpack, Luther lies down beside Hank atop a bedspread patterned with a map of the constellations. The boy sleeps on his side, his back to the intruder. Luther watches him for a moment under the orange gleam of a night-light, wondering what it must feel like to have a son.

Because he's dreaming, the boy's neck snaps more easily than his little brother's.

Luther rises, unzips the backpack. He takes out the gun, the handcuffs, the tape recorder, Orson's bowie. The gun is not loaded. Silencers are hard to come by and under no condition will he fire a .357 at two in the morning in a neighborhood like this.

Slipping the handcuffs into his pocket, he moves back into the hall and arrives at last in the threshold of the master bedroom where Zach and Theresa Worthington sleep.

In the absence of a night-light the room is all shape and shadow.

He would prefer to stand here, watching them from the doorway for an hour, glutting himself on anticipation. But this isn't his only project tonight and the sun will be up in four hours.

So Luther sets the tape recorder on a nearby dresser and presses RECORD. Then he thumbs back the hammer on the .357 and strokes the light switch with his latex finger though he does not flip it yet.

Zach Worthington shifts in bed.

"Theresa," he mumbles. "Trese?"

A half-conscious answer: "Wha?"

Luther's loins tingle.

"I think one of the kids is up."

CHAPTER 13

Elizabeth Lancing couldn't sleep. She'd gone on her first date with Todd Ramsey tonight and a spectrum of emotions swarmed inside her head, giddiness to guilt. Todd had taken her to a French restaurant in Charlotte called The Melting Pot. Initially she'd been horrified at the prospect of making conversation over three hours of fondue, but Todd was charming and they'd fallen into easy conversation.

They started out discussing their law firm where Todd just made partner and Beth had been a legal administrator for five years. At first they resisted the gossip, but Womble & Sloop was a rowdy firm and the fodder was bottomless and irresistible. This transitioned into a brief exchange on their philosophies of employment and how neither of them knew anyone whose work afforded absolute fulfillment. They posited finally that the ideal job did exist but that finding it was such an excruciating chore most people preferred instead to suffer moderate unhappiness over an entire career.

Toward the end of dinner, as they dipped melon balls and strawberries into a pot of scalding chocolate, the conversation took an intimate turn. They sat close, basked in prolonged eye contact, and compared only the idyllic slivers of their childhoods.

Beth knew that Todd had been recently divorced. He was well aware that her husband had disappeared seven years ago through some mysterious connection to Andrew Thomas. But neither came within a hundred miles of the other's baggage.

After dinner Todd took her home. It was eleven o'clock, and cruising north up a vacated I-77 Beth watched the pavement pass, mesmeric in the headlights. Riding with Todd, she felt foreign to herself in a fresh and frightening way. Like the start of college and autumn. Not a thirty-eight-year-old single mother of two.

She came very near to holding his hand.

She wanted to.

Had he reached out she would not have pulled away.

But the part of her that had lived ten years with another man and borne his children and experienced the loss of him quietly objected. So she kept her hands flat against her newly-purchased sleek black A-line, partly out of fear, mostly out of respect, thinking, *Next time perhaps but not tonight, Walter.*

Now Beth had climbed out of bed and come downstairs where she stood at the kitchen sink looking through the window at the black waters of Lake Norman, the moon high and lambent, an ivory sun in a navy sky.

The lake was no longer smooth. An easy wind had put ripples through that black plate of water and disturbed the reflection of the moon. Beth could hear the fluttering leaves and see them spiraling down out of sleeping trees into the frosting grass.

Next door, the Worthingtons' rope swing had begun to sway—some wayward specter revisiting a childhood haunt at this wee hour of the morning.

The clock on the stove read 1:39.

She took a glass from the cabinet and filled it from a bottle of water. Following those wonderful glasses of Shiraz that had accompanied her supper, she was parched and downed the glass in one long gulp.

Instead of returning to bed, Beth walked through the dining room into the den and curled up on the sofa beneath an afghan. She wasn't remotely tired and this exacerbated her realization that it was now Monday and she would be staggering into work in six short hours.

Moonlight streamed through the French doors leading out onto the deck where the shadows cast by Adirondack chairs lengthened as the moon moved across the sky.

She wore an old satin teddy Walter had given her years ago for Valentine's Day. Because all the lights were off downstairs, when she crinkled the fabric the blue crackling of static electricity was visible as it danced in the satin.

She ruminated on Walter. He was more vivid in her mind than he'd been in a long while. What she felt toward him wasn't sadness or nostalgia or even love. It was beyond an emotion she could name. She thought of him now as light and time and energy—a being her earthbound soul could not begin to comprehend. Did he watch her now? she wondered. From some unfathomable dimension? She had the warmest inkling they would meet again as pure souls in the space between stars. They would communicate their essences to each other and luminously merge, becoming a single brilliant entity. This was her afterlife, to be with him again in some inconceivable form.

Beth heard the footfalls of one of her children upstairs. Rising from the sofa, she walked into the foyer, the hardwood floor cool, dusty beneath her bare feet. She climbed the carpeted staircase to the second floor and upon nearing the top felt the insomnia begin to abate and her eyes grow leaden. She was tired of thinking. Perhaps she would sleep now.

The stairs bisected the second-floor hallway.

To her left the corridor extended past two linen closets and Jenna's bedroom and terminated at the closed door of the bathroom, behind which John David urinated hard into the toilet.

Beth went right toward her bedroom at the opposite end of the hall. Passing another pair of closets and the playroom, she approached the open doorway of John David's bedroom. Before leaving on her date with Todd she'd made J.D. promise to clean it up.

She stopped at his doorway and peeked inside. Though it was dark, she could see that the floor was still buried in clothes and toys. J.D. and Jenna had been playing Risk since they came home from church. The game board rested at the foot of the bed, framed by dirty blue jeans.

Beth drew a sudden breath.

John David was sleeping in his bed.

She heard the bathroom door creak open.

Turning, she looked down the corridor.

With the bathroom light now switched off she could only see the silhouette of a tall dark form standing in the bathroom doorway.

So it was Jenna in there.

"Hey, sweetie," Beth called out—but her voice betrayed scraps of doubt.

The form at the other end of the hallway did not move or respond.

"Jenna? What's wrong, Jenna?"

Beth's heart thudded against her sternum.

Behind her John David mumbled incoherently. She closed the door to his bedroom, a salty metallic taste coating her throat with the flavor of adrenaline and dread.

She was ten steps from her bedroom door.

Gun in closet. Top shelf. Nike shoebox. Loaded?

Stepping out into the middle of the hall, she began to backpedal slowly toward her room, squinting through the darkness at the motionless shadow, thinking, *I haven't fired that gun in seven years. I don't know if I remember how.*

Her hand grasped the doorknob. She turned it, backing through the threshold into the master bedroom.

The shadow remained at the other end of the hall.

Phone or gun?

She could scarcely catch a sufficient breath. Some part of her wondered, prayed that this was a recurrence of one of those awful dreams she'd suffered in the wake of Walter's death.

Much as she hated to let that thing out of her sight, she was impotent without a weapon. Beth turned and moved deftly to the bedside table. She lifted the phone. *Jesus, no.* The line was dead and her cell phone was downstairs in her purse.

Beth slid back the door to the closet as the unmistakable resonance of thick-soled bootsteps filled the hallway.

She hyperventilated.

Do not faint.

Standing on her tiptoes, Beth reached for the top shelf and grabbed the shoebox with her fingertips and pried it open. It contained a box of bullets but the .38 was gone. She noticed other boxes on the floor at her feet—he'd been rummaging while she was downstairs.

The footsteps stopped.

The house was silent.

A wave of trembles swept through her, sapping the strength

from her legs, forcing her to the floor. The thought of her children stood her up again and she walked to the doorway of her bedroom and peered down the hall.

It was empty now.

"I've called nine-one-one on my cell phone!" she yelled. "And I'm holding a shotgun and I'm not afraid to use it!"

"Mom?" Jenna called out.

"Jenna!" Beth screamed.

In a knee-length flannel nightgown her daughter stepped from her bedroom into the hallway. Jenna was taller than Beth now, prettier. She'd inherited her daddy's good looks and athleticism, missed her mother's plainness.

"Why are you yelling, Mom?"

"Get back in your room and lock the door!"

"What's wrong?"

"Now, goddammit!"

Jenna ran crying into her room and slammed the door.

"I don't want to shoot you but I will," Beth hollered at the darkness.

"How can you shoot me when I have your gun?" a calm masculine voice inquired.

The shadow emerged from the playroom and walked toward her.

Beth flicked the light switch on the wall.

The hallway lit up, burning her eyes and flooding the shadow with color and texture.

The man who approached her had long black hair, a face whiter than a china doll, and smiling red lips. He tracked boot prints of blood across her hardwood floor. It speckled his face, darkened his jeans and long-sleeved black T-shirt.

Beth sank down onto the floor, immobilized with terror.

Luther came and stood over her, said, "I haven't hurt your children and I won't long as you're compliant."

Beth saw the ivory-hilted knife in his right hand. It had seen use tonight.

Jenna's door opened. The young girl poked her head out.

"I'm all right, baby," Beth said, her voice breaking. "Stay in your room."

Luther turned and gazed at the teenager.

"Obey your mother."

"Why are you doing this?" Jenna cried.

"Get in your room!" Beth yelled.

"*What is happening?*"

"Get in your room!"

Jenna's door slammed and locked.

When Beth looked back up at the intruder she saw he'd traded his knife for a blackjack.

"Turn around," he said. "I need to see the back of your head."

"Why?"

"I'm going to hit you with this and I'd rather it didn't smash your face."

"Don't you touch my children."

"Turn your head."

"Swear to me you won't hurt—"

Luther seized her by the hair and whacked the back of her skull.

CHAPTER 14

According to the official Web site *www.wafflehouse.com* the thirteen hundred Waffle Houses in the United States collectively serve enough Jimmy Dean sausage patties in twenty-four hours to construct a cylinder of meat as tall as the Empire State Building. And in one year they serve enough strips of Bryan bacon to stretch from Atlanta to Los Angeles seven times.

Luther recalls these amusing factoids while cruising down the off-ramp of I-40, exit 151, in the city of Statesville, North Carolina. Though it's 4:13 A.M., two establishments remain open for business. There's the never-closing Super Wal-Mart on his side of the underpass and the wonderful Waffle House—just a left turn at the stoplight and two hundred yards up the street. Its lucent yellow sign cheerfully beckons him. He smiles. He hasn't enjoyed that smoke-sated ambience in a while.

Luther pulls into a parking space and turns off the '85 Impala. In addition to stinking of onions, the car has been running hot, and he worries it won't endure the remainder of his journey. With respect to his sleeping cargo, breaking down would be an unthinkable disaster.

Intricately patterned frost has crystallized on the windshield of the car beside his, a web of lacy ice spreading across the glass. Touching the fragile crystals, he shivers and takes in the predawn stillness of the town. From where he stands the world consists of motels, gas stations, fast food restaurants, the drone of the interstate, and the sprawling glowing immensity of that Super Wal-Mart in the distance, set up on a hill so that it looks down upon its town with all the foreboding of a medieval stronghold.

Luther heads first into the bathroom. Though his work clothes rest safely in a trash bag in the backseat, he hasn't had the opportunity to wash up. His hands and face are bloodspattered and he watches the water turn pink and swirl down the drain.

Even at this hour of the morning, Waffle House is buzzing, the bright light from the huge hanging globes bouncing off a murky cloud of cigarette smoke. The grill sizzles on without respite, the smell of the place a potpourri of stale coffee, smoke, and recycled grease.

A waitress moseys over to Luther's booth.

"Know what you want, sweetie-pie?"

Though still perusing the illustrated menu, he knows exactly what he wants.

"Vanilla Coca-Cola. Sausage. Bacon. Grits. Scrambled Eggs. A stack of pancakes. And more maple syrup. I'm going to use a lot more than what's in that dispenser."

The waitress chuckles. "We don't serve pancakes."

Luther glances up from the menu.

"Is that a joke?"

"Umm, this is the *Waffle* House. We serve *waffles*."

She's being friendly, flirtatious even, but Luther doesn't catch this. He feels only humiliation. The waitress is a young thing. Very pregnant. He thinks that she might be pretty if her teeth weren't crooked. Her nametag reads Brianna.

"I hate waffles, Brianna."

"Well, there's other stuff than that, darlin'. Fr-instance, my favorite thing is the hash browns. If you get em' triple scattered all the way you never had anything so good."

"All right."

"So you want to try it?"

"All right."

"And you still want all that other stuff, too?"

"Yes."

When Brianna the waitress is gone, Luther leans back against the orange-cushioned booth. He tries not to dwell on how severely disappointed he is that the Waffle House doesn't serve pancakes. How did he miss that? The waitress probably thinks he's stupid now. Perhaps she should join the others in the trunk.

Numerous signs adorn the walls. While he waits for his Coke he reads them:

Cheese 'N Eggs: A Waffle House Specialty
You Had a Choice and You Chose Us. Thank you.
Bert's Chili: Our Exclusive Recipe
America's Best Coffee

By the time his food arrives the first inkling of dawn is diffusing through the star-filled sky.

"You tell me how you like them hash browns," Brianna says. "Pancakes, that's a good one."

The triple scattered all the way hash browns taste like nothing Luther has ever eaten. The bed of shredded fried potatoes is covered in melted cheese, onions, chunks of hickory-smoked ham, Bert's chili, diced tomatoes, and slices of jalapeno peppers. He likes it better than pancakes and when Brianna brings him a refill of Vanilla Coke he thanks her for the recommendation. No longer is he ashamed for ordering pancakes in a restaurant specifically called Waffle House.

Luther sips the Vanilla Coke, briefly at peace, watching the sky revive through the fingerprinted glass.

Things are progressing famously.

How could the death of the Worthingtons and the kidnapping of both Karen Prescott and Elizabeth Lancing not grab Andrew's attention, wherever he is hiding?

As he starts to leave, Luther notices a man of sixty-five or seventy facing him two booths down, his sallow face frosted with white stubble, eyes bloodshot and sinking, staring absently out the window, a cigarette burning in his hand.

There is a transfer truck parked outside and based on the man's J.R. Trucking hat and hygienic disrepair Luther assumes he's the truck driver.

He senses the man's loneliness.

"Good morning," Luther says.

The trucker turns from the window.

"Morning."

"That your rig out there?"

"Sure is."

"Where you headed?"

"Memphis."

"What are you hauling?"

"Sugar."

The old man drags on his cigarette, then squashes it into an untouched egg yolk.

"Gets lonely on the road, doesn't it?" Luther says.

"Well, it certainly can."

He doesn't begrudge the man's curt replies. They don't spring from discourtesy but rather a desolate existence. Had he more to say he would.

Luther slides out of the booth, zips his sweatshirt, and nods goodbye to the trucker.

The man raises his coffee mug to Luther, takes a sip.

At the cash register Luther pays for his breakfast and then gives Brianna the waitress an additional ten-dollar bill.

"See that old man sitting alone in the booth? I'm buying his breakfast."

And Luther strolls out the front door to watch the sunrise.

CHAPTER 15

Pulling out of the Waffle House parking lot, Luther can hardly hold his eyes open. It's Monday, 6:00 A.M., and since Friday evening he's managed only four hours of sleep at a welcome center outside Mount Airy, North Carolina.

He takes the first left onto Pondside Drive, a residential street so infested with trees that when he glances up through the windshield he sees only fragments of the magenta sky.

He follows Pondside onto Cattail, a street that dead-ends after a quarter mile in a shaded sequestered cul-de-sac, its broken pavement hidden beneath a stratum of scarlet leaves.

Luther kills the ignition and climbs into the backseat.

Lying down on the cold sticky vinyl, he takes out the tape recorder, presses PLAY, and drifts off to the recording of Mr. Worthington begging for the lives of his family.

When he wakes it's 11:15 A.M. and the crystal sunlight of the October morning floods the Impala, the vinyl warm now like a hot water bottle against his cheek.

In downtown Statesville he picks up Highway 64 and speeds east through the piedmont of North Carolina and the catatonic towns of Mocksville, Lexington, Asheboro, and Siler City.

The sky stretches into infinite blinding blue.

Near Pittsboro, 64 crosses the enormous Lake Jordan, its banks bright with burning foliage. Luther cannot remember ever being so joyful.

By midafternoon he's hungry again.

At a Waffle House in Rocky Mount, North Carolina, he orders his new favorite dish: hash browns, triple scattered all the way, and a cold Vanilla Coke. Through the window his view is of a tawny field turned gold by the leaves of soybean plants.

Halfway through lunch it dawns on him.

He was careless at the Worthingtons'.

He left something behind.

CHAPTER 16

When Beth awoke she thought she was dead and gone to hell but it wasn't the inferno she expected. The image of hell she entertained derived from a painting she'd seen recently at the North Carolina Museum of Art.

The 1959 painting was called *Apocalyptic Scene with Philosophers and Historical Figures*, an oil on Masonite board by the Reverend McKendree Robbins Long.

The painting depicts a cavernous chamber and a legion of hopeless souls being herded by demons toward the obligatory lake of fire. Among the philosophers and historical figures are the faces of Einstein, Freud, Hitler, Stalin, and Marx. Others cling horrified to the rocky bank, still in their evening wear, as if seized from a lavish ball. A horde of men and women fall naked from the ceiling toward the burning lake and in the unreachable distance, visible to all, two luminous angels hover around a white cross—a constant torturous reminder of the love the damned have spurned.

My hell is worse, Beth thought, *because it's real.*

Her head ached terribly in this empty darkness and she possessed no recent memory. The faces of Jenna and John David flashed in her mind, and as she pictured the three of them lounging on the pier something shattered inside of her that could not be reassembled.

She sat up suddenly, smacked her forehead into the soundproofing, and fell back onto a limp hand.

"Who's there?" she shrieked.

Nothing answered.

She located the hand in the dark and squeezed it.

"Do you hear me?" she whispered, thinking, *If that's a corpse I'll fucking lose it.*

A half-conscious female voice mumbled, then gasped, jerked away from Beth.

"My name is Beth. Who are you?"

A voice croaked back, "Karen." It sounded as if she spoke through clenched teeth.

"Is this hell?" Beth whispered.

"It's the trunk of that psychopath's car."

Everything came rushing back in a fury of consciousness.

"Where are my children?" Beth asked.

"Your children?"

"Did he hurt them?"

"I don't know."

Crying now, Beth tried to shove the fear down in her craw, into that calloused niche she'd found when her husband was murdered.

He only took me. That animal did not hurt my children. Please God You did not let that happen.

———

Lying on their sides, facing each other in absolute darkness, the women held hands. They could each feel the exhalations of the other—warm comforting breath in their faces.

The car was in motion again and the force of inertia tossed them about in the dark at the slightest change in speed or direction. As the pavement screamed along beneath them they snuggled closer. Karen stroked Beth's hair and wiped her wet cheeks. She wished she'd just lied and said that her children were safe.

Hours later, the car came to a stop, the engine quit, and the driver side door opened and closed.

Karen strained to listen.

Footsteps faded.

As she held Beth she concentrated on the scarcely audible sounds beyond their black cage—the continuous slam of car doors, the starting of engines, crying children, and the unmistakable squeak of shopping cart wheels rolling across pavement.

"We're in a parking lot," Karen whispered.

Three doors slammed nearby.

A voice came through: "Shannon, quit primping. You look fine."

"She doesn't want to disappoint Chris," another voice taunted.

"Fuck you and fuck you."

"Help!" Beth screamed. She jerked away from Karen's embrace and put her lips against the foam. "Help me! PLEASE!"

"Be quiet!" Karen hissed. "He'll kill us if we—"

"PLEASE! PLEASE! MY KIDS NEED ME!"

Karen wrapped her arms around Beth, put her hand over the woman's mouth, and pulled her back onto the filthy carpet.

"It's okay, sweetie. It's all right," she said, Beth shaking violently in her arms. "It's gonna be all right. But you can't—"

The voices passed through from outside again.

"There is nothing in that trunk, Shannon. You're crazy."

"It sounded like a dog barking. What kind of sicko leaves his dog in the trunk?"

"Who cares? Chris is waiting."

Beth elbowed Karen in the ribs, broke free, and screamed through the soundproofing until she thought her larynx would rupture.

When fatigue finally stopped her, all was silent again save her frenzied panting and the shudder of her heart.

CHAPTER 17

Luther dislocates a buggy from a caterpillarlike row and rolls it past the enfeebled greeter of the Rocky Mount Wal-Mart.

"How are you today, sonny?" the blue-vested old man asks him.

"Pretty fucking great." And he is. He adores Wal-Mart.

Luther heads first to the CANDY/SNACKS aisle where he places ten bags of Lemonheads into the buggy. Tearing open one of the bags, he drops three yellow balls into his mouth and begins to suck. On average he consumes two to three bags per day. The way he eats the candy is to suck off the tart lemon coating and spit out the white pit.

His teeth are rotting out of his head.

The candy is all he really came for, but it occurs to him that a digital camera might be a fun way to memorialize what he's going to do with Karen. So Luther pushes the buggy into ELECTRONICS.

Against the back wall two dozen televisions of varying size show the same muted cartoon. He is overstimulated with a din of obnoxious sound: bland sedating elevator music pours throughout the store from speakers in the ceiling; a rap song blares from a nearby display stereo; explosions, machinegun fire, and screams of suffering emanate from a video game.

Luther stops to examine the face of the small boy who holds the controller and stares at the images of gore and violence on-screen. The boy plays the game with rapt engagement and the glaze in his eyes reflects a mix of concentration and awe.

Leaving his buggy in the CD aisle, Luther walks over to the counter. He kneels down and peers through the glass at several digital cameras.

After a moment he rises, clears his throat.

The salesclerk sits on a stool, a telephone receiver held between his shoulder and ear. According to the name tag on the blue vest his name is Daniel. Daniel is tall and thin with short bleached-blond hair and slim black sideburns.

"I'd like to see the Sony Cybershot P51."

Daniel closes his eyes and holds up one finger.

Luther waits.

He begins to count silently.

When he reaches sixty he says again, "I'd like to see the Sony Cybershot P51."

"Megan, could you hold on a sec?" Now holding the phone against his chest: "Sir, could *you* just hold your horses there for a minute?"

"I've already held my horses for a minute, Daniel. I'd like to see that camera right now."

Luther feels the blood of humiliation coloring his face. Daniel brings the receiver to his ear again, steps down off the stool, and turns his back to Luther.

"Megan, I'm gonna have to call you back. I'm sorry . . . Yes,

I do think Jack is being unreasonable, but—" Daniel laughs. "I do, yes."

Daniel continues to talk.

Luther again counts to sixty.

Then he returns to his buggy and pushes it out of ELEC-TRONICS. He rolls the buggy outside without paying through the chromed brilliance of the crowded parking lot to his gray Impala. He loads his bags of candy into the backseat and climbs behind the steering wheel. From a notebook in the passenger seat he tears out a clean sheet of paper, on which he scribbles *OUT OF ORDER: DO NOT ENTER!* Then he takes a roll of Scotch tape from the glove compartment, crams several handfuls of Lemonheads in his pocket, and walks back into Wal-Mart.

Luther arrives at the service counter in SPORTING GOODS.

The clerk is a stodgy woman with black-rooted red hair.

"Babs, I'm in the market for a baseball bat," he says.

"Oh, I'm sorry, honey. We don't carry those 'cept in summer. But we just got our huntin' merchandise in if you're—"

Walking away, Luther pulls his hair into a ponytail and takes a camouflage baseball cap from an aisle of hunting apparel in case the cameras are watching.

For the next two hours he loiters on the outskirts of ELEC-TRONICS. As Luther watches Daniel flit around ignoring customers, he sucks through Lemonheads until he has a chemical burn on the roof of his mouth.

Daniel finally leaves ELECTRONICS and ambles to the front of the store.

Luther follows him outside where Daniel leans against a Sam's Choice drink machine and smokes two cigarettes while staring contemplatively out across the parking lot. It's six o'clock in the evening and the light is bronze. Luther stands near the automatic doors, his attention divided between Daniel and the red sunset.

He feels an erection coming.

By the time Daniel reenters Wal-Mart, Luther is swollen. He follows the clerk to the back left corner of the store, then down a bright empty corridor. Daniel digs his shoulder into a door and disappears into a restroom. Luther reaches the door, pulls the sheet of paper from his pocket, and tapes it over the 🚹.

Luther enters.

Three stalls, two urinals.

Dropping to his knees, he sees the pair of legs in the last stall and smiles.

They are alone. He could not have planned this any better.

Luther walks into a vacant stall. He reaches down, lifts the right leg of his gray sweatpants, and unbuttons the strap of his leather sheath. After setting the knife on the toilet, Luther takes off his sneakers and socks, pulls down his gray sweatpants, his underwear, and removes his sweatshirt and T-shirt.

This is going to be messy, and walking through Wal-Mart in blood-drenched clothes is not a wise thing to do.

Taking the knife, he emerges naked from the stall and turns the two faucets wide open. The soft roaring echo of water pressure fills the room. He flushes the urinals, the toilets in the first two stalls, and starts both automatic hand dryers. Finally he flips off the light and opens and shuts the bathroom door as though the janitor had left.

Daniel curses, the toilet paper dispenser barely audible over the babble of running water and rushing air. The blackness is complete except for a razorthin line of light along the base of the door.

Luther stands beside the light switch stroking himself.

He inhales deeply, at home in darkness.

Daniel's toilet flushes and as the zipper on his jeans ascends Luther grips the knife.

He would have preferred to spread Daniel's brains across the wall with a Louisville Slugger, one judicious *thwack*. But the blade will do. In the car he settled on a name for his knife: Zig, short for Ziegler, Andrew Thomas's middle name.

Luther hears the creak of the stall door swinging open.

Hesitant footsteps approach and eddies of Daniel's cologne sweep over him.

He feels Daniel beside him now, the clerk's hand on the cinderblock wall, groping for the light switch.

The knife feels coldly sublime in his palm.

Suddenly the restroom is awash in hard fluorescent light.

Daniel's eyes register first bewilderment, then terror.

Now the blade moving, two graceful strokes—one to silence, one to open.

Daniel sits in a warm expanding puddle, fingering the gorge in his abdomen, unable to make utterance.

"Now you sit there and think about what customer service means."

Luther reenters the stall and quickly dresses.

Then he hits the light and is out the door, one more cairn for this trail he's blazing.

CHAPTER 18

Upon regaining consciousness, Karen's first thought was that she was no longer in the trunk. Though she couldn't see, her present blindness owed to the blindfold tied around her head. She felt a cold wind in her face and an erratic source of light struggled through the oily-smelling cloth that masked her eyes.

Karen did not remember being moved. For all she knew she was dreaming again though the chill metal against her cheek seemed convincingly real. She tried to move but could not, her hands and feet now bound with thick rope. The numbing grogginess of thirst weighed down her head.

Footsteps approached, the tip of a boot now inches from her face. She smelled the grass and dirt that clung to it—raw and earthy.

"Good. You're conscious."

The voice contained no reverberation. She was outside.

"Where am I? Please take off the blindfold."

"We better leave that on for now. I tell you, you're a heavy gal. If I sound winded, it's because I just carried you up two hundred fourteen steps."

A prickling crawled through Karen's spine. "Where is this?" she asked.

"Don't you see the light? Even through the blindfold I don't know how you could miss it."

"I don't under—"

"That light is magnified by a First Order Fresnel Lens, operational since October First, Eighteen Seventy-two. Karen, let me quell your fear." The man sat down beside her. "I brought you here to let you go." Karen began to cry, filling with the purest relief. "But I have to hold on to the Widow Lancing. You remember her from the trunk?"

"Yessir."

"See, the only reason you're being released is because I flipped a coin. You were heads. It landed on heads. You get to live."

"Why are you doing this?"

She smelled his lemony breath in her face and his words came very even and very quiet.

"You think this is all about you, you arrogant twat?"

"No, I—"

"I only took you and Elizabeth Lancing to get someone's attention. Can you guess who it is?"

"I don't know."

"You should know. You've fucked him. Well, I'm just making an assumption there but—"

"I don't know who you're—"

"Andrew Thomas."

"What do you want with him?"

"Seven years ago, Andrew shot me, left me to die in a snowy desert."

"I'm so sorry."

"Don't be. What I've got planned for him is going to make it all worthwhile. One last thing. Think hard before you answer. Do you believe you're an evil person?"

"No, I'm—"

"Why not?"

Her captor's breath warmed her mouth as she thought of all the charitable acts she'd performed in the last year—Wednesdays in the soup kitchen on 54th, the new writers she'd guided to publication, the angel tree at Ice Blink.

"I'm a decent person," she said.

"And me? From what little you've seen. Am I evil?"

"No sir. I don't believe you are. I don't know you. I don't know what sort of parents you come from. I don't know if tragedies have happened to you. I'm sure things have caused you to behave . . ."

"Destructively."

"Yes."

"Is anyone evil, Karen?"

"People get damaged. They malfunction. But no, I don't believe in evil."

"I see. Thank you for talking so candidly with me."

The blindfold was removed.

Karen stared through iron bars across a half mile of pines and marshland and dunes to the Atlantic. From this height and distance the ocean was mute though in the light of the yellow moon she could make out the ragged thread of surf extending for miles down the coastline.

Her captor was gone.

She managed to sit up and saw that she occupied a small observation deck encircled by iron railing. At her back a ladder climbed the last six feet of the tower up to the lantern room of the Bodie Island Lighthouse.

Its beam was blinding. It flashed on for 2.5 seconds. Off 2.5

seconds. On 2.5 seconds. Off 22.5 seconds. This rhythm repeated, dusk to dawn, and she could not behold the mighty lens as it magnified its 160,000 candlepower beacon out to sea.

Karen strained against the rope, but the knots held. As she dragged herself around the platform, her eyes followed the ribbon of Highway 12 as it skirted beach and marsh and finally, three miles south, traversed the troubled waters of Oregon Inlet onto Pea Island. From there it would be sixty miles of desolate sound and seashore and tiny beach communities and then Cape Hatteras and Ocracoke and the Core Banks.

But she didn't know place-names.

She didn't even know she was in North Carolina or that her captor had cut two locks with a bolt cutter in the oil room and carried her up a rickety spiral staircase to the top of this 131-year-old lighthouse.

How the hell am I gonna get down from here? Fuck it, I'll find a way. Flag down a car. Get to an airport. Call Scott Boylin, have him wire some money. It will feel so sweet to be back in my apartment again. First thing I'll do is listen to Ashley Chambliss and drink an entire bottle of that chardonnay and I won't even feel guilty about it. Everything will be different now. I'll be a better person. Publish better books. Stop living on autopilot. This experience might actually turn out to be a—

Rounding the base of the lantern room, she froze.

Oh God, why is he still here and squatting over a pile of rope?

The man with long black hair looked over his shoulder and smiled.

"Be right with you, Karen."

When he turned and stood she saw that he held a noose by its coil.

He came forward as she tried to crawl the other way and slipped the noose around her neck. Then he hoisted her up over his shoulder and set her down on top of the railing facing him.

Unable to muster a scream, Karen glanced over her shoulder, felt a needling in her stomach. Far below she saw the adjoining oil room at the granite foundation of the lighthouse. She saw the roof of the nearby Keeper's Quarters and the visitor parking lot. Westward beyond the marsh, she took in the waters of the Pamlico Sound and farther on the blinking red lights of radio towers on the mainland.

"This is a black and white banded lighthouse," the man said. "I've measured out the rope so you'll hang in the middle white band facing the visitor's center. Imagine the face of whoever finds you first. Maybe some minivan family from the Midwest, with lots of little ones."

He laughed.

Karen looked at the skein of climbing rope at his feet and the bulky knot he'd tied to the railing. He held her by the waist belt of the bathrobe she'd worn since her abduction.

She sought out reason in his eyes and found it. They were not wild or impassioned but black and serene. And if they burned, it was a smoldering like embers.

Now only clutching her with one hand, he brushed his black hair from his eyes.

Karen felt gravity pining for her, a waterless undertow.

She upchucked on his windbreaker, but he did not let go.

"Karen," he said. "Now do you believe?"

He released the belt of her robe, watched her fall.

She screamed for two seconds; then the rope silenced her.

Back and forth she swung, still fifty feet above the lawn, a pendulum for the lighthouse.

CHAPTER 19

At two in the morning the Impala streaks south on Ocracoke Island, a ribbon of land less than a half mile wide. To the west the Pamlico Sound yawns out into darkness. Oceanside the Atlantic shines like black blood under the jaundiced October moon.

In the trunk, Elizabeth Lancing sleeps and she does not dream.

Behind the wheel the smiling driver is tired and happy, the window down, his hair whipping across his pale face. He inhales deeply, the tepid air redolent of kelp and saltwater and driftwood and the carcasses of fish on tide-smoothed sand.

At last he sees it beyond the dunes that now hide the sea—his hometown, a faint incandescence on the black horizon.

And he wonders, *Old Andrew, since I've shown you the way, will you come?*

VIOLET

CHAPTER 20

The last Wednesday of each month is unfailingly baked spaghetti night at Lighthouse Baptist Church. It is tradition, a comforting inevitability for this Christian community.

The congregation slowly progressed from the kitchen into the fellowship hall much as it had done every Wednesday evening for the past twenty-two years. Each churchgoer carried a paper plate laden with baked spaghetti, a yeast roll, a salad of wet lettuce and shredded carrots, and a Styrofoam cup of sweet tea.

They dined with their brothers and sisters in Christ at the circular foldaway tables, happily consuming the insipid meals, the fellowship hall resounding with myriad conversations and rampant children, while praise music flowed from speakers on the stage, an auditory warmth. Through tall windows the dying sun funneled weaker and weaker, now only a suggestion of purple in the late October sky.

Violet King sat at a table with her parents, Ebert and Evelyn, and a friend of her parents named Charles. Charles was thirty, single, and on fire for Jesus. Violet disliked the way he looked at and spoke to her, as though he were privy to some secret she had not disclosed, as though he were something more than a shallow acquaintance.

Charles had been monopolizing the conversation for the last five minutes, narrating his attempt to witness to a "troubled black youth."

But Violet wasn't listening. She just stared at the cube of baked spaghetti on her plate.

". . . and I told him, 'Jesus died for *you*, little fella.'" Charles's bottom lip had begun to quiver, his voice gone soft and earnest with emotion. "And you know what he said to me? It'll break your heart, Ebert. He said, 'How come God loves me?' And I told him, I said . . . You with me, Violet?"

Violet looked up into those small lonely eyes across the table. "Yes, I'm with you, Charles."

"I told him, 'God loves little black boys just as much as He loves little white boys.'"

A four-year-old boy ran over and stopped in front of Violet, a chocolate icing ring around his smiling little mouth.

"You're pretty," he said, then ran away shouting, "I did it, guys! I did it!"

The young woman laughed.

"Where's Max, Violet?" Charles asked.

"Same place he was when you asked me a week ago," Violet responded, but she did not say it bitterly. "He's coaching cross-country this fall. They had another meet today."

Is that all right with you, you freaking weirdo?

"Just don't want to see him backsliding on us. You start skipping Wednesday nights, what's next?"

"My son-in-law ain't no backslider, Charles," Ebert said. "You know I wouldn't tolerate that. Ain't that right, baby?"

"Yes, Daddy."

Violet smiled at her father, a big brawny man, white-bearded and bald-headed. He'd earned that shiny red dome working his dairy farm. Their table smelled faintly of manure.

As Violet sipped her tea she felt Charles eyeing her. She often caught him staring, especially during Sunday sermons. He was always chiding her about her "boy haircut," said women were supposed to have long and flowing hair, encouraged Violet to let her blond locks grow out.

Her pager buzzed against her hip and she glanced down at her lavender skirt.

When she saw the number she stood up.

"Mom, if Max comes, tell him I'll be right back."

"Everything all right, Vi?"

Evelyn stared up at Violet through cloudy blue eyes that picked up the gray in her hair.

How can you sit here with this whacko? "Yes ma'am."

Violet walked out of the fellowship hall into the corridor of classrooms. At the end of the hallway, the double doors had been thrown open and she could see into the new sanctuary where the music director was furiously arranging chairs in the choir loft in preparation for the practice that would immediately follow the fellowship dinner. She didn't feel up to singing tonight. She wanted to go home, crawl into bed with a pint of Cherry Garcia, and watch television, preferably a Ken Burns documentary on PBS.

With the commotion of the feasting congregation now a whisper, Violet stepped into a dark classroom and closed the door behind her.

The pager vibrated again.

She rummaged her purse for the cell phone.

CHAPTER 21

Violet turned around in the cul-de-sac and parked her Jeep Cherokee on the curb. The dashboard clock read 7:15. There was no tinge of luminosity in the sky excepting the blurry pinpoints of starlight that obscured when you looked straight at them. Turning off the engine, she stared at the chaos in the distance, filtering out the dazzle of flashing lights so she could imagine this hysterical street as it must've seemed that night.

Tranquil.

Ordinary.

Safe.

She absorbed her surroundings—the young pine forest across the street from the lakefront houses, the cul-de-sacs at each end, the road that dead-ended into Shortleaf Drive, the number of houses between cul-de-sacs (eleven) and that serene black lake.

Violet did not speculate or theorize. With the investigation only in its infancy it wasn't useful to do so. All she knew was that a family of four had been slain in that brick ranch forty yards down the street. Coupled with the other murders—the clerk knifed to death in a Rocky Mount Wal-Mart and the woman hanged from the Bodie Island Lighthouse—this had been one of the bloodiest weeks in North Carolina since the Civil War.

As she opened the door and stepped out into the autumn evening she couldn't help thinking, *Most investigators never encounter anything like this.* And then: *You are not equipped to handle it.*

Her legs gave out and she leaned against the Jeep.

Closing her eyes, she took a long calming breath, whispered a prayer, and started walking toward the flashing blue lights.

The perimeter of the Worthingtons' half-acre lot had already been roped off with crime scene tape. Violet counted three police cruisers, an ambulance, a van, and two unmarked cars parked along the curb across the street.

A uniformed patrolman stood at the foot of the driveway, guarding the perimeter.

"Hi, Reuben," she said.

"Viking? *You* were on-call for this one?"

"Yep."

"Lucky you. That house next-door is where we had the kidnapping on Monday. These are the neighbors we could never get to answer the door or the phone."

"You're kidding me. You were first car?"

"No, Bruce was. He's over talking to Barry."

Violet stepped under the tape and walked down the driveway toward her sergeant, a wide massive man with the girth of an oak tree and a voice as deep as her daddy's. He was talking to a patrolman when she walked up between them.

"Hey, guys."

Her sergeant looked down at her and shook his head.

"You sure caught it this time, Viking," he said as though it were her fault. "I'm gonna go talk with Chip and the boys. Bruce can tell you what you got."

"You been in yet, Barry?" she asked.

"No. We just got the search warrant. Bobby's executing it right now."

"CSI ready to start videotaping?"

"I think so."

"Would you ask them to hold off a sec? After I talk with Bruce, I'd like to do a quick walk-through."

Sgt. Mullins gazed down at her for a moment. He rarely smiled. Standing under his undecipherable scowl always made her feel eight years old again. She knew exactly what he was thinking because she'd thought it, too: she was incapable of handling this.

As Sgt. Mullins lumbered off toward the white-jacketed CSI techs, Violet glanced over her shoulder at a woman who stood weeping in the street at the edge of the Worthingtons' lawn.

She turned back to Bruce.

He was a year younger than Violet, just a year out of the academy on uniformed patrol. They'd attended the same high school though they hadn't known each other then. But Violet remembered him. He looked much the same—tall, slender, slightly bugeyed, with a fearful nervous mien.

She pulled a notepad and pencil from her purse as Bruce stared at the woman crying in the street.

"Bruce?" His large eyes came to Violet. "You all right?" Bruce took a deep breath. "Tell me what I got." They were standing by the Worthingtons' minivan and Bruce leaned against the back hatch. "No, Bruce, don't."

He stood back up, pointed toward the street, said, "That woman up there crying—name's Brenda Moorefield. She lives three houses down. Earlier this afternoon—"

" 'Bout what time?"

"Between three-thirty and four. She came over and knocked on the Worthingtons' door. Apparently their children play together, and Mrs. Moorefield hadn't seen the Worthington kids in two days. She had a key to the house and since their cars were in the driveway but they weren't answering the phone or getting the mail, she decided to go in.

"She was halfway through the foyer when she smelled them. Came right out, called nine-one-one. I arrived a little after five.

"You've got one boy under the breakfast table in the kitchen. The other kid's in his bed. I didn't see any blood near the children. Zach and Theresa Worthington are in their bed . . . it's bad. I couldn't stay in that room very long, Vi. I'm sorry, I just—"

"It's okay, Bruce. Not your job. What are the kids' names?"

"Hank and Ben. They were eleven and seven. Ben's the one under the table."

"Okay, mobile command should be here any minute. Reuben's got the perimeter. I want you to go over and calm Mrs. Moorefield down. I'm gonna go in, see what I got before CSI starts taping. I'd like to talk with Mrs. Moorefield while they're doing their thing, so make sure she doesn't leave."

As Bruce headed back up the driveway, Violet rubbed her arms. She'd left her Barbour coat in the fellowship hall at church and a chilly breeze was blowing in off the lake, dislodging dead leaves from the enormous oaks in the front yard.

She took a moment to gather herself, then started toward the front porch where a gaggle of noisy lawmen awaited her on the steps. They intimidated her, but she could handle them.

What troubled her more was what waited for her inside the house.

CHAPTER 22

Violet kicked off her heels and slipped her tiny feet into the cloth bootees. Then she squeezed her hands into a pair of latex gloves and stood up.

Standing by the Worthingtons' front door, the officer in charge of the scribe list wrote down her name and time of entry. Since this would be a cursory walk-through she was going in alone. A crime scene is a delicate ecosystem and the more people come and go, the more evidence they disturb.

"I'll be quick, guys," she said.

"Hey, Viking, want some Vicks?" one of the techs asked her. "From what Bruce says, they're pretty juicy in there."

"No, I'll be fine."

Sgt. Mullins said, "I've called Rick and Don. They're gonna come out first thing in the morning."

"Good. That'll move things along. We can each take a room."

Armed only with a flashlight, a notepad, and a pencil, Vi entered the home of Zach, Theresa, Hank, and Ben Worthington and closed the door behind her. Standing in the foyer, she noted two sounds: the rush of central heating and the voices of the lawmen standing on the front porch. It felt good to be out of the cold though she knew the warm air would only magnify the smell.

The house was dark, in the exact condition Bruce had found it.

Vi walked into the dining room. She hadn't breathed yet and her eyes made slow progress adjusting to the darkness. At the dining room table she stopped, letting form and detail vivify in the shadows.

Then she took an unflinching breath.

Sweet. Rich. Rot.

Some putrid aberration of macaroni and cheese.

So keen she could taste it.

She sniffed again, letting the scent of decay engulf her. During her second month in Criminal Investigations Division she'd caught her first suicide—two summers ago on a sweltering July afternoon, a seventy-four-year-old man suffering with Alzheimer's had put a twelve-gauge under his chin. He was found a week later in a small trailer without air-conditioning. Though his smell was horrific, she discovered surprisingly that she couldn't shun it, that she would accept, possibly embrace that awful stench out of reverence and compassion for her dead. The visceral intimacy of it inexplicably bound her first to the victim, then to the decoding of their murder.

A bright waning moon was rising over Lake Norman, its light spilling across the linoleum floor of the Worthingtons' kitchen.

When Vi saw the little boy under the breakfast table something twitched inside of her. She walked into the moonlit kitchen, knelt down by the table, and brushed her bangs out of her eyes. Turning on the flashlight, she shined it in the boy's face, then down the length of his small body. There were no visible ligature marks or bruises, but his head rested awkwardly on the floor.

Broken neck.

The flashlight beam passed slowly down his right arm and stopped at his hand, the fingers drawn into a tight fist. She shined the beam onto his other hand. Those fingers were loose, clutching what looked like a battery.

Vi walked to the back door and peered through glass panes into the moony backyard, taking in the oak, its tree house, the rope swing, the pier, the lake. Cutting off the flashlight, she walked back through the dining room into the den, her eyes now where she wanted them, accustomed to the shadows. She could've turned on the lights, but she needed to encounter the house as *he* had encountered it.

The smell sharpened in the den. She stopped and looked down at a bowl of popcorn on the floor. A videotape case sat empty on top of the television. Movie night. She walked over, glanced at the title: *Where the Red Fern Grows.*

When the telephone rang, Vi drew a sudden breath.

The answering machine picked up after two rings: "This is Theresa."

"Zack, too."

"Hank!"

"And Ben!"

Familial laughter.

A boy's voice continued: "We aren't here. Leave a message if you want."

After the beep: "Hey, y'all. It's Janet. Hadn't heard from you yet about next weekend, so I'm just calling to bug ya. Really hope you can make it. Jack and Susie send their love. Talk to you soon."

The silence resumed.

Stepping into the hallway, Vi glanced in the bathroom, then continued to the doorway of the older boy's room. She saw Hank Worthington in bed under the covers. He only looked asleep and she thought, *This house would feel so normal if you couldn't smell the death.*

At the end of the hall, the door to Zach and Theresa's bedroom stood wide open. Vi approached carefully, as though she might wake them, pulse racing, a pounding in the side of her neck.

She did not deny or curse the fear. Squatting down, she prayed, *I don't feel You in this house. Go with me into that bedroom.* She rose, felt just as alone, but walked on until she stood in the threshold of the master bedroom, eyes watering from the smell.

Vi had no tricks for steeling herself up to see innocence eviscerated. It punched the wind out of you and then you carried on or you quit. Sgt. Mullins had told her that early on. He'd been right.

With the tip of her pencil, she flicked the light switch.

The room shrieked at her and she let slip a bated whimper. Her stomach fluttered as she took three steps forward and looked straight into the worst of it.

Mr. and Mrs. Worthington stared back at her, despoiled of any scintilla of dignity.

Vi jotted on her notepad, relieved to look away.

When she finished she walked back down the hall into the foyer and opened the front door.

It felt so good to breathe fresh air again. She wanted to wash her hands for an hour.

As she stepped onto the front porch and pulled the door closed after her, she felt Sgt. Mullins and the CSI techs studying her, reading the abhorrence on her face, reflecting it in their own.

"The parents are torn up," she said to everyone. "May be a

ritual-type thing. And the boy under the table is holding something in his right hand."

One of the techs said, "You know Andrew Thomas used to live just across the lake. Bet you ten beers this was him. He's come back out of hiding. Wanted to do it with a flourish."

As Vi stepped across the sidewalk into the grass, she saw a local news van parking in the cul-de-sac.

The patrolman stood in the street with his arm around Brenda Moorefield and as Vi walked toward them, cold again, she called her husband and told him not to wait up.

CHAPTER 23

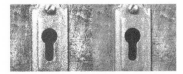

On the day he planned to interview Andrew Thomas, Horace Boone woke to the frozen pitiless darkness of his singlewide shithole on the outskirts of Haines Junction. The kerosene heater had gone out again during the night and despite five layers of quilts and blankets he lay on the mattress on the floor, shivering uncontrollably. Having woken cold for the last two weeks, he was beginning to realize that he would not survive a Yukon winter in this rundown shelter, when the temperature fell to minus forty and the wind howled through the thin walls.

He threw off the covers and came to his feet, already fully clothed in a camouflage bib and down hunting jacket he'd purchased last week at The Woodsman, one of the local outfitters. Moving out of the tiny bedroom, he crossed the "living room" in three steps and entered the kitchen. The refrigerator was the hotspot of the trailer this morning and he pulled open the door and grabbed a carton of orange juice. Shaking it up, he took a long sip of the acidic slush and then began foraging the kitchen cabinets for his breakfast.

While he consumed a stale Pop-Tart he leaned against the sink and glanced through the living room at the wretchedness he'd called home for the last month. The mattress, the television, and that disgusting couch comprised the furnishings of his trailer. You could only sit on the left end of the couch where the springs still held weight. And if you smacked the brown cushions on a clear day, you could watch them emit a mushrooming cloud of dust into the sunbeams from their inexhaustible store.

He'd been doing most of his writing in the village at Bill's diner, sitting in a booth near the window, drinking obscene amounts of coffee. In the last two weeks he'd written the first three chapters of his book on lined college rule notebook paper. They chronicled his first encounter with Andrew Thomas at the bookstore in Anchorage, his journey to the Yukon, and his sneaking into Andrew's cabin. He kept the purple notebook with him at all times during the day and stored it in the freezer while he slept so that if the trailer caught fire his manuscript might have a chance.

On October 30, the seventh anniversary of my mother's death, I discovered that my life in Haines Junction, a life I loved madly, was over.

Just before noon I was sitting in the computer lab of the public library reading an emotional Live Journal entry from an internet friend I knew only as Tammy M. Midway through a hefty paragraph in which she analyzed her incapacity for shallow social interaction, I heard the Champagne woman sitting at the computer beside me say to her husband, "Look at that, Ralph. Andrew Thomas is back."

Adrenaline shot through me, I felt the bloodheat color my face, but when I glanced over at the couple I saw the woman pointing to a news headline on her monitor. Feeling my gaze, she looked at me.

"Horrible, isn't it?" I couldn't speak. "Says he slaughtered a whole family."

"Where?" I choked on the word.

"I'm not sure. Let me see." She scrolled to the beginning of the article. "Here it is. Davidson, North Carolina."

Something inside of me died right there. I found the Web site and skimmed the article and the names of the victims. In the third paragraph I read these words:

> The next-door neighbor of the Worthingtons, Elizabeth Lancing, was kidnapped on Monday. Though unforthcoming with details at this time, authorities have alluded to their belief that her kidnapping is related. Her husband was Walter Lancing, a former friend of the suspected serial killer, novelist Andrew Thomas, and is believed to have been one of Mr. Thomas's victims, though his body was never recovered.

My head ached and I feared losing consciousness, so I sent the article to the network printer and logged off the computer. Taking my printout, I walked out of the library into the fierce noonday cold.

I reached my Jeep, climbed inside, pored over the rest of the article.

The description of the lighthouse and what had been done to poor sweet Karen broke me.

My safe little world had just been blown the fuck apart.

On the off chance that Andrew Thomas was in fact a psychopath, Horace Boone stopped to use a payphone on the way to his cabin.

It took him a moment to recall the number.

The phone booth stood in an alley against the building that housed The Lantern. It was a clear day, blue and very cold. He looked at his watch. There was something awfully depressing about knowing it was lunchtime when the sky shone no brighter than 9:00 A.M. and wouldn't for months to come.

She answered, "Hello?"

"Mom?"

A brief pause and then, "Hello, Horace."

"Look, I should've called before. I—"

"Where are you?"

"Canada."

"Well, thanks for letting me know you're alive. I'll pass along the good news to Dad."

"Mom, stop it; just—"

"No, you don't get to not call me for two months and then be friends."

"Will you just stop talking for two seconds? Something very big has happened in my life. I can't talk about it now, but it's exciting. I just wanted to call and say I love you."

"What, are you in danger?"

"No. I don't think so. Look, I have to go. I promise I'll call you again soon."

"Horace—"

He hung up the phone and walked back to the Land Cruiser, where he sat behind the wheel for a moment, clearing his head, going once more over everything he would say to Andrew Thomas—the praise, the questions, the threat.

Then he cranked the engine and headed off toward the woods, trying to ignore the very real possibility that he would not be coming back.

CHAPTER 24

Hurtling down the dirt road toward my cabin, I discovered what an enormous coward I had become. All the way home I tried to pretend I hadn't read the news. My dream was to remain in the wilderness outside Haines Junction until the end of my days, writing for the joy of it. I'd intended to die out here, an old recluse. This last year I'd been happy for the first time since Orson and Luther ripped my life away from me. I felt at home in these woods and I had never expected to feel that again.

I reached my narrow drive and turned into the forest.

The anger subsided, but fear crept in, eroding the lining of my stomach with that old familiar ache. It conjured a parade of images I'd spent years trying to forget, and as I glimpsed my cabin through the trees something whispered, *One of them is alive.*

No. I'd watched my brother Orson take a full load of buckshot to the chest. I'd seen the vacancy in his eyes thirty seconds later, the life running out of him. I'd left him frozen on the porch of a remote desert cabin. My twin was dead; he wasn't coming back.

I parked in front of the cabin and turned off the Jeep. Staring through the cracked windshield, I thought of Luther Kite, recalled standing over him holding a twelve-gauge to his chest, my finger grazing the double triggers. But I hadn't killed him. I'd thrown the shotgun across the room and left him to die on that cold front porch, severely wounded and miles from the nearest town with no mode of transportation. *He could not have survived. He was dying when I left him. Please, God, You would not have let that monster survive.* And then this piercing thought: *What if my unwillingness to pull that trigger has cost six people, including an entire family, their lives?*

I wasn't ready to accept that. Luther Kite died with Orson in that snowy Wyoming desert. The Worthingtons' and Karen's killer—whoever had blazed that gory trail across North Carolina—was a copycat. *It's not my fault.*

I opened the door, stepped out of the Jeep, the woods cold and still.

Walking toward the porch, I wondered, *But why kill that family in Davidson across the lake from my old home? And why kidnap Beth Lancing?* As I thought her name, my self-interest evaporated and it registered for the first time that she'd been taken, that if she wasn't dead now she was in the company of a madman.

Halfway up the porch steps, a sob spurted out of me. I sat down and wept like I hadn't wept in years, hanging blame around my neck for everything that had befallen that family. The Lancings would've been better off never to have known me. I'd taken everything from them. Everything. And now, seven years after the death of Walter, their association with me continued to produce suffering. How could I not try to help Beth?

I stood up and walked into the cabin, aware that the defense mechanisms in my brain were attempting to unplug me. The immense pain I'd endured through those dark years had nearly turned me into a stoic. The tears surprised me. I'd wondered recently if I had it in me to ever cry again.

Between the time I closed the door and set the news article on the breakfast table, the decision was made and I'd acknowledged that it could only be Luther.

So I walked over to my bed and dragged a suitcase out from underneath it, shaking as I began to pack.

I was rummaging the bottom drawer of a dresser in search of an envelope of hundred-dollar bills when I heard a car approaching down my drive. Closing the drawer, I came to my feet in astonishment. In the five years I'd lived in this cabin I rarely received visitors, and I was not expecting one now.

Though it was only three in the afternoon, the sun had slipped back behind the peaks, the forest draped in an eerie twilight. I heard a door slam and through the window watched a figure step onto the porch.

There was a knock.

Taking the subcompact .40-caliber Glock from the top dresser drawer, I slipped it into the pocket of my fleece pullover and went to greet my guest.

When I opened the front door, firelight from inside the cabin streamed across the gaunt visage of a young man I'd seen around the village these last few weeks, a small kid with an acne-cratered face, swallowed in a huge down jacket. The moment we made eye contact he looked away.

"Help you?" I asked. He found my eyes again, his hands fidgeting behind his back.

"Mr. Carmichael?" he said.

"Yes?" I sensed a frightened innocence behind those twenty-something eyes.

"May I come in for a moment?"

"Why?"

"There was something I wanted to talk to you about."

He was letting in the cold, so I stepped back and ushered him inside.

The young man stood beside the breakfast table, took a good long look at me. His Adam's apple rolled in his throat and his hands shook.

I said, "Well, do I have to guess?"

"What? Oh, no."

As he leaned against the breakfast table, our eyes fixed simultaneously on the article which lay face-up, its headline in a large black font:

FAMILY SLAYING LINKED TO ANDREW THOMAS

He looked up quickly and said, "Julie Ashburn sent me out to see if you could work tomorrow night. The Curling Club is having a dinner."

I reached back, pulled my hair into a ponytail.

"What's your name?" I asked.

"Horace. I just started helping her out. Sort of a gofer. Lucky to get the job."

"Well, you'll have to tell her that I can't do it this time, Horace."

"Oh, okay. That's fine, I mean . . ." He glanced once more at the article, then back at me, becoming breathless. "I'll let her know. Should I tell her you're going on vacation? That that's why you can't?" I just stared at him and slid my hands into my pockets, fingering the cold metal of the handgun, trying to talk myself down from the paranoia. *He doesn't suspect anything. He's acting strange because he's strange. World's full of strange people. Nothing more than that. He doesn't know who I am.*

"The reason I say vacation," he continued, "you know is just 'cause I notice you have a suitcase out over on the uh, the thing over there."

"Yes, I'm going away for a little while."

"Well, okay, then I'll uh, I'll tell Julie."

He couldn't help himself. For the third time he looked at the article.

"Why don't you take it with you?" I said. "I'm finished with it. Crazy stuff, huh?"

"Yeah. It's . . . wow. Well, look, I'll uh, I'll let Julie know." He picked up the article, then said, "I'm very sorry to bother you."

As Horace walked by and opened the front door, I realized how paranoid I'd become. He stepped out into the afternoon darkness and I lingered in the doorway, watching him climb into a Land Cruiser and head back up the driveway. The noise of its engine soon faded into woodland silence and there was nothing but the whisper of wind in the firs.

I walked back inside to finish packing, my thoughts returning to how I would find Luther Kite in this wide wide world.

Driving home through the cold Yukon darkness, Horace Boone could hardly contain his joy. Having read Andrew Thomas's manuscript, *Desert Places*, he understood perfectly well what was happening: on the supposition that Andrew was telling the truth, Luther Kite had survived the desert, was now alive and wreaking havoc, and Andrew was going to find him. Though it would devour all his savings, Horace would follow.

This was as much of a story as any writer could dream of.

I lay awake in bed, the sleepless hours ticking away. My suitcase was already packed in the Jeep and when I woke in the morning

I had only to walk outside, climb behind the wheel, and drive away. Whitehorse, Yukon, was 158 kilometers to the east. There I'd catch a flight to Vancouver and from Vancouver on to America. In a storage locker in Lander, Wyoming, there were things that might help me find Luther Kite—my brother's journals containing poetry, photographs, even a record of his and Luther's activities. I'd put it all in storage after fleeing Orson's cabin seven years ago because some of it incriminated me.

Now something was needling me about Luther and how I would find him. It seemed I'd read somewhere in Orson's journals that he'd grown up on an island.

There was a cracking in the distance. I knew this sound.

My first autumn in the Yukon I woke in bed one night petrified by a mysterious cracking in the forest. Unable to fall back asleep, I dressed and crept through the trees, arriving at last at a frozen pond where a bull moose was stamping his hooves into the ice. I'd watched him finally break through and dip his muzzle into the frigid water for a drink.

Hearing that sound again, I imagined it to be a goodbye of sorts and it threatened to unglue me. But I wouldn't cry anymore tonight. I'd loosed all the tears I was going to shed and now existed in a state of shock—shock that I was willingly leaving my harbor to sail back into madness. It was the uncertainty that haunted me, mostly for Beth Lancing, selfishly for myself—as I lay in bed watching fireshadows dance along the rafters of my precious home, I couldn't purge the thought that I would never see this place again.

CHAPTER 25

Early Friday morning Vi pulled into the driveway of her new home and turned off the car. The far left window on the façade of her house glowed and through half-drawn blinds she saw her husband rising out of bed. She climbed out, shut the door, sat down on the back bumper of the Cherokee. She glanced at her watch. It was one minute before five, which meant she'd been awake now for forty-six hours.

Dawn was imminent. She gazed out across the treeless subdivision, hushed and still. The drone of the interstate reached her from beyond the field, a quarter mile away, hidden behind a sliver of pines. There was never a moment in Arcadia Acres when the interstate fell silent. But she loved its transient undertone, found comfort in it. And she relished the ordinariness of this neighborhood. When Vi looked down Briar Lane she didn't see a street of soulless homogeneous starter homes. She saw herself and Max earning an honest living. Because Vi wasn't raised on entitlement she aspired to simple things—a family, comfortable home, occasional vacations to Gatlinburg and Myrtle Beach, finding an identity in her community, her church, her precinct.

In the cold misty silence of Arcadia Acres she meditated on the blessings in her life. After the crime scene she'd just processed she needed this stabilizing solace.

On the way to the front door she gathered up the broken necks of Ben and Hank Worthington, the evisceration of their parents, the shock of Jenna Lancing, and shoved it all into an insensate alcove she'd been conditioning in the back of her mind. This was the hardest part—walking into a warm peaceful home after thirty-five hours in hell. It was unbearable to Vi that such disparities could exist and she wondered, *Which is the illusion?*

Her husband was standing in the foyer in his briefs when she stepped inside. The aroma of newly ground coffee beans was strong, and as the front door closed Max came forward, arms opening for an embrace. But Vi put her hand on his chest and shook her head.

"It's all over the news," he said.

She walked past him and turned left into the hallway, still lined with unopened boxes.

"Don't you wanna talk, sweetpie?" he called after her.

When she reached their bedroom she set her purse on the dresser and sat down on the edge of the giant waterbed, only slightly smaller than the dimensions of the bedroom.

Her eyes closed. She could've fallen asleep sitting up.

When she opened them Max was kneeling beneath her. He slipped off her heels, massaged her feet. Then he unbuttoned her lavender jacket, grabbed it by the cuffs, and said, "Hold your arms out." Vi closed her eyes, held out her arms. Max tossed her jacket into the corner and while he undid the buttons on her blouse she drifted off. He told her to hold her arms out again, then to stand up. Max unzipped and unclipped her skirt. It dropped to the floor. He worked her hose down her legs and pulled them off her small feet. From his shirt drawer Max took a soft gray Mooresville Cross-Country T-shirt. Then he unhooked his wife's bra and slung it across the room onto the accumulating heap of clothes.

"Arms up."

He slipped the T-shirt over her head. Then he turned back the comforter and helped guide her legs underneath the covers. Two days without shaving had turned them imperceptibly rough like ultra fine grit sandpaper.

"Thirsty, angel? Need anything?"

"No," she whispered, nearly gone.

"Why won't you talk to me?"

" 'Cause I'm so tired I can't even think, Max. Stop it."

Max sat on the edge of the bed and stroked her hair while she fell asleep.

When Vi awoke it was dark again. Her eyes focused on the wooden cross hanging on the wall beside the doorway. It was the only adornment they'd put up since moving into the house last week. Her father had carved it from an oak branch and presented it to her three Christmases ago.

She heard Max in the kitchen. Pots clanged and the sweet warmth of baking bread flowed into the bedroom from the hallway.

Vi climbed out of bed and walked into the tiny adjoining bathroom. She stripped her shirt and panties and started the shower. She sat down in the bathtub, letting the water rain down upon her head and diverge into hot rivulets that descended the contours of her body.

Mindlessly she watched the water swirl into the drain and she did not rise until the shower had begun to cool.

Max was lying in bed when she emerged from the bathroom, towel-wrapped, her skin still steaming. Normally she'd have asked him to leave the room while she changed. The week before their wedding, Vi's mother had advised her never to dress in front of her husband. Too many free peeks and Max would take for granted the beauty of his bride.

Vi dropped her towel and donned a pair of royal blue sweatpants and an undershirt she'd owned since high school.

"I made dinner," Max said while Vi towel-dried her hair. "I made the Irish soda bread you like."

That was a first.

Vi threw the towel into the bathroom and climbed onto the bed. She lay flat on her back beside Max without touching him. He still wore his navy sweat suit from cross-country practice and smelled of running outdoors in the cold, his plentiful, curly black hair in a sweaty tangle.

Max sat up and said, "I'll bring your dinner back here."

"Just lay with me."

Max laid back down. They didn't move or speak for a while.

"I talked to this little girl," Vi said finally, staring into the ceiling. She spoke at hardly more than a whisper. "Thirteen years old. Name's Jenna. Wants to be an Olympic swimmer. Four days ago, in the middle of the night, Jenna watched a man with long black hair beat her mother unconscious. That man had just come from the next-door neighbors' where he'd broken the necks of two little boys and murdered their parents.

"While her mother lay unconscious in the hall, this thing broke into Jenna's bedroom. She was hiding in her closet. He threw open the doors, told her to get on the bed. She said he spoke very softly. Said he was covered in blood. Thought it was her mama's.

"Jenna got on the bed thinking she was going to be raped and killed. You know what he did? Tucked her in. Pulled the covers up around her neck, his face just inches from hers. She said he smelled like lemons. He told her, 'I have to take your mommy with me.' Said it very softly. Then this monster told Jenna he'd drown her in the bathtub if she got out of bed before sunrise.

"He left her room and went and talked to her brother. Jenna stayed in bed until the sun came up. When she walked out into the hallway, her mother was gone.

"She told me all this, sitting in the Cherokee. Never cried. But she's very worried about her brother. He won't talk to anyone. Their father was killed by Andrew Thomas. Now the mother's probably dead. And we may not catch this guy, Max."

"But you know it's Andrew Thomas. I mean, who else would've pushed his old girlfriend off that lighthouse?"

"Of course we think it's him, but the evidence isn't there yet. The physical description of the perp from that terrified little girl doesn't really fit Andrew Thomas. We got faint boot prints in the Worthingtons' backyard. Reports of a gray Impala in the neighborhood on Sunday afternoon. The only promising piece of evidence is a laser pointer we pried out of Ben Worthington's right hand. CSI lifted a partial and latent prints is checking it out. It's the only hope we've got at this point. And even if it turns out it belongs to Andrew Thomas, we still have to find him, and he's managed to hide for seven years."

"You gonna be able to detach from this? I mean, how long till I have my wife back? I can't go for a week without you—"

"He murdered an entire family, Max. Children, you know? Tore up the parents something fierce. Since before we got married, my period has started every twenty-eight days between two and five o'clock in the afternoon. My body's an atomic clock, and right now, I'm two days late. This didn't even happen when Papaw died."

Max rolled over on top of Vi, held her face between his palms.

"I know what would take your mind off this," he whispered, planting delicate kisses along her eyebrows. "Wanna play?"

He had the long lean body of a runner and it fit perfectly between her legs. She sensed him swelling against her through his nylon pants, felt lewd for wanting him while the slaughter of the Worthingtons consumed her.

"I still have the smell of that family in my nose," she said. "How can you even—"

Max slid her sweatpants below her knees, kissed her inner thigh, and moved up slowly with his tongue.

"You just tell me when to stop," he said, "and I'll go get your dinner."

He went back to work. She did not tell him to stop.

CHAPTER 26

On Halloween I flew into Rock Springs, Wyoming, rented a car, and by sunset was cruising north up Highway 191 into the unending bleakness of the high desert plain.

At dusk I pulled over at an abandoned gas station in Farson where 28 crosses 191 and runs northeast around the southern terminus of the Wind River Mountains for seventy miles to the city of Lander, my destination. Stepping out of the car, I walked across broken faded pavement into the middle of 191 and gazed north and west into the evening redness.

I wondered if my brother's cabin still stood in this wasted country. Just thirty miles north I imagined I could feel it, a dark presence on the horizon exhuming memories I would not acknowledge. The wind was calm, the highway empty. The silence and loneliness of the desert bore down on me, matching my spirit.

At an elevation of 7,550 feet I crested South Pass. Through the driver side window I could see the lavender foothills of the Winds. When I swallowed, my ears popped.

The highway descended at a gentle grade. A brown sign informed me that I was now in grizzly bear country.

The moon came up, lit the hills.

I drove through downtown Lander, a small town that in the summer months served as a port of entry to the eastside of the Winds. But now that the range was snowmantled and inaccessible most businesses had closed for the winter leaving the streets of Lander forlorn and listless.

Brawley's Self-Storage Co. was located off 287, two miles north of town. I pulled up to the gate several minutes past eight o'clock and punched in the access code. The facility was dark and deserted. As I entered and the gate rolled shut behind me, I recalled the last time I'd come here, after fleeing the cabin seven years back, in that state of shock and dread. At the time I didn't think I'd last through Christmas. My life was over in every way imaginable and the first enticing whispers of self-destruction had begun to germinate in the weakened tissue of my psyche.

I drove through the empty rows of storage buildings for five minutes until I located mine.

It was colder when I stepped outside, the moon still rising, the snowfields glowing high on the distant peaks. I unlocked the door and stepped into the hallway of small storage lockers. Mine was a 3' by 4' on the bottom row. I'd rented the space for nine years at a cost of $1,200.

Kneeling down, I removed the padlock and pulled open the door.

Dust plumed.

I coughed.

The overhead light had burned out in the corridor and the moonlight that streamed in through the doorway did not provide adequate illumination. So I dragged the filthy suitcase out of the locker. I walked back outside, set it down on the hood of the Buick.

I unzipped the suitcase.

They moved me in a terrible way, these artifacts of Orson. Sitting down on the hood, I lifted a manila folder and a notebook from the stash. Despite what I would have to pay for looking at his photographs and reading his words, I intended to examine everything, to immerse myself once more in my brother's depraved world, to learn what I could of his accomplice, Luther Kite, and where he might possibly be.

CHAPTER 27

The starting gun for the girls' race fired as Vi opened the back hatch of the Cherokee and grabbed the folded blanket she always brought to Max's cross-country meets.

She followed the trail to the start/finish line, staring through the tall limbless loblollies of MacAnderson Park at the field of runners dashing up the first hill of the 3.1-mile course. The cheers of the spectators faded as the runners moved out of sight.

It was the first Monday of November, a mild one, the sky unblemished and sapphire, the leaves a week beyond peak—red into crimson, gold into russet. The air stank of pine needles and exhaust from the tailpipes of the yellow buses that had carried the six cross-country teams of the Foothills Athletic Conference to this championship meet.

Vi walked over a footbridge and made her way toward the circle of blue and white uniforms near the start line. Max stood in running shorts and a tank top amid eight lanky boys, charging them for this last race of the season. He'd woken her this morning practicing his pep talk as he shaved in the bathroom.

Stepping out of her heels and spreading the blanket across the grass, she listened to Max, tickled at his excitement.

"This is a special day, gentlemen. You each have the opportunity to make history for your school. Now I know we aren't favored. I know y'all think the Raiders over there are an awesome squad—and they are—but anything can happen at a conference championship. What's the most important thing? Somebody tell me."

"Having fun?" offered the smallest boy on the team.

"Well, yeah. But *after* having fun."

"Breathing," said Patrick Mullins, truest athlete of the bunch and oldest son of Barry Mullins, Vi's sergeant in Criminal Investigations Division. Patrick would be attending Davidson next year on a track scholarship.

"That's it," Max said. "Breathe, gentlemen. That's all I want you to think about out there. Filling your lungs with sweet oxygen. Now it's thirty minutes till the gun. Go warm up." As the boys took off from the start line Max jogged over to Vi's blanket.

"You came," he said.

"Wouldn't have missed it."

That wasn't entirely true. She would've missed it had Sgt. Mullins not left a message on her cell phone saying he needed to see her at the cross-country meet to "discuss things."

"You look cute, honey," she said. "Just don't let your package hang out of those itsy bitsy shorts."

Max grinned, said, "Violet King, you better watch that mouth." He leaned down, kissed her, and ran off toward the footbridge to rejoin the team. As Vi watched him go, someone called her name.

"Violet! Hey, sweetie, how *are* you?"

She saw Judy Hardin walking toward her from the scoring

station. Judy was a magpie, the loquacious mother of Josh Hardin, a junior and the second fastest runner on the team behind Patrick. As Vi rose and met Judy in the grass, the tall redhead bent down and hugged her crushingly around the neck.

She wore a sweatshirt with "MOORESVILLE MAMA" in block letters across the front. "Go Blue Devils!" was stenciled on each cheek with glittery blue face paint.

"So you finally came to a meet," Judy said. "Big day for the Blue Devils, huh?"

"Sure is. You know Max is—"

"Josh could hardly sleep last night. You know he's got a pretty good shot at making all-conference today. That's what everyone keeps telling me. Yeah, I'm so nervous for him. I feel like *I'm* running, you know? Isn't that crazy?"

"It is nerve-racking being a—"

"Well, don't you look darling in your suit?" Judy took the cuff of Vi's black blazer and rubbed the wool between her fingers. "Is this like official detective wear?"

"Oh, no, it's just—"

"So tell me, does it just totally blow your mind that you're chasing Andrew Thomas? I mean, whoever thought that you, little Violet King, would be mixed up with that monster? I taught you in Sunday school for heaven's sake, and you could be famous when this is all said and done! You better not forget me when you write your book and movie and do the whole—"

"I don't really think of it like that, Judy."

"And I see you on the news every night. I mean, you never talk or anything, but they always show you at that poor family's house." Judy winked and nudged Vi with her elbow. "So can you give me some inside scoop? Oh, you know I'm only kidding! You thought I was serious! Ha-ha! I know you can't talk about the details of the case! I'm not naïve!"

Vi saw Barry Mullins coming toward them. She wished he would walk faster.

"Judy, I'm sorry, I have to—"

"And Max is so good with the boys. Josh was telling me the other day that he liked Coach King so much better than that weirdo who coached last year. I mean—"

"Hello, ladies," Sgt. Mullins rumbled. It was the first time Vi had felt relieved to see her boss. "Sorry to bust up your conversation, but Judy, I need to speak with Violet privately."

"Uh-oh. Gotta have a powwow about the big case?"

Sgt. Mullins only smiled and Vi smiled and Judy's smile mutated into chagrin.

She slunk back toward the scoring station.

"Walk with me, Viking."

The sergeant and his investigator strolled through the grass beyond the start line. The leaders in the girls' championship were coming down off the first mile of the course and Vi listened as someone called out the mile-split for each runner.

In a fatherly fashion, Sgt. Mullins took hold of her arm above the elbow.

"I just talked to Bradley," Sgt. Mullins said. "We got an AFIS hit off that partial."

"You're kidding."

"Came back with a Luther Kite. White male. Thirty-two years old. Last known address is his parents' house, Thirteen Kill Devil Road, Ocracoke, North Carolina. Ever been to Ocracoke?"

"No sir."

"Well, we're going tomorrow."

"We?"

"Yes ma'am."

"I'll go beat out a search warrant. I mean we've got probable cause just with the partial. Then we show Jenna and John David Lancing the AFIS photograph, maybe get an ID. That right there's the foundation of our case."

"Ease down, Viking. We just want to talk to the parents. For all we know, they haven't seen their son in years. Last thing we need to do is bust in there with a SWAT team and tear the place apart. You could forget any help from them after that."

They walked again. Vi smiled at the flushed face of each high school girl who ran by.

"Great job," she said to a Mooresville runner named Holly.

"So how you holding up, Vi?" Sgt. Mullins asked. It took her aback. She'd never discerned anything approaching concern from her sergeant. For the two and a half years she'd worked in CID he'd maintained a hard unreadable veneer. This shred of kindness moved her and she stopped and looked up at him.

"I'm all right, sir. Thank you for asking." Sgt. Mullins stared down at her, stroking his thick dark mustache. She saw the doubt resurfacing in his eyes.

"You want to take it away from me, don't you?" she said. "You don't think I can—"

"Viking, I wouldn't take you off this case if you begged me. Now don't make me regret letting a woman handle this."

Sgt. Mullins walked away and Vi stood watching the race.

Across the creek, Max led the team in jumping jacks.

A runner limped by, stricken with cramps, red-faced and crying.

Vi wished Sgt. Mullins had taken her off the case and she burned with self-hate and shame.

CHAPTER 28

In a manila folder entitled "THE MINUTES" I came at last to the following string of journal entries.

It was 1:30 A.M. and my eyes burned with strain.

With the moon directly overhead I lay back against the cold windshield and read Orson's tiny scrawl in the minor light.

> *Woodside, Vermont: November 1, 1992*
>
> Sat in my booth at the pub all afternoon, read the most atrocious collection of papers I've ever had the misfortune to grade (coffee better today). Highlight was the piece on gladiators. Curious amount of detail on the lunch interlude executions. Well researched. Author thoroughly interested in his subject matter. Hmm. Awarded him a C+, because, let's face it, it was still a real piece of shit.

<u>Woodside, Vermont: November 6, 1992</u>

Called on our execution expert in class today. Never do that again. He turned red, wouldn't answer me, look at me. Stopped him on the way out of class and apologized for embarrassing him. What a peculiar kid. Asked him if he liked beer. He said no. Coffee? No. Finally, just asked what the fuck he did like, and he smiled sheepishly, said pancakes. We're having pancakes tomorrow.

<u>Woodside, Vermont: November 7, 1992</u>

Met this Luther kid at the Champlain Diner. Had breakfast for dinner. Think he was suspicious of why I wanted to see him outside of class. For the first twenty minutes I bored him to tears with a slew of questions, like where he was from, where he lived in Woodside, if he liked school . . . he was having a terrible time, so I mentioned how much I'd enjoyed reading his term paper. That brightened him up, started asking all sorts of things about the gladiator fights, Caligula. Told him about my thesis, shared some of my theories. He was very impressed. We were waiting for the waitress to bring the check when this woman passed by our table. Real pretty thing. Watched Luther watch her, and I saw it. Hard to put into words. Let's just say I sensed something in him, in those three seconds his eyes followed the movements of this Woodside knockout. When he looked back at me, I couldn't help but smile. His black eyes had become . . . reptilian. I thought Luther was going to say something, but he just blushed.

He'll do.

<u>Woodside, Vermont: December 9, 1992</u>

Last day of classes. Haven't spoken to Mr. Kite in a month. On the way out of class, told him I looked forward to seeing him next semester. Said he wasn't coming back. Flunked out. That shy, ashamed, little boy again. Made sure to get his home address. Maybe I'll take him to the desert next summer.

Ocracoke Island, North Carolina: June 11, 1993

Been following LK around this island for two days. What fun! Lives with his parents in an old, stone house on the sound. Last night at 10:30, he went for a walk by himself. If he goes again tonight, I'll take him.

CHAPTER 29

In Swan Quarter Vi boarded the last ferry of the day. Once the vessel had cleared the pilings, she grabbed the loaf of moldy bread Max had suggested she take and stepped out of the Cherokee.

She strolled back to the stern where a flock of chatty gulls tailed the boat. As the wharf and timber pylons diminished in the wake, Vi untwined the twist tie and pinched off a chunk of bread. The moment she extended her arm a fat gull swooped down and grabbed her offering in its beak.

As she fed the birds and watched the coastal plain of North Carolina shrink into a fiber of green, she thanked God for the people she loved. She prayed for Max, for her parents, for strength, and lastly for her sergeant's recovery.

Barry Mullins had taken his son, Patrick, out for barbecue after winning the cross-country championship last night. They were both in the hospital this morning with food poisoning, so Vi would be interviewing the Kites on her own.

A little boy came and stood beside her. She noticed him watching and asked if he'd like to feed the seagulls. When he nodded she handed him a piece of bread.

"Just lift it up like this. They'll come right down and steal it."

The boy lifted the fuzzy-blue bread and gasped when a gull snatched it. He looked up at Vi and grinned. She gave him the rest of the loaf and walked to the bow.

It was near dusk now and when she looked west she could no longer see the mainland. Eastward, the Pamlico Sound stretched on into a horizon of gray chop with no indication of the barrier islands that lay ahead.

Again she thought of the woman who'd been hanged at the Bodie Island Lighthouse. The image had been with her all day thanks to a tasteless photograph she'd seen on the front page of a tabloid. She wondered if praying for the dead made any difference.

Clutching the railing, she stared down at the water racing beneath the boat.

The engine clatter, the cry of the gulls, the briny stench of the sound engulfed her.

On the assumption that prayer was retroactive, she closed her eyes and prayed for the fifth time that day that the woman hadn't suffered.

The sun sank into the sound.

Vi checked her watch, saw that she'd been on the water now for more than two hours. The village couldn't be far. As the sky and sound turned the same sunless shade of slate, she imagined Max or even Sgt. Mullins standing here beside her in the mild headwind. She wouldn't mind her sergeant's patronization right now and she thought, *I was doing fine until the sun went down. Just like staying with Mamaw and Papaw when I was ten and the home-sickness that set in after dark and the crying on the phone begging Daddy to come get me and him saying no baby you'll feel better in the morning.*

A light winked on in the east—the Ocracoke Light.

Vi turned away and walked back to the Jeep.

In her briefcase in the backseat there were photographs to memorize—bearded, bald, fat, skinny, mustached, and clean shaven—the mugs of Luther Kite and Andrew Thomas.

CHAPTER 30

One of the stewardesses on my flight into Charlotte was a North Carolina native and her southern accent moved me to tears. I hadn't heard a true southern drawl in years. It isn't the back-woods sheep-fucking twang Hollywood makes it out to be. A real North Carolina accent is sweet and subtle and when you haven't heard one in seven years, it sounds like coming home.

My flight landed in Charlotte Douglas International Airport just before midnight and by 1:00 A.M. on Tuesday I was hurtling north in a five-speed Audi with I-77 all to myself. I thought be-ing home again would flood me with nostalgia, but as I cruised through the piney piedmont darkness my only sensation was the ulcer that had burned in my gut since leaving Haines Junction.

At Exit 28 I left the interstate, and driving the familiar back-roads toward Lake Norman started catching glimpses of the water through the trees. When I finally saw my mailbox in the distance and the tall pines that lined my old driveway like sentries, I pulled over onto the side of the road and turned off the engine.

I walked along the shoulder of Loblolly Lane until I reached the mailbox. My gravel road had been paved, and two hundred yards away at the end of the drive cars were parked in front of my house, their chrome reflecting the warm illumination of a porch light. It astounded me that someone had the gall to take up residence in the home of a suspected serial murderer. How did they sleep at night? Did it never occur to them that Andrew Thomas might one day come home? I'll bet they got my place for a steal.

I jogged a ways down the drive but then thought better of it. Stopping on the smooth blacktop, I inhaled the scent of pines and remembered walking up this drive with Beth and Walter ten Decembers ago, placing *luminarias* in preparation for a Christmas party.

As I stared at my old home, part of me thought, *Fuck this place. I'm not that man anymore.* But the other part of me wanted to stand on the deck and see Lake Norman again and the blue light across the water at the end of Walter Lancing's pier, wanted to pretend he could just stroll into 811 Loblolly Lane and climb the staircase up to his old bedroom. And when he woke in the morning maybe he'd be that writer again. Maybe he'd have his name back. Maybe his mother and Walter would be alive and the events of seven years ago nothing more than the plot of his latest novel.

He'd just wanted the sensation, however fleeting, of being Andrew Thomas the Almost Famous Writer, when that name was the best thing he owned.

In the morning I took I-40 through Raleigh, then Highway 64 into eastern North Carolina and the flattening coastal plain, through towns called Tarboro, Plymouth, and Scuppernong. At sunset I crossed the Alligator River, then the sounds of Croatan and Roanoke. The eastern fringe of North Carolina had softened into marsh and swamp as it dissolved into the Atlantic.

Sixty-four ended at the Outer Banks in the town of Whalebone, and from there I glimpsed the Bodie Island Lighthouse to the south rising up out of the pines. Coupled with Orson's journal entries, the fact that my former fiancée was found hanging from that lighthouse erased any doubt I may have had about whether Luther Kite was currently in operation somewhere on the Outer Banks.

I took Highway 12 south for seventy miles through the beach communities of Rodanthe, Little Kinnakeet, Buxton, and finally Hatteras Village, the end of the line.

I caught the 9:00 P.M. ferry to Ocracoke Island and as the noisy engines gurgled through the water I walked up to the starboard.

I'd never been to Ocracoke. According to a brochure I'd picked up at a gas station in Buxton, it was a skinny island, sixteen miles long, less than half a mile wide in places. Its seven hundred residents inhabited a village at the south end on a small harbor that faced the sound. The brochure had bragged that it was the quaintest remotest village in all of the Outer Banks.

In light of Karen's very public execution, an unsettling possibility occurred to me as the ferry crossed Hatteras Inlet and the full devastating reality of what I was doing set in: *What if my coming to the Outer Banks isn't a surprise at all for Luther but precisely what he wants me to do? What if those murders were for me? What if they were bait?*

Now the ferry neared the tip of Ocracoke, the wind whipping cold and salty in from the sea.

I leaned against the railing and stared out into the soundside darkness.

OCRACOKE

CHAPTER 31

At 6:00 A.M. Wednesday on the third floor of the Harper Castle B&B, Violet knelt over the toilet in her suite, wondering if it was the flounder she had last night that was ravaging her stomach. After fifteen minutes of dry heaves she went back to bed and slept until ten o'clock.

She felt much better when she woke again. Turning over onto her left side, she stared through the window at the bay around which the village of Ocracoke had been built. In the windless cloudy melancholy of the morning, Silver Lake Harbor maintained a veritable supernatural stillness.

As Vi rolled up her sheer black hose she noted the cheerful island décor of the tiny room—the pastel painting of a five-masted schooner in rough seas above the headboard, the coral wallpaper patterned with little white sand dollars. *Max would love this place*, she thought, placing a small tape recorder into her purse and fastening her shoulder rig: a holstered .45 Smith & Wesson with a twin magazine-carrier. Max had surprised her with the horsehide holster last February on Valentine's Day.

Vi primped in the bathroom, dusting her cheeks with blush and adjusting a purple suede headband that matched her suit. Then she grabbed her purse and headed downstairs through the sprawling wood "castle," across oak floors, between walls of cypress, into the dining room, lured by the promise of a complimentary continental breakfast.

The buffet had been heavily grazed. She chose one of the three remaining bran muffins and filled a glass with cranberry juice. Except for the snoozing old man (his mouth dropped wide open, an *Ocracoke Observer* still in his grasp), the dining room was empty.

Vi sat down at a table near the window so she could look out across the small harbor, lined with hoary docks. On the opposite shore the Swan Quarter ferry churned through the narrow outlet into the open waters of the Pamlico Sound, bound for the mainland with its cargo of departing tourists.

Vi glanced at her watch: 10:50. Max's planning period. She took out her cell and called him. She got his voicemail, left a brief message: "Hey, baby. Just wanted to check in. I'm getting ready to go interview the Kites now. Hope you're having a good day. I'll call you tonight. Love you."

From the outside the Harper Castle B&B looks childish and fanciful with its gabled roofs, asymmetrical right wing, and imposing façade of seven dormers. Vi looked out the window of her Cherokee up to the fourth-story cupola, the penthouse of the establishment, and wondered what a night up there might cost. Maybe she could convince Max to bring her back for their anniversary next June. There was so much she wanted to see—the lighthouse, the British Cemetery, the Banker ponies, Portsmouth Island.

She turned out onto Silver Lake Drive, the road that circumscribed the harbor. A guidebook to the island had warned of traffic jams in the village during the summer months, but this bleak November morning it seemed every bit its reputation as the most sequestered outpost on the North Carolina coast.

At the corner of Silver Lake and Highway 12, a man was selling conch shells out of his truck bed for five dollars apiece. Vi would've pulled over and bought one, but she already felt guilty for sleeping late and Sgt. Mullins would be expecting her full report this evening.

Though the island of Ocracoke is less than a mile and a half across at its widest point, it took Vi thirty-five minutes to find the mailbox of Rufus and Maxine Kite. She couldn't see their house from the dead end of Kill Devil Road, their drive being a private overgrown affair that wound for a hundred yards through a stand of live oaks.

As she proceeded down the narrow drive, Spanish moss draped from the overhanging branches and swept across the windshield, its tuft of gray green filaments a living curtain. Though only ten minutes from the harbor (tourist garrison of the village) it felt much farther, seeming to exist in its own timeless universe.

Driving through these sad old trees made something sink inside of Vi. This unpillaged tract of land radiated a sleepy southern gloom and it pervaded her soul.

The dirt road emerged from the thicket and there stood the sound and the gray of the sky and the deeper gray of the crumbling granite that comprised the prodigious home of Rufus and Maxine Kite, a gothic residence that looked as though it belonged on a dreary English moor.

There was no driveway. Wild beach grass had overrun the lawn and two ancient live oaks guarded the house, their gnarled branches nearly touching the disintegrating masonry of the third floor like arthritic fingers.

Remnants of a stone path, broken by roots, meandered between the trees to the front door.

The house was three stories of rock, as if God had cast off a gigantic block of stone, dropped it on the edge of the sound. Great chimneys spiked like horns from each end.

Vi thought the edifice resembled some alien skull, its teeming windows like hollowed eye sockets, portals into darkness.

CHAPTER 32

Vi parked under one of the oaks beside the only other vehicle on the premises, a rusting Dodge pickup truck that might've been sixty years old. As she followed the path toward the front door she gazed up at the tall black windows and the cupola.

The house oozed vacancy.

A twinge of fear and guilt shook her. She'd promised Sgt. Mullins she'd hook up with local law enforcement, get the sheriff, or at least a deputy to escort her on the Kite interview. But the last thing she wanted was some good old boy from down east tagging along, patronizing her. She was fully capable of handling this on her own.

Vi stopped at the door, smoothed herself, ran her fingers through her short blond hair, and knocked.

Something scurried through the grass behind her.

Turning, she saw an emaciated gray cat streak up the nearest oak. It settled on a disfigured limb and watched her through large yellow eyes. She'd seen another cat skulking the parking lot of the Harper Castle. According to the concierge, Ocracoke was rampant with feral felines.

When Vi turned back she started.

The door had been opened and in the threshold stood a tall old man, his kind face brimming with years and creases. Slightly hunched, he looked down at her through sunken black eyes, his white hair long but scarce.

"Who are you?" he asked.

Vi reached into her purse, withdrew her badge, and held it close so he could see.

"Sir, my name is Violet King. I'm a detective with the Davidson Police Department. May I speak with you?"

Rufus Kite looked up from the badge and beamed a toothless smile.

"Come in, young lady."

As Vi entered the house of Rufus and Maxine Kite she reached into her Barbour coat and unsnapped the latchet on her holster.

After Rufus closed the front door it took a moment for Vi's eyes to acclimate to the dimness. The effluvium of mildew permeated the home—a bouquet of age, neglect, rotting mahogany, wet stone. Her heels slid on the dusty floor.

Rufus helped her out of the coat and hung it on a tottering coatrack beside the door. Then he led her through the dusky foyer into the living room and offered her a seat in an armchair beside a massive dormant fireplace.

Rufus eased himself down onto a crushed velvet couch, once gold, now a badly-faded flaxen. Light trickled through those tall windows, weak and dismal.

"Beautiful!" Rufus yelled.

"What?" a voice carried down the staircase.

"We have company!"

"Be right down!"

"Would you care for anything to drink or—"

"No, thank you." Vi was sinking into the armchair, so she scooted forward onto its ottoman. "I'll wait for Mrs. Kite," Vi said. "So I don't have to start over."

"Of course." Rufus smiled, all gums. Vi smiled back. Rufus reached into the patch pocket of his flannel shirt and took out his teeth. He slipped them in and smiled again. "Your first visit to Ocracoke?"

"Yessir. Y'all have a lovely island."

"Ocracoke is quite a place. Particularly this time of year when the dreadful tourists are gone. How old are you if you don't mind? I can get away with inappropriate questions at my age."

"Twenty-six."

"My goodness, you're just a baby."

Footfalls on the steps drew their attention to Maxine Kite, carefully making her way down the creaking staircase. At the bottom of the steps she stopped to catch her breath and straighten the scallop-edged collar of her canary sweatshirt with an appliqué bunny rabbit on the front.

Vi rose and walked back into the foyer, her stomach cramping at the prospect of telling this frail elderly woman what her son was suspected of doing.

At sixty-two inches, Vi rarely had the occasion to tower over anyone, but she found herself looking down into the sweet somewhat startled eyes of Maxine Kite.

When Vi had introduced herself and helped Maxine over to the couch beside her husband, she returned to the ottoman.

"Mr. and Mrs. Kite, would y'all mind if I recorded our conversation?" Vi asked, pulling the tape recorder from her purse.

"Actually, I would," Rufus said, "since we don't know what this is all about."

"Oh. Okay." Vi dropped the tape recorder in her purse and

crossed her legs. "When was the last time either of you saw or spoke with your son, Luther?"

Rufus and Maxine glanced at each other. Then Rufus squeezed his wife's hand and looked back at Vi.

"We haven't had contact with our son in seven years."

"Do you know where he is?"

"No ma'am."

"Where did you see him last?"

Rufus leaned back into the couch and put his arm around Maxine. She laid her head on his chest and stared into the hearth as he stroked her bony shoulder with thick liver-spotted fingers.

"I love my boy," Maxine said. "But he isn't like most people, see. He drifts around. Doesn't need the same things we need. Like family and—"

"Stability," Rufus cut in. "He never wanted to settle down. Wasn't for him. And he knew it. He certainly knew it. That's admirable in a way. To know your mind right off."

"He's a good, good boy. Happier on his own, I think. A true loner. Did he do something, Miss King?"

Vi sighed. The stench of fish flowed into the living room from the kitchen.

"Thing is, we aren't sure yet. We lifted Luther's fingerprints from a crime scene, so we'd just like to talk with him and—"

"What sort of crime scene?" Maxine asked.

"That's uh . . . I'm not allowed to divulge that at this point. So where did you see him last?"

"Here," Maxine said. "It was Christmas Eve and we hadn't heard from him in a while, but that wasn't so strange. After he quit school, we never saw much of him." The old woman brushed a wisp of white hair from her cheek, which still rested against her husband's chest. "Rufus and I were in the kitchen peeling shrimp. We always have a special supper on Christmas Eve. I heard logs shifting in the fireplace, rushed out here, and there was my boy, standing by the hearth, poking the fire. He asked me, 'All right if I spend Christmas with you, Mama?' "

Maxine smiled, her eyes gone heartsick, swallowing as if she had a lump in her throat.

"He left the next morning," Rufus said. "We haven't heard from him since. Sometimes, I think he's dead."

"No, he isn't dead, Sweet-Sweet. Luther just doesn't reckon time the way we do. I think seven years to him don't mean a hill of beans. He'll come home again when it pleases him. That's just his way."

"Did Luther have any close friends in Ocracoke?"

"Luther was never interested in making friends. Like I said, he's a loner."

"No, Beautiful, remember Scottie?"

"Manning?"

"No, Claude and Helen's boy."

"Who's this?" Vi asked.

"Fellow named Scottie Myers. A real local. Lives over on Back Road. Used to be a fisherman when you could make a living at it. I think he waits tables at Howard's now. He and Luther are the same age. When they were in high school the two of them used to go crabbing with Claude on the weekends."

"I don't think they were that good of friends, Rufus."

"Well, I'm just trying to help Miss King. I mean, is that helpful to you?"

"Oh, absolutely. Now you said he worked at Howard's? What's that?"

"It's a pub on Twelve where all the locals go. And a fair number of tourists, too. Bring your appetite." He spread his thumb and index finger an inch apart. "The fried oysters are yea big."

"Sweet-Sweet, I'm tired," Maxine whined.

"Miss, I don't know if you have more questions, but maybe we could finish this—"

"I could come back tomorrow."

"It'd have to be later in the afternoon," Maxine said. "After five o'clock."

"That's fine." Vi smiled. "Well, look, y'all have been so helpful. I know this wasn't easy."

Rufus said, "Our pleasure."

Vi came to her feet and lifted her purse.

"Y'all have one of the most interesting homes I think I've ever seen. When was it built?"

"Eighteen-seventeen," Rufus said. "One of the oldest structures on the island. You can see the lighthouse and the sea from the cupola."

Vi slipped her purse over her shoulder.

"Would I be imposing to ask for a tour of this magnificent house?"

"Perhaps another time, Miss King," Maxine said. "I was on my way to a nap when you knocked."

Rufus kissed his wife's forehead and struggled to his feet.

"Let me walk you to your car," he said. "I'd give you the tour myself, but I'm breading four flounders in the kitchen, and they're liable to spoil on me if I keep dillydallying."

As Vi opened the door of the Jeep and tossed her purse into the passenger seat, Rufus said, "Miss King, I just wanted to thank you."

"What for?"

Rufus leaned against the dirty Jeep.

A raindrop splattered on Vi's cheek.

"Not telling my wife the nature of the crime scene. Maxine isn't well. She didn't need to hear about it, and I'm grateful to you. You said you're from Davidson, North Carolina?"

"Yessir."

"I know why you're here. Did my boy . . . he kill that family?"

Vi shut the door, reached out, touched Rufus's arm.

"Mr. Kite, we really don't know at this juncture. That's the truth." Rufus nodded, patted her hand. "But would it surprise you if he had?"

The old man exhaled a soft whimper.

"Come back tomorrow," he said, then walked away through the weeds toward the water.

As she drove away from that morose eroding home, Vi watched Rufus Kite in the rearview mirror. Through falling mist she could see him standing on the bank, staring out across the leaden sound.

CHAPTER 33

My vision faded in upon the cottage-cheese ceiling paint of my little room. It was Thursday, my second morning in Ocracoke, and I'd been roused from sleep by the whine of a vacuum cleaner in the adjacent suite.

This was the sixth morning I'd woken in an unfamiliar place. Back home the first things my waking eyes beheld were the support beams of my cabin—a recurring comfort that soothed me like the familiar respiration of a sleeping spouse. It pained me not to see those rafters, that instead of my home in the Yukon wilderness I was coming to consciousness in this cheerless overblown room with its sand dollar–patterned wallpaper, mawkish painting of a ship in stormy seas above the headboard, and clear glass lamp on the chest of drawers, its base filled with seashells.

Someone knocked on the door and called out in a Spanish accent, "Housekeeping!"

I stumbled out of bed and yelled back through the door, "Not today, thank you!"

From my third-floor window I glanced out upon the harbor and the village. The rainfall that had whispered throughout the night had ended and Silver Lake Drive showed patches of dry pavement.

I'd sadly learned yesterday that the free continental breakfast offered each morning was not worth the energy it required to walk downstairs to the dining room and claim it. And since I'd gorged myself on fifteen-cent shrimp and beer last night at a restaurant called The Pelican, I decided to just skip breakfast and get on with it.

I rented a bicycle from the Harper Castle office and set out from the inn under a moody cloud deck that looked pregnant with rain. In the raw and blustery morning I pedaled the ungainly bike alongside the harbor. Across the water, the ferry rammed into the pylons as it tried to dock. I could hear the gulls crying from half a mile away, those ferry leeches.

When I glanced back I could now see the lighthouse peeking above the oaks. Only sixty-three feet high, it rose humbly above its community, a whitewashed brick tower that had stood its ground since 1823, second oldest beacon in the country.

That old timer was selling shells again at the corner of Silver Lake and Highway 12. I smiled and nodded to him as I passed by, but he returned my friendliness with a glowering stare.

After several blocks of restaurants and cottages and B&Bs, I turned onto Old Beach Road, then Middle Road, and found myself once again in the residential quarter of Ocracoke.

These yaupon and live oak–lined streets seemed all that remained of the island's soul.

I came at last to the termination of Kill Devil Road, a worn-out street, cracked and embedded with oyster shells, more than a mile from the nearest residence.

Yesterday, after leaving my car several hundred yards up the street, I'd trespassed through the Kites' grove of live oaks, right up to the edge of the wood. Lying down in the sand and slimy leaves, cold drizzle soaking in, I'd watched the stone house as the afternoon darkened into evening.

No one came.

No one left.

When night set in I crept up behind one of the contorted live oaks in the front yard and peered through the windows into the living room. Yellowmadder firelight lit the mahogany walls and the feeble frames of an old man and an old woman, statuesque on their old couch, staring into the fire.

After an hour of watching them sit there, inert, I crawled back toward the wood, fully concealed in the luxuriance of weeds that had subjugated the front lawn. As I walked back to the Audi, my course of action became clear and though I hated the idea, though it entailed a major gamble, it was my only option.

So now, a day later, I pedaled beyond the mailbox of Rufus and Maxine Kite, down the dirt road that led to their soundside home. Queasy and cotton-mouthed, I hadn't tried anything like this in years. My life in northwestern Canada had been based upon the eradication of risk and I feared I'd lost the nerve for this sort of thing.

A wet veil of Spanish moss brushed through my hair as I exited the grove of live oaks. Through swaying beach grass I rode on, disregarding my palpitant heart, the Pamlico Sound now in full gaping view behind that ancient house of stone.

A heady north wind blew in from the sound.

Whitecaps bloomed in the chop.

That old Dodge pickup truck, parked yesterday under one of the oaks, was gone.

I left the bicycle in the grass beside the wrought iron railing and ascended four steps to the stoop, wishing I had the cold reassuring weight of the Glock in the pocket of my leather jacket. But in all likelihood I wouldn't need it. From what I'd observed yesterday, Rufus and Maxine Kite suffered lives of lassitude and seclusion.

As I knocked against the door I caught the scent of woodsmoke. Looking up, I saw a thin gray cloud rising out of the granite chimney.

I knocked again.

A minute passed.

No one answered.

Reaching down, I palmed the tarnished doorknob, surprised to feel it turn in my grasp.

The wide oak door swung inward.

CHAPTER 34

I stepped inside the house of Rufus and Maxine Kite and closed the door behind me. Having had no prior intention of entering this house uninvited, the part of me grown intolerant of risk screamed to leave.

I called out, "Is anyone home?"

To my immediate right an archway opened into a long living room with a hearth at the far end, on the grate of which glowed a bed of bright embers.

A grandfather clock loomed in a nearby corner. Its second hand twitched every four seconds.

I glanced left into the dining room, the table set for three. When I touched the saucer at one of the place settings my finger disturbed an alarming layer of dust. It had settled in the bottoms of the wineglasses, on the surfaces of each plate, even upon the yellowed tablecloth.

Strings of cobweb were everywhere.

I proceeded deeper into the house, past a staircase that climbed into darkness. The foyer narrowed into a corridor and under the stairs I noticed a little door in the wall.

The air grew damp and stagnant, fraught with the odor of must.

I entered the kitchen.

Through the windows behind the sink I could see the sound. On the breakfast table a row of grayish blue fillets and a thin-bladed filleting knife had been left out on a cutting board beside a glass mixing bowl half-filled with cornmeal.

Standing over the sink, I looked into the weedy backyard that sloped down to the water. There was a plot of tilled earth near the house that might've once been a shade garden, though nothing grew there now.

A thoroughly rotten dock stretched out into the sound. Its collapse seemed inevitable when the next storm blew in.

Leave and come back. You should not be here like this.

I started back toward the front door.

A tiny old woman stood in the kitchen doorway.

She appeared to have just woken, her pearly mane in such extraordinary disarray it seemed to be more the result of an explosion than a nap. I could see the silhouette of her spindly frame behind the threadbare fabric of her nightgown.

Barefooted, she walked into the kitchen, opened a cabinet, took down a tin of ground coffee.

"Sleep all right?" she asked.

"Um, I uh—"

"You're in my way. Go sit down."

I took a seat at the table as she filled the coffeepot with water from the faucet.

"Now this isn't that fancy shit. So if you've turned into one of those dandies who has to have their coffee soaked and freshly ground and God knows what else, tell me now."

"Maxwell House is fine."

Mrs. Kite noticed the fillets on the cutting board.

"God*damn* him!"

She set the coffeepot down hard on the butcher block countertop and pointed at the raw fish.

"Rufus is going to ruin our lunch. You can't leave fish out. You CAN'T! LEAVE! FISH! OUT!" She sighed. "Your coffee will have to wait, Luther."

Sitting down across from me at the breakfast table, she picked up one of the fillets.

"I don't believe it," she said. "There's no chili powder in this cornmeal. You know, I'm starting to think your father doesn't know how to fry bluefish. And be*sides*, you're not supposed to *fry* bluefish."

She dropped the fillet and stood up. From the spice rack on the counter she plucked a small plastic bottle and returned to her chair. When she'd shaken half the bottle of chili powder into the cornmeal and stirred the mixture with her finger, she looked up at me, bewildered.

"Who are you?" she asked, a completely different person.

"My name's Alex. Alex Young. I came here to—"

"Who let you in?"

"You did, Mrs. Kite. I knew your son, Luther, at Woodside College."

"Luther? He's here?"

"No ma'am. I haven't seen him in a long time. We were friends at school. Is he in Ocracoke right now? I'd really like to see him."

As the wave of lucidity engulfed her, her eyes traded confusion for sorrow. She pinched the bridge of her nose between her eyes as though her head hurt.

"I'm sorry. Sometimes my brain gets scrambled. What's your name?"

"Alex. Do you know where—"

"And you were friends with my Luther?"

"Yes ma'am. At Woodside. I came here to see him."

"He's not here."

"Well, do you know where he is? I'd love to—"

"I haven't seen my son in seven years."

Her eyes blinked a dozen times in rapid succession. Then she grabbed a handful of cornmeal, sprinkled it onto a fillet, and began patting it into the meat.

She slammed her hand down on the table and my heart jumped.

"Luther, ass out of the chair, bring me a glass of water."

I got up and walked over to the sink. It overflowed with smelly dishes.

"When are you heading down to Portsmouth?" she asked as I washed a dirty glass.

"I don't know."

I filled the glass from the tap and offered it to her.

"What's this?" she asked.

"You asked for a glass of—"

"The hell I did. Get that out of my face." I set the glass on the counter. "If you *are* going down to Portsmouth today, I want you to go before it gets late. You got no business being out on the water after dark. And let me tell you another thing. I want the lodge left in immaculate condition. Your father and I are thinking of going down next weekend, and I don't intend to spend my time cleaning up your shit."

She started on another fillet and as I watched her in the dreary natural light of the kitchen I thought of my grandfather, Alexander, stricken with Alzheimer's in his late seventies. I knew the symptoms well and in the course of five minutes it had become clear to me that some form of dementia was ravaging the brain of Maxine Kite. It appalled me that she'd been left alone.

I started for the doorway.

"Where you going?" she asked.

"The bathroom. Mom."

Leaving Luther's mother to her bluefish, I stepped out of the kitchen into the dark corridor. A door stood cracked at the end and as I walked toward it the house resumed its unnerving silence.

I could no longer hear Mrs. Kite in the kitchen or the moan of the wind outside.

At the end of the hall I pushed open the door and entered a small bookless library. A dying fire warmed the study, its barren bookshelves gray with dust.

An old and soiled American flag was displayed behind glass on one wall. It was shopworn, nearly colorless, riddled with holes made from fire, and so defiled I felt ashamed for looking at it.

On the stone above the hearth, a photograph caught my attention. It had been framed and mounted. Approaching the fire, I looked up, surprised to see that it was a photograph of the Outer Banks, taken from a satellite. I recognized the long skinny isle of Ocracoke by the harbor at its southern tip.

Of greater interest, however, was the collection of uninhabited islands a few miles south across the shallow inlet. I read their names: Casey. Sheep. Whalebone. Portsmouth.

Portsmouth. Turning away from the photograph, I felt the prickling exhilaration of discovery. But my heart stopped as my gaze fell upon the wall opposite the hearth.

The black soulless eyes of Luther stared back at me, grotesquely caricatured by the amateurish rendering. Though he was only a teenager in the oil painting, the vacuum in his eyes was unmistakable, a haunting prophecy of what he would become.

I hurried out of the study, crept past the kitchen where Mrs. Kite was still preparing her fish, and moved quietly through the foyer back out into the cold misty morning. Lifting the bike out of the grass, I mounted the wet seat and pedaled away between the live oaks.

CHAPTER 35

It started to rain on the way back to the Harper Castle—a metallic soul-icing drizzle. Riding into the parking lot, I threw down the bicycle and unlocked the trunk of the Audi. I opened the suitcase holding Orson's journals, and as I stood shivering in the steady rain came at last across the passage that had been chewing at my subconscious for six days, since my first encounter with it at Brawley's Self-Storage Co. in Lander, Wyoming.

When I'd finished reading over Orson's journal entry, I tingled with relief and fear.

I could feel it in my bones.

I had found Luther Kite.

> *Wyoming: July 4, 1993*
>   *Independence Day. Luther and I drove down to Rock Springs this evening to drink beer at a bar called The Spigot. Met this kid named Henry, a young man about*

*Luther's age. Shared a few pitchers with him. Said he was
working a ranch up near Pinedale for the summer. He got
"tow up" as they say 'round here. When he went to the
bathroom to puke, Luther asked if we could take him
home. Isn't that cute? He thinks of the cabin as home.*

*Well, it's 2:00 A.M., and Henry's in the shed right now,
sobering up for what will undoubtedly be the worst, longest,
and last night of his short life.*

*Luther's getting changed into his work clothes, and I'm
sitting out here on the front porch where the moon is full
and bright enough for me to journal by its light.*

*Tonight, on the drive back to the cabin, Luther invited
me to come spend a few weeks with him in Ocracoke over my
Christmas break. Wants me to meet his folks. Said they
have this lodge on a remote island that would be
perfect for the administration of painings.*

Yeah, he calls them painings. I don't know.

*There he goes, down to the shed. On account of it being
Luther's last night in Wyoming, he asked me if he could
have Henry all to himself. By all means, I said.*

I've probably done too good a job on this one.

Drenched and shivering, I biked over to the Community Store on Silver Lake Harbor and walked to the shack at the end of the dock.

The door was closed, but I heard the static of a weather radio spilling through the walls. The sign over the door read TATUM BOAT TOURS.

I knocked and waited.

A quarter mile across the water I saw the ridiculous façade of the Harper Castle and the Ocracoke Light beyond in the foggy distance.

The door finally opened and a white-bearded old salt looked

me up and down. He smiled and spoke in a coastal Carolina accent laced with Maine: "You're a sight there."

"Charlie Tatum?" I asked.

"All my life."

"Mr. Tatum, I was wondering if you could get me over to Portsmouth this afternoon?"

I glimpsed all the mercury fillings in his molars as he laughed.

"On a beautiful day like this?"

He motioned to the harbor, gray and untrafficked and filling with cold rain.

"Well, I mean, I know the conditions aren't ideal, but—"

"Day after tomorrow, probably the next time I'm going out. Besides, you don't want to visit Portsmouth when it's like this. Supposed to rain a few more hours as this low passes offshore. I was just listening to the forecast when you knocked."

"Mr. Tatum, I have to get to Portsmouth this afternoon."

"It'll still be there on Saturday."

Beth Lancing might not.

"Yes, but—"

"And look, forget the rain, come three o'clock this afternoon, that wind's gonna turn around and start blowing in off the sound at thirty knots. Three-, four-foot seas we're talking. Ain't safe in that boat." He pointed to the thirty-foot Island Hopper moored to the rotting timbers of the dock. "Ya, you don't want to be out there in that. For damn sure."

"Mr. Tatum—"

"*Cha*lie."

"Charlie. What do you charge for a boat ride to Portsmouth?"

"Twenty dollars a person."

"I'll give you two hundred to take me this afternoon."

He stared at me and blinked.

"Can't do it," he said, but his hesitation convinced me that he had a price.

"Five hundred dollars."

He grinned.

"Seven fifty."

He laughed.

"All right," he said, "but if it's all the same to you, I'd prefer we get you over there soon as possible. Before this wind turns around."

I wiped the condensation off my watch.

"It's one o'clock now," I said. "I'll be back in two hours."

As I walked back down the dock I noticed something following me in the water—a brown ramshackle pelican, grounded with a mangled wing. He watched me through small black eyes and I wondered what he thought of his old flying days, if he missed them, or just wrote them off as dreams.

CHAPTER 36

Back at the Harper Castle I took a hot shower and did not leave the steamy bathroom until the chill had been thoroughly driven from my bones. As I sat on the bedspread, tying the laces of my soggy tennis shoes, it dawned on me that I was utterly unprepared for my trip to Portsmouth.

I knew nothing of the island, had inadequate clothing for this raw November weather, and I was hunting for a madman without a weapon of any sort (my alias, Vincent Carmichael, didn't possess a gun permit, so it had been far too risky to smuggle my Glock, even in pieces, with my checked luggage).

I headed downstairs through the lobby and out the rear exit into the muddy parking lot. According to the visitor's guide, there was a bait and tackle shop on Highway 12 at the north end of the village that stocked the supplies I would need.

Three minutes later I pulled into the parking lot of Bubba's Bait and Tackle. A hundred yards farther up the highway, the village abruptly ended, and as I stared through the rain-beaded glass I could see where 12 continued on and on for the full thirteen remaining miles of Ocracoke, accompanied only by the sound, the dunes, and the sea.

The store was a tumult of overstimulation—three sea kayaks, a blue marlin, and a red canoe hung from the ceiling. Along the back wall stood a phalanx of fishing rods. Reels shined under glass at the front counter. I noticed an aisle devoted solely to tackle boxes, another to waders.

A T-shirt had been tacked to the wall above the register:

FISHED ALL DAY AT OCRACOKE INLET

AND ALL I CAUGHT WAS A BUZZ

A rotund young man dressed in camouflage, his bottom lip swollen with tobacco, emerged from behind the counter and asked if he could help me with anything. I recognized the rural distrust in his eyes and smelled the wintergreen Skoal.

"Are you Bubba?" I asked.

"I'm Bubba's boy. My name's Brian."

I told Brian I was going to Portsmouth this afternoon, that I might be spending the night, and that I'd be willing to purchase anything that would keep me from freezing my ass off in this bitter rain.

"You going to Portsmouth in a nor'easter?" he said. "Who'd you find to take you?"

"Just show me some camping gear, okay?"

Forty minutes later I stood at the counter, Brian behind the register, ringing up an ungodly assortment of camping equipment. He'd talked me into Moonstone raingear, a three-season, two-man tent by Sierra Design, a Marmot 30°F sleeping bag,

Nalgene water bottles, a WhisperLite stove, MSR fuel bottles, a PUR water filter, Patagonia fleece pants and jacket, Asolo boots, and the kicker, a 5500 cubic inch internal frame backpack by Osprey, just to catalogue the substantial purchases.

"Sell any maps of Portsmouth?" I asked as he swiped my credit card and handed it back to me. He reached under the counter, set one on the glass.

"Oh, I'm sorry. That fucked up the total, didn't it?"

Brian chuckled. "Mister, you just spent," he glanced at the receipt as it printed out, "a little under fifteen hundred dollars. The map's on me."

He tore off the credit card receipt and handed it to me.

I signed it, said, "I was hoping to eat a hot meal before I head out. Can you recommend something?"

"Right across the street. Place called Howard's. If you don't eat there at least twice when you come to Ocracoke, you've wasted your trip."

"I'll check it out." I handed back the receipt and looked down at the heap of gear on the floor. "Brian," I said, as he opened a can of Skoal and chose an earthy pinch, "you're telling me all this equipment is going to fit into that backpack?"

He shook the pinch of tobacco in his hand, inserted it into the pocket between his lower teeth and gums, and licked his tongue across his bottom lip.

"Oh sure," he said.

"Care to show me how?"

CHAPTER 37

Though Violet longed to tell him in person, she didn't know if she could hold out that long—through interviews with Scottie Myers and the Kites and reporting to Sgt. Mullins and the subsequent nine-hour return trip to Davidson. So as she sat in the Cherokee in the parking lot of Howard's Pub, she took out her cell and dialed Max's mobile.

He won't answer, she thought as the phone rang. It was Thursday afternoon, 2:15, which meant that sixth period had just begun—eleventh-grade honors English, his favorite class. Max was finishing up a unit on Poe (he always taught Poe in the vicinity of Halloween). She'd seen him reviewing his heavily-underlined text of "The Black Cat" the morning she left for Ocracoke.

It came as no surprise that Max didn't answer. He'd probably turned off his phone during class, but she wasn't so desperate yet as to leave voicemail. So instead she dropped the phone in the passenger seat, and sitting behind the wheel, rain pattering on the roof, rehearsed various ways of telling him.

Max, I'm pregnant . . . Max, we're pregnant . . . You're going to be a daddy . . . Max, I'm going to be a mommy . . . You know how before on the pregnancy tests, only one line appeared? Well, there were two today, baby.

Glowing, joy flushing her cheeks, she thought, *How strange to be on this dreary island, under these awful circumstances, when I come upon the happiest moment of my life.*

Even the rain turned beautiful. Even a nearby Dumpster. And especially that bathroom sink in her suite at the Harper Castle, upon which she'd set the pregnancy test and watched it declare her a mother.

She praised God and basked in euphoric eddies that kept coming and coming, eroding the lies she believed about herself—*you wouldn't be a good mother; you're just a child; you are unworthy, undeserving.* She saw her insecurities in plain unflinching light, glimpsed their cowardice, their impotence, their hiding places. She waxed powerful, immune, and it occurred to her, *Life could be so amazing if I always felt this way, if I weren't saddled by my dread of failure.*

Opening the door and stepping out into the rain, she encountered the sweetest image of all—the enormous calloused hands of her daddy, cupping his squirming grandchild.

Vi walked into Howard's Pub into the smell of frying fish and old smoke. The teenage hostess came out from behind the bar where she'd been watching a soap opera on one of the half-dozen televisions.

"Hello," she said, taking a menu from the podium. "One for lunch?"

"Actually, I'm here to see Scottie Myers. I understand he's working today?"

"He's in the kitchen. I'll get him for you."

As the hostess left to find Scottie, Vi strolled into the main dining room to absorb this unassuming pub that had been recommended to her five times since her arrival in Ocracoke. In one corner she spotted a Foosball table. In another, a dartboard. Pennants for every major collegiate and professional sports program hung from the wood beams of the ceiling.

A screened porch adjoined the dining room where a long-haired man, the pub's sole customer, occupied a table under one of the glowing space heaters.

Howard's exuded the energy of an old baseball mitt, this local hub that never closed, not even for Christmas or hurricanes. Even on a cold and rainy afternoon like this when the pub was dead, she could hear the laughter and the salty yarns told over shellfish and pitchers of beer. They had accumulated in the smoke-darkened walls, on the smooth floorboards, in the dinged furniture. Howard's had a warm history. You could feel it. People wanted to be here. It was a loved place.

A lank man in his mid-thirties emerged from the swinging doors of the kitchen. As he approached Vi, he wiped his hands off on his apron. She noted the fish guts smeared on the cloth and hoped he wouldn't offer his hand.

"Help you with something, Miss?"

"Mr. Myers?"

Scottie stroked his dark mustache and cocked his head.

"Yes, why?"

"My name's Violet King. I'm a detective from Davidson." She reached into her purse, flashed her credentials. "May I ask you a few questions?"

"Something wrong?"

"Oh, no sir. You haven't done anything." She smiled and touched his arm. "Let's sit down. Won't take but a minute."

They sat down at the corner of the bar and Vi came right out and asked him if he knew Luther Kite. Scottie had to think for a moment, stroking his mustache again and staring at the impressive train of beer bottles, nearly two hundred strong, lined up on the glass shelves where the liquor should have been.

"Oh yeah," he said finally. "I remember him. He do something?"

"Well, I can't really go into that, but . . . Do you know where he is right now?"

"Sure don't. I hadn't seen him in, God, ten years maybe. I didn't even know him that well when I knew him. Know what I mean? He was one of those quiet, loner types. Me and him used to go crabbing with Daddy back in high school. That's the only reason I knew him. Daddy gave him the job. We weren't friends or nothing. Fact, I didn't like him. That whole family's strange."

"Mr. Myers, anything you could tell me about him would be a great help."

"I don't know what to tell you. I don't know him any better than I know you. Who said I knew him so good?"

"His parents."

"Well, sorry I can't help you."

Scottie glanced up at a nearby television. On the screen, an immaculately groomed couple stood in bathrobes kissing in low-light before a fireplace. He looked back at Vi and grinned.

"So how old are you?" he said.

"Twenty-six."

"And you're a detective already? You're just a young'n. You get hit on a lot, Miss King?"

"Sometimes."

"I bet you do. Yes indeedy."

Vi noticed the shift in his eyes. What had been fear at first was now pursuit, lustful interest.

"Thank you for your time, Mr. Myers." Vi stepped down from the barstool.

"I think it's great what you've accomplished and all," Scottie said. "You're good at your job. I can tell. Don't you ever take any shit from a man, okay? We underestimate you. Had lunch yet?"

"No, but—"

"Then why don't you have lunch on me. My treat."

"Oh, Mr. Myers, you don't have to do that."

"No, I want to. I wish my little sister were here to meet you. Be good for her. She's married to a real son of a bitch who don't think women can do nothing. You like oysters?"

"Um, sure."

"I'm gonna go shuck a few and bring you an appetizer. Take a look at the menu and decide on a main course. See that string hanging from the ceiling over there?" He pointed to an alcove across the room. "There's a ring on the end of it. What you do is you take the ring and stand back and try to catch it on the hook in the wall. Everyone who comes to Howard's has to play 'Ring on the Hook.'"

Scottie headed back to the kitchen and disappeared through the swinging doors. Vi glanced at her watch. She had almost two and a half hours until her second interview with the Kites and she'd been so excited this morning after taking the pregnancy test that she'd forgotten to eat.

So she walked over to the alcove and played "Ring on the Hook" while she waited for lunch. She didn't feel guilty for loafing. The trail was frigid and it looked more and more as if Luther Kite hadn't set foot on this island in a very long time. Besides, this was Ocracoke, the antithesis of haste, the sort of island where you stay indoors on a rainy autumn afternoon and turn idleness into a virtue.

CHAPTER 38

The waitress promised me that the oysters I'd ordered had been harvested from the Pamlico Sound early this morning. I asked for a double Jack Daniel's, neat, and was informed that Hyde County was "semidry," in other words, no liquor-by-the-drink. So I settled for a glass of sweet tea and leaned back in my chair, relishing the radiant drafts from the space heater and this last interlude of solace.

I'd chosen a table on the screened porch of Howard's Pub so I could dine alone and listen to the rain falling on the bamboo that cloistered the building. Having already changed into my long underwear and fleece pants, I was ready to depart for Portsmouth as soon as I finished my meal.

I took out the map, unfolded it across the table, and skimmed the brief history of Portsmouth. Much to my surprise I learned that it had once been inhabited. During much of the eighteenth and nineteenth centuries it was the main port of entry to the

Carolinas and correspondingly the largest settlement on the Outer Banks. In 1846 a hurricane opened up Hatteras and Oregon Inlets to the north. Deeper and safer than Ocracoke Inlet, they became the favored shipping lanes. With its maritime industry doomed, Portsmouth foundered for the next hundred years. The two remaining residents left the island in 1971 and it had existed ever since in a state of desertion, a ghost village, frequented only by tourists and the National Park Service.

From what I could discern from the map, the island consisted of beaches, extensive tidal flats, and shrub thickets throughout the interior. There were several primitive trails through the wooded regions and twenty structures still stood on the north end of the island, remnants of the old village. Hardly a substantial landmass, it barely warranted mapping—just a sliver of dirt separating the sound from the sea. If Luther was there, I'd find him.

The door to the main dining room creaked open and a young woman bundled up in a Barbour coat stepped onto the screened porch. She took a seat at a table across the room, beneath the other space heater.

When our eyes met, I smiled and nodded.

She smiled back.

A Southerner, I thought. Who else smiles at strangers?

A waitress brought her a plate of oysters Rockefeller for an appetizer and the little blond read the back of the menu while she ate. She couldn't have been older than twenty-five. I wondered if she lived on the island and, if not, what she was doing on Ocracoke alone.

I turned my focus back to the map and studied the topography of Portsmouth until the waitress brought my plate of fried oysters with sides of coleslaw and hushpuppies. As she walked back into the dining room, I glanced across the porch at the adorable blond.

She gazed back at me with a look of captivation.

Her eyes averted to her menu, mine to my map.

I hadn't been hit on in years and it felt amazing, particularly coming from this gorgeous young woman.

I picked up an oyster and took a bite. Excellent—briny and crisp.

A chair squeaked.

I looked up, watched the blond rise from her table and come toward me, her heels knocking hollowly on the floorboards.

She stopped at my table and smiled down at me, a lovely nervous simper.

"I'm sorry to bother you," she said. "Could I borrow your horseradish sauce?"

Her accent was unmistakable. She hailed from my old stomping ground, the piedmont of North Carolina.

"Sure. I'm not using it."

As she lifted the bottle I noticed her chest billowing beneath her coat.

"I see you got the oysters, too," she said, then took a sudden breath.

"Wonderful, aren't they?"

She brushed her short yellow hair behind her ears, her eyes moving across the map of Portsmouth, then back to me again.

"Are you from Ocracoke?" she asked.

"Oh, no. Just visiting."

"Me, too," she said, still strangely breathless. "Me, too. Well, um, thank you for the ketchup, I mean horseradish."

As she walked back over to her table, I saw that a full bottle of horseradish sauce already stood uncapped beside her plate.

Thinking back to the way I'd first caught her looking at me, I finally put it all together.

That wasn't captivation.

That was recognition.

CHAPTER 39

Vi returned to her table, heart thudding against her chest, scarcely able to breathe.

Oh God. It's him. Eat something so he won't suspect you know.

She forced down an oyster and did everything she could not to look at Andrew Thomas. One of the photographs in her briefcase had been digitally enhanced to show him with long hair and an unkempt beard.

The man with gray-flecked hair sitting fifteen feet away was a dead ringer.

Scottie Myers walked onto the screened porch bearing her main course—the fish du jour, blackened dolphin. He set the plate before Vi and said, "I think you gonna like this fish better'n anything you ever ate. Go on—take a bite. Tell me what you think."

Vi managed to smile up at Scottie. She took a bite and said, "Yes, that's wonderful, Mr. Myers." *Go back inside, Scottie. Don't stay out here and talk to me. If you mention I'm a detective—*

"Yeah, I know the fisherman who caught that."

"That's wonderful," she said.

"Listen, I was thinking what we were talking about, and that Luther feller—"

"Hold that thought, Scottie," Vi said, standing up. "Would you point me to the ladies' room?"

"Oh, sure. Go through that door, and it's back there in the corner, past the pool table. You all right there, Miss?"

Vi walked through the French doors into the dining room, mindful not to rush, thinking, *I don't have jurisdiction to arrest Andrew Thomas in Ocracoke. Do it anyway? No. Call Sgt. Mullins. Tell him what's going on. Then nine-one-one. Get Hyde County Sheriff's Department down here. Hold him at gunpoint while you wait. You have to walk back in there packing. Throw down on him. Freeze! Police! On the floor! Make him cuff himself to the space heater.*

She entered a filthy bathroom, the walls adorned with NASCAR memorabilia. Her hands trembled so much she could barely get a grip on the zipper. Standing in front of the cracked mirror, she unzipped the Barbour coat, her shoulder rig now exposed, the satin stainless .45 gleaming in the hard fluorescent light. She reached into her pocket for the cell phone, but it wasn't there. In her mind's eye she saw it in the passenger seat of the Cherokee.

It's all right. He doesn't suspect anything yet. Just walk outside and call Mullins from the Cherokee. No, Andrew Thomas will see you leave and he didn't see you pay. He might bolt. Get him on the floor first. Then have Scottie call from the restaurant's phone.

This man has been on the run for seven years. He's a monster. He's desperate. Probably armed. Breathe, Vi. Breathe. You've been trained for this. You can do this.

Unsnapping the holster latchet, she pulled out her .45 and chambered the first round. She took three deep breaths and waited twenty seconds for her hands to stop shaking.

Then, gripping the gun in her right hand, she slipped it into her coat and stepped toward the door.

Vi cracked it open and glanced through the dining room onto the screened porch.

Her stomach dropped.

Andrew Thomas had left his table.

She opened the door and started for the porch.

Something threw her back into the bathroom and slammed her against the wall.

Time slowed, fragmented into surreal increments: the door closing, lights out, trying to scream through the hand covering her mouth, reaching for the gun (no longer there), the coldness of its barrel behind her left ear, lips against her right ear, then whispering she could hardly hear over the williwaw of her own hyperventilation.

"Have you called anyone?"

She shook her head.

"You know who I am?"

She shook her head.

"Don't lie to me."

She nodded.

"Put your hands behind your back. If you make a sound, you'll never walk out of this bathroom."

Andrew Thomas found the handcuffs in her coat pocket and cuffed her hands behind her back.

"What's your name?"

She had to think about it for a moment.

"Violet." The voice didn't sound like anything that belonged to her.

"We're going to walk out of here together, Violet."

He dug through her purse, found the car keys.

"Which one is yours?"

"The Jeep. I'm a detective, sir. You'll be in a world of trouble if—"

"I'm already in a world of trouble. When we get outside, I'll
open the door for you. You get behind the wheel."

Her hands were going numb as Andrew Thomas zipped the
Barbour coat up to her chin. In the darkness she felt the barrel of
the .45 jab into her ribs.

"Feel that? Anything goes wrong, the first bullet is yours.
The rest are for whoever else gets in my way, and their blood
will be on your hands. I don't want to hurt anyone, but I will, and
without hesitation, because I have nothing to lose. We clear?"

"Yessir."

He opened the door and pushed her out.

As they walked through the main dining room, Andrew put
his arm around her.

Vi looked straight ahead, praying that Scottie Myers or the
hostess or one of the waiters would be standing near the front
door. They'd see the terror in her eyes; they'd stop this from
happening.

Crying now, she prayed, *Please God let someone be standing by
the register.*

She heard laughter in the kitchen, loud gleeful laughter, but
no one saw her walk outside with Andrew Thomas, down the
steps, into the cold rain.

The foreknowledge of her imminent death proved the hardest truth she'd ever faced. It weakened her knees and she fell,
bawling, as Andrew dragged her toward the Cherokee, the wet
gravel skinning her knees through the hose.

She'd failed miserably and would soon pay for it, along with
Elizabeth Lancing and all future victims of Andrew Thomas.

Only as she glimpsed her oncoming death did she realize that
she'd never believed in it. Dying was something that happened
to other people. The unlucky and the old.

But she believed in it now because once she got into her Jeep with Andrew Thomas no one would ever see her again. Last year she'd told a class of high school freshmen to fight with everything they had to keep from getting dragged into an attacker's vehicle. She should've made Andrew Thomas shoot her right there in the parking lot.

But she climbed into her car at gunpoint for the same reason most people in that circumstance do—because she was afraid, because she didn't have the guts to risk dying now, even though getting into the Jeep with him all but guaranteed the lonely horrible death to come.

PORTSMOUTH

CHAPTER 40

The detective pulled into a parking space at the Community Store on Silver Lake in proximity to Charlie Tatum's dock. I sat directly behind the driver's seat as the young woman shifted her Jeep Cherokee into PARK and turned off the engine. She'd cried all the way from Howard's Pub and she was still crying when she gave me the car keys and laid her head against the steering wheel.

While she wept, rain hammered the roof and streamed down the glass.

The .45 trembled in my grasp.

"What's your name again?" I asked.

"Violet," she whimpered.

"Sit up, Violet. I want you to stop crying."

Violet wiped her eyes and glanced at me in the rearview mirror. I scooted over into the middle seat and told her, "Put your hands on the steering wheel and don't let go."

"I'm pregnant," she pleaded, her face starting to break all

over again. "I just found out this morning. If you kill me, you'll be—"

"Shut up. I don't care. Give me your wallet and your badge." She reached into her purse and handed them over. "The phone, too. You have a pager?"

"Not with me." She lifted her cell phone from the passenger seat. I took it out of her hand, dropped it on the floorboard, and stomped it into bits with the heel of my boot. Then I opened her wallet and scanned the driver's license. She was from Davidson, North Carolina, my old home, and only twenty-six years old.

"I told you not to let go of the steering wheel. Did you follow me here?" I asked.

"No."

"No?"

"I swear."

"Then what the fuck are you doing on Ocracoke?"

"I came here to find a man named Luther Kite. His parents live here, and it was his last known—"

"Are you investigating the murder of that family in Davidson?"

"Yes. Along with the kidnapping of Elizabeth Lancing."

"Boy, you have really fucked things up for me."

The dashboard clock read 3:05. It would be getting dark soon and Charlie Tatum was expecting me.

Through the windshield I saw him exit the shack at the end of the dock and step down into his boat. Its motor subsequently purred in the water.

When I looked back at Violet her neck was craning. She eyed the gun. She'd probably never had a loaded firearm pointed at her.

"Well, here's the deal," I said to Violet. "We're taking a boat ride. You're my wife, and your name is . . . Angie. Don't talk. Don't cry. Once we get on the boat, you just sit there and stare at the ocean, like we're fighting."

"Where are we—"

"And let me tell you something. This old man who's giving us a ride . . . his life is in your hands. Because if you start crying and freaking out and he gets suspicious, I'll just shoot him and dump him in the sea. You understand that?"

"Yessir. You don't have to hurt anyone."

"That's up to you. I've been hiding for seven years. I'm not going to prison."

Reaching into the way-back, I grabbed up her red poncho and a pair of small damp hiking boots. Then I dragged the backpack I'd purchased from Bubba's Bait and Tackle into the backseat.

"Here." I handed her the poncho and boots. "It'll be wet and cold where we're—"

"You going to hurt me?" she asked.

I wanted to say, *No, you're safe. Everything you know about me is a lie.* But only fear would get her to that island. She had to wholeheartedly and simultaneously believe two things: first, that I would execute her at the slightest resistance, but secondly, that she still had a chance of surviving this.

So I lifted the .45, aimed it between the seats, and threatened her with terrible things.

CHAPTER 41

We sat on a bench seat along the gunwale. I put my arm around Violet and cuddled with her as Charlie Tatum piloted the Island Hopper away from the dock into the middle of Silver Lake. The deck reeked of mildew and the discarded sunspoiled viscera of fish.

"That wind's already turned on us," he warned. "It's gonna get rough as hell once we clear the harbor."

Silver Lake was empty. I saw the motels and B&Bs along the shore, tendrils of smoke climbing out of several chimneys.

The rain intensified.

I wondered for a moment if I were mad for doing this, then thought of it no more.

We chugged through the Ditch and I stared beyond the narrow outlet into the sound, its waters roiling in the fierce north wind. Emerging from the harbor, Charlie leaned into the throttle. As the ferry lurched forward in a sprint for open water, he pointed to Teach's Hole, a cove in the murky distance that the pirate Edward Teach (a.k.a. Blackbeard) had used for a hideout prior to his beheading in 1718.

Passing the southern tip of Ocracoke, we finally reached the inlet, where ocean and sound collided in a series of deadly shoals and currents. Waves pounded the sides of the boat and spindrift whipped off the whitecaps. We were exposed now to the full force of the nor'easter, the rain driving sideways into the plastic drop curtain with such fury we could see nothing of Ocracoke, its lighthouse, or the blue water tower just a few hundred yards back. The howling grayness enveloped everything, reducing our world to a cold angry sea.

The boat rose to the crest of a wave and slammed down into its trough, nearly jarring us from the padded seat. Charlie looked back at me and shook his head.

"Worse than I thought!" he yelled above the roar of the motor. "We got no business being out here in this! I don't know if I can dock her!"

I glanced down at Violet. Her poncho was drenched, her hands cold and red. She stared out to sea as she'd been told. Her lips moved. I wondered if she was praying.

When I gave her a gentle squeeze she looked up at me. So delicate.

"Cold?" I asked. She nodded. I pulled the arms of her poncho down over her hands and almost told her that she was safe.

We struggled on through the chop.

Waves swelled.

Violet trembled and I stared ahead into the deluge and the cold chaotic nothingness of the storm and the sea, as scared and alive as I'd felt in a good long while. But I didn't savor the adrenaline. I'd have taken the boredom and solitude of the Yukon wilderness any day.

We'd been on the water for twenty minutes when Portsmouth

appeared suddenly in the gray distance. Several wooden structures stood near the bank and they looked long deserted. Glimps-
ing the ghost village through the pouring rain and the scrub pines
flailing about in the wind like an army of lunatics, I filled with
foreboding. This north end of the island looked utterly haunted.
Had I not known the history of Portsmouth, one glance at those
abandoned dwellings would have told it all.

My dread was palpable.

I didn't want to set foot on that island.

It was forsaken.

CHAPTER 42

I tossed my backpack to Charlie, stepped up on the gunwale, and climbed onto the dock.

The wind gusted, then died down as I heaved the pack onto my shoulders.

"I think y'all are nuts for doing this," the old sailor said, rainwater spilling over his hood, running down his face into his bushy white beard.

The sea was rowdy.

It banged the boat into the beams.

"We'll see you tomorrow afternoon," I said.

"Hope so. Let me give your wife a hand up. I got to get back to the harbor 'fore this gets any worse."

"Mr. Tatum, just a moment. These buildings from the old village are publicly owned. Correct?"

"Yes. The village proper is on the National Register of Historic Places."

"Are you familiar with the entire island?"

"Most of it."

I glanced back at Violet. She hadn't moved.

"I'm looking for a lodge of some sort. Something someone still owns. I don't think it would be a part of the village."

"Well, there's some old hunting lodges down past the middle village ruins."

"Where's that?"

Charlie pointed shoreward.

"The ruins are about a half mile south of Haulover Point."

"Where's Haulover Point?"

"You're standing on it. You'll see the trail when you reach the end of the dock. I can't believe you're gonna camp in this shit."

"Look, I have to be back at work in three days. I've planned this trip all year, so I don't have the luxury of waiting out the storm."

He grinned, shook his head, wiped rainwater from his eyes.

"Well, she don't seem too happy about it."

"No, Angie would rather be back at the inn. You get home safe."

Charlie patted my shoulder and stepped past me to the edge of the dock.

The detective rose to her feet, rattled, shivering.

"Give you a hand there, sweetie-pie?" the old sailor asked.

Violet stood at the end of the dock, watching the Island Hopper dwindle away into the savage sea. The groan of its motor carried poorly in the wind and before long the only sound derived from the storm—waves sloshing about and raindrops pelting the rotten boards beneath our feet.

"We need to go," I said.

The young woman turned and glared at me, crying again. Then she started walking and I followed her down the long dock.

We stepped ashore onto a sandy path and hiked alongside a

creek. In the distance, rundown buildings of varying dilapidation teetered amid the scrub pines.

Wet marsh grass bent and rustled as it moved in slow vegetative waves all around us.

Violet walked fast.

Her boots splashed through puddles.

She sobbed.

The path branched. We could push south into the interior of the island or veer left, across the creek, into the ghost village.

Violet stopped and faced me. She couldn't stop shaking.

"I'm s-s-s-so c-c-cold."

We needed to continue south toward the middle village ruins, but I doubted if Violet had the strength. She looked hypothermic.

In the village I noticed the spire of a small church poking above the pines.

"We're going to get you warm," I said.

We proceeded across a bridge toward the church. It rained so hard now I could hear nothing above the relentless pattering on my hood. I glanced at my watch. Four o'clock. We'd have a premature dusk with this ominous cloud deck.

One of the brochures had used the adjectives "quaint" and "enchanting" to describe Portsmouth Village, but I found nothing remotely enchanting about this place. It was a dismal graveyard in the throes of decay. Had I visited the island as a carefree tourist on a pleasant summer afternoon, perhaps my impression would've been more cheery. But now it seemed we'd entered a village of corpses, some dolled up and embalmed with fresh paint and new foundations, the majority left to rot and collapse in the marsh grass.

I wondered why people came here, what they hoped to see. There was no mystery, no explanation to be found in these ruins. Towns degenerate. People leave. They die. Their dwellings crumble. That's *the* storyline, the only plot there will ever be. Here is the house of Samuel Johnson. He was a cobbler. In 1867 he died. So will you. So what. It isn't news. Just the way of things.

We arrived at the steps of an old Methodist church, a small gothic chapel in pristine condition compared to the ruined homestead just across the muddy path.

I tried the door and it opened.

I ushered the detective inside and closed the door behind us.

The silence in the nave was awesome. I could smell ancient dust on the pews. Rain ticked the windowpanes. Floorboards creaked under our weight. Walls creaked as the wind pushed through them.

I led Violet to the front pew and helped her out of the dripping poncho. I told her to sit down. She was in shock, no question, her black skirt and blouse soaking wet.

I unsnapped the hip belt of my Osprey backpack and leaned the pack against the pew. Unzipping the bottom compartment, I pulled out the compressed sleeping bag. Then I unrolled the air mattress across the floor and laid the sleeping bag on top of it.

I knelt down before Violet.

"Hey." I patted her knee. She looked at me, eyes glazed. "Violet, we need to get you out of your wet clothes." She shook her head, teeth chattering. "Can I help you take them off? Here, let me—"

"No!"

She tried to jerk away.

I grabbed her arms.

"Stop it!" I said. "I'm not going to hurt you. I am not. Now I know you have no reason to believe that, but you also have no choice."

She just stared at me.

I let go of her arms, untied her boots, and helped her stand. She undid the clasp on her skirt and it dropped. I peeled off her wet hose, then unbuttoned her blouse and tossed it to the end of the pew. I removed my raingear and fleece jacket. I offered her my fleece and she took it, motioning for me to turn away while she put on the soft jacket.

I guided her over to the sleeping bag. I don't know why she trusted me. The shock, probably, her thinking fuzzy. I closed the air nozzle on the Therm-a-Rest and unzipped the mummy bag. She climbed inside and I zipped her up.

She still shivered. I lay down beside her on the cold boards.

We were quiet for a while.

I listened to the storm raging and watched the sky entering twilight through those arched windows. I stared up into the airy ceiling of the eighty-nine-year-old church. Simple lovely architecture. Sitting up on one elbow, I gazed down into Violet's blanched face.

"Getting warm?" I asked.

"Not yet."

My gun . . . her gun lay on the nearby pew. It was getting dark fast.

"Don't be scared," I said. She watched me. I couldn't determine the color of her eyes in the fading light. Green perhaps. Emerald.

The wind shrieking now.

"Violet, I'm not going to hurt you. I swear I won't. You know I'm Andrew Thomas, don't you?"

God, it felt strange to say that name aloud. It had been *years*.

She nodded that she knew. Her shivering had abated.

"I would never have hurt anyone in Howard's Pub. I have to tell you that. You have to believe me. I wouldn't have hurt Charlie either. Or you. But I had to say those things, because you put me in a difficult position.

"I don't know what you think of me. What you've read or seen on the news. But I'm going to tell you this, and I'm only going to say it once. I am not what you think I am. I did not do those murders seven years ago. I did not kill my mother. You and I came to the Outer Banks for the same reason."

"Is Luther Kite the murderer?" she asked, her voice still enervated and slurring.

"He was involved with some of the murders, but I don't know to what extent. My brother, Orson Thomas, was the real killer."

I closed my eyes. Tears welling. Rain sheeting down the glass. Dusk outside. Dusk in the chapel. This thing gnawing my guts out for seven years and now I'm on the verge of telling a petrified twenty-six-year-old cop who I've essentially kidnapped.

I got up and walked between pews to a window. Nothing human moving through the village, among the house skeletons, the trees still manic, the grasses waving, pools forming on the lawn, creeks flooding, the Ocracoke Light winking on across the inlet, and a knot in my stomach that waxed with the darkness.

"Andrew?" she called out. I looked back—she was just a shadow on the floor now, the chapel draped in gloaming. "Please talk to me."

I returned to Violet and sat down on the front pew.

"You afraid of me?" I asked.

"Yes."

"I want to tell you what happened to me."

"I want to know."

I suspected she was just trying to pacify me, but I told her anyway. All of it. Even what had happened in the desert. I don't know if she believed me, but she listened, and by the end of my narrative my voice could scarcely sustain a whisper. When your sole verbal communication is infrequent chitchat with strangers, your voice atrophies from disuse.

But she listened. I didn't ask if she believed me. I'm tempted to say it didn't matter, but that isn't accurate. Rather, what mattered most was that the truth had been told by me to someone.

You cannot imagine the release.

CHAPTER 43

Violet sat up now in my sleeping bag, propped against the railing that separated the pews from the altar. I'd managed to fire up the camping stove, a propane-fueled WhisperLite. It stood in the aisle, a pot of water coming to a boil over its hissing blue flame.

I ripped the tops off two pouches of Mountain Pantry lasagna and set the freeze-dried dinners beside the stove. Then I took the potgrab and lifted the lid. A billow of steam moistened my face. I set the lid down, lifted the pot, and poured the boiling water into each pouch.

After the lasagnas had stewed for ten minutes we dined. The church completely dark now, I found a candle in my first-aid kit, lit it, and placed it on the floor between us.

"Not bad, huh?" I said.

"It's good."

The rain had let up. The wind was easing. A cloudy night on an island without electricity is total darkness.

"How long you been a cop?" I asked.

"Year and a half."

I put the hot pouch down and took a drink of water from the Nalgene bottle.

"Back in the car you said you were pregnant."

A quick intake of breath. Stifling of tears. Violet looked at the floor while she spoke, her voice newly wrecked.

"Look, I can't do the personal thing right now, okay? Unless you want me to just fall completely apart, please . . ."

I looked at her in the candlelight. Beautiful. Still a kid. Could've been a grad student somewhere. She wiped her cheeks on the sleeves of the fleece jacket. I wondered if she had any idea of how far over her head she was.

She finished off the lasagna and, reassuming that budding official tone, became the cop again: "You said we came to Ocracoke for the same reason. You mean Mr. Kite?"

"Yes. I came here to find him. That woman they found hanging from the Bodie Island Lighthouse—I knew her. And Beth Lancing, the Worthingtons' neighbor who was kidnapped—she's the wife of that very dear friend I was telling you about—Walter. I believe Luther murdered that family just to bring attention to Beth Lancing's abduction. And he hanged Karen Prescott from the lighthouse for the same reason. Those murders were so public. He wanted me to find out. He knew I'd know it was him. That wasn't a mindless killing spree. I think those murders were executed in such a way as to lead me to him, or his general vicinity. And that's what's scaring me right now. You see, my biggest fear is what if Luther knows I'm here?"

"What do you mean 'here'? In this church?"

"No, Ocracoke. God help us if he knows we're on this island."

"Andrew, why *are* we on this island?"

"Well, now that you're in my life, that's an interesting question. You feel any better?"

"I'm warm now."

"And your poncho's dry. I've got spare fleece pants and long underwear in my pack." I looked at my watch. "It's a quarter past seven. Rain's let up. Yeah, we should get on with it."

"With what?"

"I'm fairly confident Beth Lancing is somewhere on this island. Luther, too."

"Oh, no, Andrew, let law enforcement handle this. We could call them in—"

"What about me? I'm wanted."

"Of course I'd—"

"Of course what? You'd tell them how I'm really innocent and—"

"No, I wouldn't do that. It wouldn't matter what I—"

"Then what?"

"You'd have a day in court."

"A day in court. Think that's what I need?"

"You need something. Don't you want to settle all this crap you've been through? Put it to rest, one way or another? Find some peace?"

"I've already found my peace, Violet. My home is far out in a beautiful wilderness. And I'm as happy there as I have any right to be. It's paradise—"

"Sounds a little escapist to me, Andrew."

"Well, the world, human nature as I understand it, based on what I've seen, is well worth escaping. But I don't expect you to understand that." I came to my feet. Shadows and candlelight waltzed across Violet's face, the only warmth in the church. "And besides, what if settling 'all this crap' means I go to prison?"

"Are you guiltless?"

"I don't deserve prison."

"How do you know what you deserve?"

"You're a naïve little girl," I said. "You think if you always try to do the right thing, it'll all work out in the end. You think that don't you?"

"It's called hope. What if I do?"

"I *hope* you're never faced with some of the decisions I've had to make. Where you lose everything no matter what."

I grabbed her .45 from the pew and shoved it into my waistband. We'd be leaving just as soon as I repacked the Osprey.

"You need that optimism," I said. "It protects you from the horror you see. Was what Luther did to the Worthingtons anything less than pure brutality?"

"No. It was awful."

"Did you fabricate a silver lining there?"

"If they had their faith, I believe they're in heaven."

"I'm sure that's just what Mr. Worthington was thinking as Luther Kite butchered him. 'Boy, I'm glad I have this faith.'" I glanced up at the wooden cross mounted to the wall behind the altar. "You're a Christian?" I asked.

"Yes."

"Tell me. Where is God now? Where was He when Luther savaged that family?"

She glared at me, her wet eyes shining in the firelight.

"I don't know."

CHAPTER 44

Moonless and windless, the island brooded: cold, dark, silent. Having left the backpack in the church, we followed the path back to the old general store and turned at the junction onto a southbound trail that would lead us to the middle village ruins in the island's interior.

We traversed Doctors Creek, passed an abandoned school-house, and entered a thicket of live oaks.

Violet walked ahead of me.

The only sound came from the *swish* of wet Gore-Tex, the *splat* of our boots in mud.

The trail narrowed.

We didn't talk.

All around us the undergrowth rioted, impenetrable, in a state of unkempt anarchy, live oaks dripping, wet branches clawing at our arms and legs. I could hardly see Violet and she could hardly see the path before her. Occasionally she'd veer from the trail into a shrub, sigh, and right herself. I debated going back for the headlamp but decided against it. We'd already hiked at least a quarter of a mile and according to the map the ruins weren't far ahead.

As we pushed on into the interior, I realized that I was trusting Violet to guide us, my eyes fixed on the backs of her boots.

I couldn't decide if I was more afraid of finding or not finding Luther.

At last we emerged from the thicket and arrived at the edge of a vast marsh.

I whispered for Violet to stop.

We'd reached the ruins.

Just off the trail I noticed what was left of a house—a crumbling stone chimney surrounded by a pile of rotten boards. Other remnants of the village were scattered throughout the neighboring wood. A brick chimney sprouted up from the middle of the marsh, no trace of the house it had warmed more than a century ago.

I told Violet to keep walking.

The trail followed a slim land bridge across the wetland. As we walked, distant splashes and squawks rang out across the water.

Well, there's some old hunting lodges down past the middle village ruins.

I kept hearing Charlie Tatum's voice and thinking of that passage from Orson's journal:

> *Said they have this lodge on a remote island that would be perfect for the administration of painings.*

We reentered the thicket on the other side. Scrub pine instead of live oak. A roomier wood.

The trail split and Violet stopped.

"Which way?" she whispered.

"I'm not sure. Let's keep walking south."

"What are we looking for exactly?"

"A lodge of some sort."

"I don't think anyone else is on this island, Andrew."

"Yeah, I'm starting to wonder that myself."

We continued southward, the air now perfumed with wet pine and cold enough to cloud our breath.

It was just after nine o'clock when the trail ended, having deposited us on the bank of a wide slough that separated Portsmouth from Evergreen Island. I remembered this feature from the map and my heart sank. If the Kites' lodge stood on Evergreen we'd have to bushwhack east for half a mile and bypass the slough via the tidal flats that connected these barrier islands. It would take all night.

Eastward, I could see where the backwater eventually emptied after several hundred yards into the flats. The sea lay hidden behind distant dunes.

"Look," Violet whispered.

I turned, gazed back into the wood.

"Do you see it?"

A speck of orange light twinkled somewhere in the pines. It could've been a ship on the sound. It could've been ball lightning.

"Let's go," I said. "Pull your hood down so you can listen."

Violet rolled her hood back and pushed her hair behind her ears.

Leaving the path, we struck out into the pines in search of the light. The suction of our boots in the mud seemed positively deafening and the light grew no closer. I had an awful premonition that it would suddenly wink out, stranding us in the pathless dark.

We walked on, faster now between the pines, and for the first time that orange luminescence seemed closer.

I took the .45 from the inner pocket of my rain jacket.

"I see it," Violet said.

We crouched down in a coppice of oleander.

Tucked away in some live oaks at the terminus of a black creek stood a little wood lodge. A lantern or candle (some source of natural firelight) glowed through the only window. A boat was moored to the small dock.

"Is that it?" she asked.

"I have no idea."

We walked on. I was soaked with sweat underneath my rain gear.

Within twenty yards of the lodge, I pulled Violet behind a tree and whispered in her ear: "Wait here and don't move."

I drew back the slide on the .45 and moved quietly toward the structure.

Halfway there I stopped to listen.

The wind had died, the silence absolute save the knocking in my chest.

I crept to the window, but because the lodge had been raised several feet off the ground on four-by-fours I couldn't see inside.

Three deliberate breaths and I walked around to the steps leading up to the front and only door.

At the top I glanced over my shoulder, saw Violet still hunched near the tree.

I put my ear to the door, listened.

Not a sound.

I grasped the doorknob and turned it as slowly as I could, a line of icy sweat trilling down my left side.

With the tip of my boot I nudged the door and let go.

It swayed partly open.

Hinges squeaking.

The only movement inside came from fireshadows on the walls and ceiling.

The furnishings were scanty—a ratty futon, a card table bearing dirty plates, a bowl of pistachio shells, a jug of water. The place stank of scorched eggs and spoiled fish. A candle, almost burned down to the brass, had been set on the windowsill, the sole source of light.

I steadied my hands, knelt briefly on the stoop to rest my trembling knees.

Then I stood, stepped through the threshold, kicked the door all the way open.

Sweet Jesus.

Movement in the right corner.

I swung around, nearly shot Beth Lancing, duct-taped to a folding chair, eyes gone wide with horror, head shaking, hair in shambles, cheeks marbled with bruises and mud.

Lowering the gun, I stepped toward her, reached to pull off the tape covering her mouth, but stopped.

"Beth," I whispered, "J.D. and Jenna are safe. I'm here to take you home to them. Don't scream when I take the tape off."

Frantic nodding.

I ripped off the tape.

"Andy, he's waiting for you."

"What?"

"A man with long black—"

From the woods, Violet screamed my name.

Footfalls pounded up the steps to the lodge.

Before I could move, the door slammed shut.

CHAPTER 45

I called out to Violet as I jerked on the door.

It wouldn't open.

Outside, Violet screamed.

I ran to the window, glimpsed a long-haired shadow sprinting into the woods. Taking the candle from the sill, I set it on the floor and busted the glass out with the handgun.

The window was too small for me to crawl through. Violet could've done it.

I charged the door and rammed it with my shoulder. It barely moved, the wood an inch thick, probably padlocked from the outside.

I lifted the candle and put it on the card table. There was a boning knife on a dirty plate and I took it, walked around to the back of Beth's chair.

"I'm gonna cut you loose," I whispered.

"Where'd he go?"

"I had a detective with me. A young woman. I think he went after her."

"She have a gun?"

I pointed to the table. "That's it."

I sliced through the duct tape, freed her wrists, then her ankles.

Beth stood and faced me, haggard, half-naked, clothed only in a torn teddy.

I took off my rain jacket and fleece and wrapped her in them.

"I didn't murder Walter," I said.

"Just get me out of here."

"I'm not sure how."

"Shoot the door."

I took the .45 from the table, pressed the magazine release. It popped out. I counted the rounds.

"Nine bullets," I said. "I'll waste three on the door, but that's it."

I shoved the magazine back in.

"Wait," Beth whispered. "What if he doesn't know you have a gun?"

"So?"

"So let him think it. He unlocks the door—bang, bang."

"Okay. Let's sit. I don't feel safe standing up."

I thought of Violet, fighting for her life out in those woods, couldn't imagine that young woman surviving Luther. My fault if she died.

Candlelight bathed the walls. It was freezing in here and I had no idea of what to say to Beth.

My best friend's widow.

So much history between us, so many unanswered questions, I just sat there beside her and tried not to let the weight of it all crush me.

"Has he hurt you?" I asked.

"No. Not bad. Where are we?"

"The Outer Banks. Been in this lodge the whole time?"

"No, just tonight. I don't know where he kept me before that. All I remember is darkness and stone. What's today?"

"Thursday, sixth of November."

"Ten days."

"What's that?"

"How long I've been apart from my kids."

She shivered. The candleflame shivered.

We sat in silence.

She said finally, "Tell me how he died."

"Beth—"

"I want to hear it, Andy, and I want to hear it from you. But first, pass me that jug on the table. He gave me a few sips earlier, but I'm still so thirsty."

I fetched her the half-empty jug. She took a long pull, then gave me the water.

I flicked off the cap and we sat in the corner, passing the jug back and forth.

The water was cool and faintly sweet.

Finally, I dove in—told her about Orson and the desert and the threat he made against her family, her children. I told Beth about how Walter and I went and found Orson and kidnapped him from his home that Friday evening seven years ago.

I said, "So we drove out into the countryside with my brother in the trunk. Already dug the hole earlier that evening. We dragged Orson out and put him in the backseat. We needed to find out where Luther was—that's the man who just kidnapped you. Orson had sent him to find you.

"When Orson came to, he riled Walter, talking about what Luther was going to do to you and the kids. Walter wanted to shoot him, Beth. Right there. He lost his head. But I knew if we didn't find out from Orson where Luther was, you and the kids would be dead. No question."

I swallowed, growing colder, Beth's eyes never moving from my face. Even in the poor light she seemed to have aged more than seven years since I last saw her.

"Walter pointed his gun at Orson. I told him no. He wouldn't listen. He was so mad. It was a stupid fucking thing to do, but I pointed my gun at Walter. Told him, God I remember it so well, 'You kill him, you kill your family.' Out of nowhere, Orson kicked the back of my seat and my gun went off. He was gone instantly, Beth. Swear to you."

She closed her eyes.

She let out an imperceptible sigh, then was quiet.

All I could hear was the wind stirring the pines.

The silence became oppressive.

After a long time, she whispered, "You buried him?"

"I'll take you to the spot when we get out of this."

"I hate you, Andy," she said. Her voice was thick with tears. "Do you know how much I hate you?"

"Yeah. I do."

She leaned into me and I put my arm around her.

As she quietly wept, the candle expired and the lodge grew so dark I could see only the navy black of the sky through the window.

Iced updrafts rising through slits in the floor.

I waited, thinking my eyes would adjust, but they never did.

"Andy," she whispered. Her voice sounded strange and faraway, as though she were calling out to me from the bottom of a deep well.

"What?"

"Something's not right."

"What are you talking about?"

"My head . . . I feel dizzy . . . it's . . . so heavy all the sudden."

Now that she mentioned it, my head felt weird, too.

Maybe we were just hungry.

But when I glanced down at the empty jug between my legs, it dawned on me what had happened.

"Oh, Beth, I think we fucked up bad."

CHAPTER 46

Vi leaned against the live oak as Andrew stepped into the lodge. She watched the black creek, lined with marsh grass, meandering west between the pines. Had the night been clear, she'd have seen where it widened to join the sound.

On the periphery of vision something moved.

She saw a black shape emerge from the woods and move quickly toward the lodge.

At first she thought it was a deer, bounding. Then her blood froze as though she'd glimpsed a demon, watching in silent terror as it reached the steps.

She screamed, "Andrew!"

The thing with long black hair slammed the door to the lodge and padlocked it as Andrew shouted her name.

Then it looked right at her.

Vi reached instinctively for the .45, felt her bony hip.

Before she could even stand, the shadow had descended the steps and was running toward her.

Vi shrieked, sprang to her feet, and bolted into the woods, tree trunks screaming by, her animal panting drowning even the sound of her predator's footsteps.

She ran and ran and did not look back, expecting at any moment to feel a hand come down on her shoulder and drive her into the ground.

The grove of live oaks turned back into thicket.

She tripped on a dead vine.

Fell.

Chest heaving now against the ground.

In the distance she heard her pursuer flailing about in the thicket.

It stopped.

She held her breath.

Silence.

Her ears adjusting.

Now she could clearly hear the sound of its panting. Much closer than she thought.

She prayed the woods were as dark to it as they were to her.

When her heart quieted she could hear her eyes blinking and nothing else.

A moment passed; then came the rustling, like footfalls on brittle leaves.

Craning her neck, she looked back, saw the shadow stepping gingerly through the thicket.

It stopped fifteen feet away, just a bush between them.

Vi wondered if it was enough to hide her.

The thing walked toward the bush, so close now she imagined she could smell it.

The brush shifted beneath her, made a crackling she thought was deafening.

The monster twitched, pushed its hair behind its shoulders.

It stood motionless for what seemed hours.

Listening.

Then abruptly it turned and started back toward the lodge.

Vi couldn't bring herself to move even when the sounds of its thrashing had grown indiscernible from the *snaps* and *creaks* of the island's other nighttime murmurs.

She didn't want to budge. Ever.

If I move, he'll hear me, come back, find me, kill me. But I have to get off this island.

She lay in the thicket for another hour, praying for the will to stand and push on.

Vi had been making her way through the woods for thirty minutes when she stopped and sat down in the undergrowth. Closing her eyes, she pinched the bridge of her nose, trying to faze out the adrenaline and the panic. She wanted to boil the moment down to the facts and proceed from there. That's what a strong cop would do.

She took several deep breaths, then stood up again and continued on, flinging the possibility from her mind that she had miles and miles of this thicket still ahead of her.

In keeping with the trend of her day, things degenerated. The undergrowth became so dense she was spending thirty seconds on each step, untangling the vines from around her ankles, whacking the labyrinth of limbs out of her way.

When she failed to unwind one persistent vine she found herself lying facedown in mud.

She did not get up.

She lay there and cried, then filled with anger at the tears, and resisted allowing the totality of this "fucking bad fucking day" to envelop her. *You can't think about it. It's too much. Just get up and do your job, Viking. It could be worse. A lot worse. You could be dead. Now. Get. Up.*

She struggled to her feet. Waded on. Mad. Weak. Right on the verge.

Ten steps later she broke out of the thicket. From claustrophobic vegetation to the sprawling spaciousness of a tidal flat, the wind spilling over the distant dunes, carrying the briny reek of the sea. Eerie black plants rose out of the alkaline soil—salt-sculpted formations, otherworldly and demonic, like the remnants of some nuclear apocalypse.

The flat extended north to south as far as she could see and she tore across it, her boots sinking in the mud, the wind chilling her down, arms pumping, swallowing great mouthfuls of air.

She ran and ran.

The moon, only a sliver of it, materialized behind a ragged gauze of cloud.

God, it was cold in the clearing night. A star appeared here and there, and still she ran, straight ahead toward the small rise of dunes, though she didn't know they were dunes. She didn't know the sea lay just beyond them or that she was crossing a tidal flat. A strict mainlander, her knowledge of sea level began and ended with the Grand Strand of Myrtle Beach:

Wings.

All-You-Can-Eat seafood buffets.

Slushy lemonade vendors.

Biplanes pulling advertisement banners across the faded denim sky.

Laying out with the flabby masses and drinking limey Coronas under a twenty-five-dollar-a-day umbrella.

Walking up and down the beach at night with Max, the hazy glow of hotels and resorts marking the concave curvature of the

Carolina coast. The essence of summer. Every last week of July. That was the beach.

This was the wild. You could not walk back into a motel from this tidal flat and watch HBO.

The dunes were close now. Beach grass, cottonwood, and wormwood stabilized the mounds of white sand, glowing strangely in the moonlight.

She clawed her way to the top and there lay the sea, gleaming and foaming and drawing back into low tide. Even in the face of all she'd been through in the last eight hours, the winter beauty of this wide forsaken beach was devastating.

She scrambled down the dune onto sand that had been smoothed and hardened by the tide. Shells of mollusks and horseshoe crabs and kelp and broken sand dollars and pieces of gray driftwood lay strewn across the beach, battlefield casualties of the nor'easter.

The wind whipped out of the north, blowing white sand across dark sand and between her legs like a rushing vapor. The static whisper of sand skimming sand even beat out the crush of the sea.

Vi glimpsed a light in the north.

At this distance she couldn't be sure, but it seemed to originate from the beach.

Dead dog tired, she started walking toward the light, then jogging, then running, the shells crunching under her boots, grit watering her eyes. She doubted if she could run much farther. If that light never got closer, if it proved to be the Ocracoke Light, several miles north across the inlet, she'd find a place at the foot of the dunes to curl up and sleep through the night. Things would look better in daylight. Less surreal.

The light she'd been running toward vanished, but she saw its source.

A short ways up the beach in the soft sand beyond the reach of high tide, a white canvas tent flapped in the wind.

CHAPTER 47

As Vi approached she heard voices. A Boston Whaler equipped with a small outboard motor had been dragged up onto the beach. Fifty yards offshore, just beyond the breakers, a yacht floated in the calming sea.

She stopped outside the door of the tent and listened. A sleeping bag zipped up.

A man's voice: "I put the bucket above your head. Why don't you try and use it again before you—"

"I'm fine. I just needed to get off that boat. Oh God—"

Heaving and liquid splashing into a bucket.

"Jeez, Gloria."

More retching and splashing. The woman groaned.

"I'll dump the bucket."

Vi stepped back as the tent door unzipped.

A plume of white hair emerged from the opening and an older man holding a red bucket backed out of the tent.

"Sir?"

The man spun around, eyes wide.

"Oh jeez, oh my lord you scared me."

"It's okay, sir. I'm a police officer."

"Sam, who's out there?"

"Just stay put, Gloria."

"Who is it?"

"Jeez, Gloria! I said stay there!"

Vi stepped forward. The man girded his robe.

"Sir, my name's Violet King. I'm a detective from Davidson, North Carolina. Do you have a cell phone I could use?"

"What are you doing here?"

"That is a very long story. I really need to use a phone. It's—"

"Can't get a connection here. I've been trying all night."

"Is that your boat?"

"Yes, why?"

Vi glanced at the dark yacht offshore.

"Sir, I need you to take me to Ocracoke."

"Huh?"

"If this were a road, I'd be appropriating your Lexus. Sorry, it's an emergency."

Again from inside the tent: "Sam, what's going on out there?"

"Just a goddamn minute, Gloria! Jeez!" Sam ran his fingers through his hair. "Ma'am, we just got here. We're just getting to bed. My wife's been seasick the last twelve hours from these rough waters. I'm talking green, yacking her guts out every five minutes."

"I understand that, but—"

"We're cruising up from Jacksonville to Norfolk. We can drop you off first thing in the morning."

"I need to be there an hour ago."

"You have a badge?"

"My badge number is six-zero-nine-two. I don't have the luxury—"

"You don't have a badge? How do I know you're a cop?"

Vi took a step back, sat down in the sand, and put her head between her knees. She could've fallen asleep in seconds.

"Sir, you don't understand the day I've had."

"And you don't understand what you're asking. You want me to take you to Ocracoke in the dead of night? Across that shallow inlet? Look, we only came in this close to get Gloria ashore."

"Your wife can stay, I don't care, but you are *going* to take me to Ocracoke right now. I'm not asking."

"Did something happen on this island?"

"I'm not going into it. You just—"

"Well, you're going to have to tell me something, sweetheart."

Vi stood up.

"All right, fine. Andrew Thomas—heard-a-him? The serial killer?—is on this island as we speak. I need backup. I need—"

"Oh jeez."

Sam looked down at the bucket. He stepped toward the dunes and chucked the vomit into the sand.

When he came back he said, "You better be who you say you are. I spent a third of my pension on that yacht, and if my mate grounds her on the shoals of Ocracoke Inlet, the state of North Carolina is going to reimburse me. I guarangoddamntee you that." He turned and poked his head into the tent. "Get dressed, Gloria. We're going back to the boat."

"You are *shitting* me."

CHAPTER 48

We sat huddled together in the corner. The lodge was absolutely black.

"He put something in the jug of water, didn't he?" Beth said.

"I think so. Oh, man, if I don't get up, I'm gonna pass out right now."

I struggled to my feet, Violet's .45 clenched in my hand.

A whirlwind spun behind my eyes.

"I can't stay awake much longer," Beth whispered.

I staggered over to the broken window, peered out into the woods.

The live oaks glowed in the new moonlight, their twisted limbs lathered in electric blue. The marsh grass that surrounded the lodge stood so still it appeared frozen.

Through the fuzziness, I thought of Violet again, wondered where he'd left her, hoped the thing had been done quickly.

I felt so woozy now.

Beth was whispering my name and it sounded like "Anananandydydydy."

As I turned my head the darkness blurred.

She was slumped over, motionless in the corner.

"Anananandydydydy."

Then it occurred to me that Beth was unconscious.

The voice belonged to a man and it was coming from somewhere outside.

I looked back through the window.

A shadow appeared at the thicket's edge, its pale face glowing like a moon in the dark.

Luther.

It emerged from the woods and started toward the lodge.

I aimed the .45 through the window, then realized my hands were empty.

The gun lay at my feet.

When I bent down for it, my legs liquefied.

I stumbled backward.

Crashed into the table.

Plates shattering.

I was down on my back.

Footfalls thumping up the steps.

My consciousness twirling and falling out from under me.

The door unlocked, flung open.

And I was gone.

CHAPTER 49

As Vi stepped aboard the sixty-one-foot Queenship Sports-cruiser, *Rebecca*, she instantly understood why Gloria was green. The seas rollicked, the yacht tottering so fiercely she had to grab hold of the railing the moment her feet touched the teak deck.

The dinghy was halfway back to the beach by the time Vi had steadied herself. She watched Sam's wife run it aground and drag the Boston Whaler beyond the reach of the tide. Gloria hadn't spoken a word to her during the short boat ride to the yacht. She'd just glared. Her husband had begged her to stay on the yacht in light of the fact that a serial murderer was also on the is-land. But Gloria said in parting: "There's no way. Fact, I hope he finds me, cuts me up into a thousand pieces. Be better than this fucking nausea."

Now Sam led Vi through the curved glass curtain wall that opened from the aft deck into the salon, where she sat down at the end of an L-shaped sofa.

The interior of the yacht was spectacular—cherry wood everywhere. Italian leather. A flat-screen TV. Wet bar. Expansive windows, port and starboard.

Vi imagined that on a sunny day in the middle of the sea the view was nothing but miles and miles of sky and green water.

The ship's mate emerged shirtless from the crew quarters deep in the hull.

"Gloria no come?" he asked.

"She went back ashore, Pedro. Head on up and get us going. You know Ocracoke Inlet, don't you?"

"Yeah, I know him. Be bad tonight. Bad any night. No good idea."

"I know." Sam glanced at Vi. "Can't be helped."

As Pedro ascended to the pilothouse, Sam said, "There's the phone. I'll be up with Pedro. Shouldn't take more than twenty minutes to get there if we don't ground her."

He flicked on more lights as he walked through the galley and disappeared up the curving staircase into the pilothouse. After a moment Vi heard the engines fire up, little more than a muffled gurgle in the insulated recesses of the hull.

Her stomach lurched as the boat began to move.

She picked up the phone, then set it down.

She put her face into her hands and took long penetrating breaths.

Taking up the phone again, she dialed her sergeant's home number.

Talking with Sgt. Mullins before anyone else (911, Coast Guard, SBI) would be the smart move. He'd tell her exactly how to proceed.

A sleepy voice answered, "Hello?"

"Hey, Gwynn, it's Vi. Look, I'm sorry to be calling so late, but I need to speak with Barry. It's—"

"He's on-call tonight, and you just missed him. He had a suicide."

"Oh, well, I'll just page him then. Thanks."

Vi hung up the phone.

Her hands still trembled.

She looked down the companionway that accessed the master and VIP staterooms.

It all felt so surreal. The violence, the fear, the sudden luxury.

She thought of Max and almost called him. But the gentleness, the everydayness in her husband's voice would have broken her in two. If she didn't ease herself out of this nightmare it would shatter her.

Reaching for the phone to page Sgt. Mullins, she realized she didn't know the number for the yacht. She rose from the sofa, but the moment she started for the staircase a wave of nausea came over her.

She barely made it to the galley before spewing her lunch into the sink. Turning on the spigot, she washed the mess down the drain and splashed water in her face. Her forearms against the countertop, she held her head over the basin for ten minutes, eyes closed, praying for the nausea to pass.

Her stomach finally settled and she had just started for the pilothouse to get the phone number for the yacht when Sam came quickly down the staircase.

"We're here," he said. "Come on. I gotta get back to Gloria."

Vi followed Sam back out onto the aft deck. The night was colder, the moon now unveiled and shining down upon the harbor.

Sam offered his hand and Vi took it. He helped her step up onto the dock.

"Thank you, sir," she said. "I know this was a big inconvenience, and I hope Gloria feels better." Sam just rolled his eyes and walked back into the salon.

As Vi headed up the dock she heard the twin diesel engines come to life again. Glancing over her shoulder, she watched the yacht cruising back out into the harbor.

Vi reached Silver Lake Drive and stopped.

Sam had deposited her near the deserted Coast Guard station and the ferry docks.

The lights of Ocracoke shone and reflected in the harbor—a cold twinkling silence. It was midnight and she didn't have a key to her room at the Harper Castle B&B.

The Coast Guard station was dark.

I'll just have to wake somebody up.

She would've run, but it was all she could do to walk, her legs still burning from the sprint across the tidal flat. As she walked along the double yellow line she thought of Andrew Thomas, wondered if he'd still be alive when she saw him next.

She felt overjoyed to be back on Ocracoke. The safety was palpable. She could sense the seven hundred sleeping residents all around her.

She started to say a prayer of thanks.

A car approached from behind.

Stepping back onto the shoulder, she watched an ancient pickup truck come rumbling slowly toward her. It pulled up beside her and squeaked to a halt.

The passenger window rolled down and Rufus Kite leaned forward from the driver seat, his eyes hollowed in the absence of light—two oilblack pools.

"Miss King? Thank God."

"What are you doing—"

"Oh thank God. Everyone's looking for you."

"Who's looking for me?"

"Someone saw you with Andrew Thomas in Howard's Pub. Everyone's looking for you. Come on. Get in."

The passenger door swung open.

"I'll take you back to the house," he said. "We'll get you cleaned up. I imagine you have some very important phone calls to make."

"Well, yeah I do, but . . . No, I think I'll just walk over to the Silver Lake Inn." She motioned down the street to a three-story motel on the waterfront. "I'll wake someone up if I have to, but I don't want to trouble—"

"No trouble at all. Hop in. Besides, I don't think anyone's there, Miss King."

An odd tone in his voice. Not mere insistence.

Something rustled in the back of the truck.

"Look, I appreciate the offer, but—"

Maxine Kite sat up from the truck bed and climbed out of the back wielding a mallet. Vi was backpedaling, on the verge of running, when Maxine cracked her skull open.

Vi's knees went to jelly and her cheek hit the cold pavement, blood running across her eyelid, down the bridge of her nose, over her lip, between her teeth. She heard a door screech open, saw Rufus step down onto the road on the other side of the truck, watched his boots come toward her, wondering if this throbbing sleepiness at the base of her neck meant she was dying.

Vi rolled onto her back.

Swallowed blood.

Warm liquid rust.

The spindly branches of a live oak overhung the road. Between its limbs the night sky shone in pieces—cloudless, black, filling up with stars.

Rufus and Maxine stood arm-in-arm grinning down at her.

A walkie-talkie crackled.

Rufus pulled it from his back pocket, pressed the TALK button, said, "Yeah, son, we got her. See you back at the house."

Vi's brain told her arm to unzip the poncho and take out the gun, but she remembered that she didn't have it and besides the arm wouldn't move.

"Now that's what you call a good ol'-fashioned wallop," Rufus said and chuckled.

Then the old man kissed his wife on the cheek and leaned down toward Vi, all gums tonight.

"Her lips are still moving," he said. "Go ahead and clonk her again, Beautiful."

S W E E T - S W E E T
&   B E A U T I F U L

However, there is a locked room up there
with an iron door that can't be opened.
It has all your bad dreams in it.
It is hell.
Some say the devil locks the door
from the inside.
Some say the angels locked it from the outside.
The people inside have no water
and are never allowed to touch.
They crack like macadam.
They are mute.
They do not cry help
except inside
where their hears are covered with grubs.
—Anne Sexton, "Locked Doors"

CHAPTER 50

Four Days Later

Monday, 10:00 A.M., Horace Boone leaned back in his chair and sipped from an enormous mug of coffee, watching through the window as the sun made its brilliant ascent above the Outer Banks, whetting the sky into cloudless November cobalt.

It should've been a lovely morning, sitting in that warm sun-lit nook of the Ocracoke Coffee Company, amid the smell of fresh coffee beans and newspapers and baking pastries and the murmurs of browsing customers in the adjoining Java Books.

But Horace was a wreck.

It had been four days now since he'd watched Andrew Thomas board the Island Hopper with that pretty young woman and taxi out through Silver Lake Harbor into the sound. He'd waited and waited, staring through the windshield as the sky dumped cold unrelenting rain. An hour had passed and the Island Hopper returned without them.

By nightfall there was still no sign of them, so he made his way back to the Harper Castle B&B, had supper, and went to bed.

First thing Friday morning, he returned to the Community Store docks. The Jeep Cherokee that Andrew and the woman had arrived in was gone. Horace drove to Howard's Pub, saw that the Audi Andrew had rented wasn't there either.

Behind the wheel of his own subcompact rental, a tiny white Kia, Horace felt the hot tears begin to roll down his cheeks. Up until a few days ago he'd sensed that he was fated to tail Andrew Thomas and record his story. He'd managed to follow him nearly three thousand miles from Haines Junction, Yukon, to Denver International Airport. There, he'd lost Andrew in security, waited all weekend in despair near a stand of pay phones in the food court of Terminal B, berating himself for flushing his savings on this ridiculous endeavor. Watching the stream of travelers, he resolved to fly back to Anchorage, apologize profusely to Professor Byron, and finish his MFA in the creative writing program. This last year of his life had been derailed by a twenty-four-year-old megalomaniac who fancied he would write a book about Andrew Thomas and become famous.

As Horace gathered his backpack and came to his feet he stared down the terminal and watched in astonishment as the man he thought he'd lost glided toward him on the moving walkway. Andrew Thomas walked right up beside him, grabbed a pay phone, and with his back turned to Horace proceeded to make a phone call.

Horace felt certain he was hallucinating, but he stood there and listened as Andrew called the North Carolina Department of Transportation and inquired about the ferry schedules from the mainland to a place called Ocracoke Island. Had Horace any lingering doubt about whether fate and fortune were in his pocket, he then observed Andrew hanging up, redialing, and booking a room at the Harper Castle B&B on Ocracoke for the following week.

His rejuvenation was instantaneous.

Once on Ocracoke, Horace spent Wednesday and Thursday following Andrew's movements throughout the island—the two trips to the stone manor on the sound, Andrew's visit to Tatum Boat Tours, Bubba's Bait and Tackle, his peculiar meeting with the pretty blond at Howard's Pub, and finally Andrew and the blond's departure on that boat in the middle of a nor'easter.

Apparently they had returned late in the night and for some reason left the island. Had Horace waited by the docks he might be with them now. Instead he'd come thousands of miles only to lose Andrew permanently on a small island off the coast of North Carolina. He'd let the story of a lifetime slip away. Andrew was long gone by now, pursuing Luther Kite, in a story that Horace would never get to tell.

No question, he'd missed the party.

Horace set the coffee mug down on his little table and lifted the purple notebook containing the first four chapters of his book on Andrew Thomas. He didn't have the heart to write about Andrew this morning. Thumbing through the pages, he relived the thrill of finding him and standing outside the window of Andrew's cabin in Haines Junction, watching the master write. For a month at least, Horace had known hope.

Rising from the table, he acknowledged that this would probably be his final morning on Ocracoke. But he wasn't going to waste it as he'd done the last three days—driving aimlessly around the island searching for Andrew's Audi and that blue Jeep Cherokee. Tonight he would try one last thing and if that proved futile (as he suspected it would) he'd fly back to Alaska, beg his parents for a little money, and never again do anything this reckless and stupid.

CHAPTER 51

Beth and Violet stirred as we entered our fourth period of light.

It passed through a crack in the stone and slanted through darkness—a dusty shaft of daylight come to illuminate our miserable faces for an hour.

We sat across from one another in a cold stone room, our wrists manacled and chained to an iron D-ring, bolted to the rocky floor between our feet.

The doorway opened into a dark corridor, through which spilled the disconcerting sounds of hammering and drilling that had been ongoing without respite for what seemed like days.

I raised my head.

In the twilight I could see that the women were also conscious.

A stream of water trickled down the stone beside Violet.

Two roaches crawled through the oval patch of daylight at my feet.

A strained and hopeless silence bore down upon us.

Beth wept softly as she always did when the light appeared.

Violet sat stoical, a line of dried blood streaked from her scalp across the left side of her face.

There was nothing any of us could say.

We just stared at one another, three souls in hell, waiting for the darkness to come again.

CHAPTER 52

Luther drilled the last hole into the right armrest. Rufus was screwing a leather ankle strap into the left front leg of the chair. Because the wood was oak the old man had to lean into the Phillips head to make the screw turn.

"Lookin' good, boys."

Maxine stood in the narrow stone doorway, a glass of lemonade in each hand, the single bare light bulb accentuating deep creases in her face. "My Heart Belongs to Jesus" was spelled out in rhinestones across the front of her bright purple sweater.

Father and son laid their tools on the dirt floor. Rufus grunted as he struggled to his feet. He walked over to Maxine, leaned down, planted a kiss on her forehead. Her big baby black eyes sparkled, her only feature that showed no age.

"Bless your little heart," Rufus said and he took the glasses of lemonade from her and went and plopped down beside his son, their backs against the cool stone.

They drank.

Maxine stepped into the small room and sat in the chair.

She laid her forearms on the armrests, looked over at her boys.

"Zzzzzzzzzz!"

The old woman shook violently and laughed.

"Beautiful, you rattle that chair apart, we'll strap you in for real."

Luther finished off the lemonade, set it down.

"What's for supper, Mama?"

Maxine got up, walked over to her son, framed his face in her hands.

"Whatever my good boy wants. What does he want?"

"Boiled shrimp."

"You gonna help me peel 'em?"

"Yes'm."

Maxine gently slapped his pale drawn cheeks and lifted the empty glasses.

She said, "Boy, I thought you were gonna take care of Andrew's and that detective's cars."

"I moved them both over to the Pony Island Motel parking lot this morning."

"Ah. Good. Well, can I say for the record what a colossal waste of time y'all are spending on this chair?"

Rufus stood, pushed back his white tresses.

"Now hold on there, Beautiful. Is it a waste of time to spend hours preparing for a fine dinner? You have to think of this as a gourmet meal. It takes a little more time, but it'll all be worth it in the end. And this isn't a one-time deal. Once the thing's built, my God, it'll last forever. Besides, I'm happy. Down here working with my boy. Making memories."

Maxine said, "Well, I'm gonna go feed the guests, let them do their business. It's funny—Andrew still thinks I'm senile from that Alzheimer's bit I pulled on him."

She disappeared into the dark corridor.

Rufus gave Luther a hand, helped pull him to his feet.

"All right, son. Once you get that copper plating screwed into the arms, what say we call it a day? I'll help you and Mom peel the shrimp."

The downstairs runs the length and breadth of the 186-year-old house, unique to the island as the vast majority of residences sit several feet above ground to protect them from the flooding nor'easters and storm surges of hurricanes. Consequently, this basement has been underwater numerous times since its construction.

It served as slave quarters in the 1830s.

Servant quarters at the turn of the century.

One of the most extensive wine cellars in North Carolina in the 1920s.

A decade ago Rufus wired several rooms and passageways for electricity.

The rest are lit by candle or not at all.

The stone in one of the rooms is charred black all the way up to the ceiling.

In another the rock is stained burgundy.

Though Luther has spent a great deal of time down here, he's still prone to losing his way, particularly when he ventures beyond the cluster of rooms near the stairs, a maze of confusing corridors that were lined with wine racks eighty years ago. Broken glass and pieces of cork can still be found in some of the nooks and crannies.

Now Luther slips soundlessly through a pitchblack corridor, feeling his way along the wall. His parents are busy upstairs preparing food. He'll join them shortly.

At last his fingers register the break in the wall—the alcove where Andrew and the women wait.

Luther stops, leans against the stone, listens.

No one is talking. He hears breathing. Chains clinking.

The little blond has been chained facing the doorway. Per-haps tomorrow he'll come back when the light slips through so he can watch her from the shadows. But it's enough now to know that she sits there, just a few feet away, sharing the darkness with him.

CHAPTER 53

Horace Boone pulled off Kill Devil Road and parked his Kia in the sand behind a yaupon shrub. Reaching into the backseat, he grabbed the flashlight he'd purchased earlier this afternoon at Bubba's Bait and Tackle.

It was nearing 10:00 P.M. on a cold and glorious November Monday, the sky more milky, star-ridden, than any night in the last three years. Loading his precious purple notebook into a small backpack, he climbed out of the car, shut the door, stepped out into the road, blending seamlessly into the dark in black jeans, hiking boots, and a chocolate-colored fleece pullover.

The night was windless, the first killing frost of the season beginning to blanch blades of grass and island shrubs. He started walking, past the mailbox, down the shadowy drive, the ceiling of live oaks and Spanish moss shielding the starry sky. Horace almost turned on the flashlight but then decided it might be prudent to arrive unannounced.

He broke out of the grove and there loomed the House of Kite—crumbling masonry and rectangles of orange window-light embossed against the blackwater sound. Andrew Thomas had come here twice last week, presumably in search of Luther Kite. Before abandoning Ocracoke and his dream for good, Horace felt an inexplicable pull to see this manor for himself.

He crept along the perimeter of the live oak thicket until he faced the side of the house. The yard was a field of waist-high weeds. He dropped to the ground, crawled through them, the icy fingers grazing his cheeks.

The moon lifted out of the live oaks, lit the sound.

Horace scrambled to the corner of the great stone house. Rising, he palmed the granite, fuzzy with frosted fungi. Two steps and he peered through a tall and narrow window. The room was dark, empty. Bare bookshelves abounded. Embers glowed in a corner.

Horace crept to the other side of the stoop where he knelt finally beneath the only lighted window on the first floor.

He crouched in the sandy soil to rest.

The night aged silently.

He gazed up briefly into the stars, his breath clouding now in the damp southern chill.

When he'd caught his wind, Horace turned and faced the house.

He rose up slowly to the window ledge, stole a glance inside.

He ducked down instantly, back against the stone, replaying what he'd just seen—a living room steeped in firelight, decaying furniture, and a pale-faced man with long black hair sitting directly across from him on a couch, staring through the window into nothing.

Horace heard footsteps. He stood, peered back through the glass in time to see the long-haired man exit the living room into a foyer, where he stopped beneath a staircase. Plucking something off the wall, he reached forward, opened a little door, and stepped through into total darkness.

Two seconds later, it hit Horace between the eyes—he thought of Andrew's manuscript, *Desert Places,* and his descriptions of a man with long ebony hair and a pale "baby ass–smooth" face.

Horace smiled, but fear tempered the excitement—he'd found Luther Kite.

And it suddenly occurred to him.

What if Andrew had never left this island?

What if Andrew Thomas was dead along with the blond who'd been with him?

Horace sat down in the shadow of the House of Kite. For twenty minutes he watched the moon rise into the sky, mulling over whether he should do the safe thing—leave immediately and contact the police—or the ballsy thing that might make him famous.

By the time Luther reemerged from the door beneath the staircase, Horace had made his decision. From the window he watched Luther trudge upstairs. A moment later, the last light on the second floor went out. Now, aside from the dwindling fire-light in the living room hearth, the house stood still and dark.

Horace came to his feet, moved quietly toward the stoop, and climbed four steps up to the door, his legs gone weak and rubbery. Regardless, he reached for the doorknob. It turned, but the heavy door would not open. He leaned his weight into it, gave the wood a bump with his shoulder. It didn't budge.

Horace walked back down into the yard and jogged through the beach grass around the side of the house, the smell of woodsmoke strong at the chimney's base. There were no windows on the north end—just a wall of granite pushing into the sky.

The moon was high enough to set the backyard alight with its sickly-gleaming radiance. The Pamlico Sound stretched out before him, a black chasm, hugely silent and smooth as volcanic glass.

Horace proceeded toward a stone porch with a jaw-dropping view of the sound, climbed several steps to the back door, and looked through screen and glass into a kitchen.

He pulled on the screen door. It opened. He tried the next doorknob and though it wouldn't turn, the inner door appeared not to have been soundly closed.

He thrust his shoulder against the door.

It jarred open.

Horace stepped into the kitchen and carefully shut the door behind him.

There didn't appear to be a single light in operation in the entire house.

Nor was there any sound.

The kitchen reeked of raw fish and vinegar.

Horace inched forward. The splitting linoleum creaked.

Three more steps and he reached the intersection of two hallways, one leading to the front door, the other running the whole of the first floor into a room whose only light source emanated from the weak brown glow of those dying embers he'd glimpsed from outside.

Horace crept across a dusty hardwood floor, through the corridor that led past the staircase into the foyer.

Something popped.

Horace flinched.

It was just the fire, feeding off pockets of sap in the logs.

He entered the living room and stood before the hearth, basking his hands in the rising heat. Shadows flickered in delicate motion on the walls and ceiling. Flames hissed softly. Even through the woodsmoke he could smell the age and neglect of this ancient house.

Horace turned and let the fire warm his back, staring through the long room at the staircase. The itch of curiosity dragged him toward the foyer, away from the heat and light and sound.

He found himself standing in the darkness under the stairs, facing a locked door, the top of which came only to his eyes. From his pocket he took the flashlight. Its beam revealed a deadbolt in the door.

I saw Luther take something off this wall.

Horace shined the flashlight around the perimeter of the door. To the right of the doorframe, a shiny key hung from a nail.

He jammed it into the deadbolt.

The door swung inward and a cold dank draft swept up out of the darkness and enveloped him.

He smelled stone and water, mold and earth, as though he stood at the entrance to a cave. Though he'd yet to cut the darkness with his flashlight, there was no question in his mind that this door led to someplace underneath the House of Kite.

And the hair on his arms stood erect and some primal siren sounded in his brain, but mistaking terror for adrenaline, he walked down into the darkness because he'd never felt more alive.

CHAPTER 54

Horace kept the beam of the flashlight trained on the rickety steps. They creaked as though God Himself were standing on them—twenty-two in all—and it grew colder the farther down he went so that his breath was pluming again by the time he reached the bottom, a dusty vapor in the lightbeam.

At last Horace stood on a dirt floor.

He shined the flashlight back up the staircase. The door at the top felt miles away.

The basement lay in pure silence and blackness. Horace imagined sitting at a table in the Ocracoke Coffee Company the following morning, near a window with the early sun streaming in. He would write this scene over coffee. It would be amazing. It would be safe.

Horace swiped the beam in a slow circle to gain his bearings.

What he saw unnerved him—doorways into nothing, stone passageways, shoddy wiring snaking up the walls. He shivered, stepped back from the steps, and shined the flashlight down the widest passageway, one that ran behind the staircase into seemingly infinite darkness.

It occurred to him that a person would have to be mad to enter that tunnel, and for a moment he strongly considered heading back up the steps, through the kitchen, into the moonlit yard. The comfort of his bed at the Harper Castle B&B seemed more enticing than ever, but he steeled himself, gripped the flashlight, and proceeded into the passageway.

He progressed slowly, letting the beam graze every surface.

The corridor appeared to narrow the deeper he went.

Horace passed a doorway, shined a light through it. In the brief illumination, he glimpsed a big oak chair in the throes of construction, dripping with wires and leather restraints.

He lost his breath, leaned against the wall to get it back.

When the sound of his own panting subsided, he listened.

Water dripped somewhere in the distance, beyond the ellipse of light.

He heard something move behind him, spun around with the flashlight.

There was nothing there, but the sound repeated.

When the beam hit the floor he saw the fat rat sitting on its haunches staring at him, eyes glowing like luminescent beads.

It scampered back toward the stairs and Horace moved on in the opposite direction, the passageway now turning and branching and turning again, passing through alcoves and various rooms—one with a low ceiling, filled with empty wine racks, another with the burned and splintered remains of a bed frame. There lingered a foreboding, a dread attending these rooms and tunnels. Horace could feel it. Awful things had happened here.

He approached yet another corner, disorientation setting in. The basement seemed to extend beyond the boundaries of the house and he doubted whether he could readily find his way back to the stairs.

At the corner he stopped, shined his flashlight through the next fifteen feet of passageway.

An icy drop of water splashed in his hair.

He glanced up.

Another landed on his nose.

Horace wiped his face, moved on.

A moment later he arrived at a fork in the passageway.

He stopped, looked back in the direction he'd come, trying to recall the turns he'd taken, resolved now to find his way back to the stairs and leave this place.

He heard something, turned, now facing the two tunnels, sound coming from the one on the left, and not the scratchy footsteps of a rat or dripping water.

As Horace illuminated the tunnel, he wondered if the beam had weakened. It seemed softer, less focused.

He ventured in.

This corridor ran straight and narrow, the sound louder now, a metallic *clink-clink-clink*.

The beam of light revealed a wide doorway ten feet ahead on the right.

The *clink* seemed to originate from there.

Horace killed the light and approached in darkness, dragging his hand along the stone so he'd know when he reached the doorway.

He soon felt the break in the wall.

The clinking stopped.

He stepped through the threshold, thinking, *Maybe I imagined it.*

His foot hit something.

Movement below him.

Chains rattling against stone.

He turned on the flashlight.

The beam lit the horrified faces of two women and Andrew Thomas, each manacled and chained to an iron ring in the center of the floor.

They looked vanquished—faces filthy and bruised, streaked with dried blood. But they were shivering and very much alive.

Horace stepped back in shock, a tentative smile parting his lips.

Rich, hero, famous, author—

Andrew Thomas said, "Who are you?"

Horace put a finger to his lips, knelt at the captives' feet, whispered, "My name is Horace Boone, and I'm here to get you out."

One of the women started crying.

The other asked, "Are you FBI?"

Horace shook his head.

"You look familiar," Andrew said.

"I followed you from Haines Junction."

Horace shined the light on the manacles that bound Andrew's wrists.

"You followed me? How did you find me in the first—"

"Let's talk about that when we're safe. Now I don't know how to get these things off."

He tapped the stainless steel manacles.

The woman who was crying said, "I pulled my hand through one of them, but I can't get the other out."

"Horace," Andrew said, "we've been hearing a lot of hammering and sawing nearby. Go see if you can find an ax or something."

Horace remembered passing the room with the oak chair. He'd seen tools scattered all over the floor.

"What time is it?" asked a quiet beaten voice.

Horace shined the light into the face of the little blond he'd seen with Andrew.

"Not even midnight," he said. "We've got time."

CHAPTER 55

The joy, the giddiness, the aching hope consumed him. Horace Boone ran through the tunnels in search of the room with the oak chair, knowing that he *should* be afraid, though excitement overwhelmed what little fear there was.

He emerged from the labyrinth on the opposite side of the staircase from which he'd entered just ten minutes ago and, plunging back into that wide passageway, soon found himself standing at the entrance to the little room with the oak chair.

He shined his failing flashlight across the floor. There were hammers, wrenches, pliers, piles of nails and screws. Stepping inside, he saw what he was looking for—a hacksaw lying on a sheet of copper.

He grabbed it and headed back toward the staircase, attempting to retrace his steps to Andrew Thomas and the women.

The light went out.

Sheer darkness.

Horace knocked it against the stone. The light came back weaker.

He moved on through the twisting tunnels, taking only one wrong turn before arriving at the alcove.

"What'd you find?" Andrew whispered.

"Hacksaw."

"Since Beth already has one hand free, cut her chain first."

"Hold this steady."

Horace put the flashlight in Andrew's hands. Then he walked over and took hold of the chain that linked Beth's manacles to the iron ring.

"Lean back," he whispered. "You got to pull it tight."

Beth pulled the chain and Horace set the blade of the hacksaw against the metal.

"Andrew," he said, poised to begin sawing, "would you grant me an exclusive interview when we get out of this?"

The second he asked, he felt dirty, and wished he hadn't.

"You get us out of this, I'll father your children."

Horace began to saw.

It was awkward at first, the chain moving so much the blade kept slipping. But once it had begun a groove in the link, the blade moved through the metal like it was rotten pine. He'd cut the first link in less than two minutes, but as he started into the next one the light died again.

"Piece of shit."

"That beam was pretty weak," Andrew said. "Might not come back on."

"I put fresh batteries in this afternoon."

Andrew flicked the on-off switch several times and the light returned, just a faint orange glow, but adequate to work by.

Horace attacked the final link.

When the chain severed, Beth fell back into the wall, a manacle still attached to her left wrist.

"Who's next?" Horace asked.

"Do him," said the little blond.

Horace handed the flashlight to Beth, told her, "Aim it here."

Andrew leaned back, pulled the chain taut.

Horace drew the blade slowly against the metal until he could feel a groove deepening. Then he sawed like mad, the friction of the blade on the chain filling the alcove with metallic screaming and the odor of heated steel.

He made it through the first link in less than a minute and had started into the second one when the blond whispered, "Wait!"

Horace stopped sawing.

They listened.

A creaking emanated from somewhere in the basement.

"What is that?" Beth asked.

Horace felt a tremor sweep through him.

"Someone's coming down the steps," he said.

As he reached for the flashlight it went out.

"Fuckin' kidding me."

Horace grabbed the flashlight, flicked the on-off button, and when nothing happened smashed it into the stone. He heard the batteries fall out and roll across the floor.

Andrew said, "Horace, you have to leave and hide. Beth?"

"I'm right here."

They were nothing now but whispers in the dark.

"Get back down on the floor and hold your hands like you're still chained."

"Who do you think is coming?" Horace whispered.

"Doesn't matter," Andrew said. "They're all psychopaths. Now go and take the hacksaw with you so they don't see it."

The creaking had stopped.

Horace reached forward, felt the side of the wall, and stepped into the passageway. There wasn't even the subtlest inference of light. Horace groped for the wall, found it, and crept away from the alcove, away from the stairs, staying close to the left side of the tunnel.

After ten steps the wall ended.

Reaching around, he found that he could palm both sides of it.

He stood at the fork in the corridor.

Gazing back through swimming darkness toward the alcove, his eyes played tricks on him, firing phantom bursts of light.

The silence roared.

He strained to listen, thought he heard things—voices, foot-steps—but it might've been his own heartbeat hammering against his eardrum.

When he saw the lanternlight on the stone he doubted his eyes. But the shadows were real, as was the sound of shuffling footsteps, and then the silhouette of a crooked old woman emerging from around a bend in the tunnel.

Horace slipped back into the adjacent corridor.

The voice he heard was soft, sweet, and utterly disarming.

"Rufus and I heard something. Y'all wanna go ahead and tell me what it was?"

"We haven't heard anything," Andrew responded.

"No?"

The old woman laughed. Horace peeked around the corner, saw her standing in robe and slippers in the threshold of the al-cove, firelight from the lantern playing on her deeply wrinkled face.

"Well, that's the funniest thing I've heard all year, because the door under the stairs was open. How do you think that hap-pened?"

"We haven't heard a thing," Andrew repeated. "I was as—"

"It doesn't matter now," the old woman said, "because Luther locked the door, so there won't be any leaving. He and Rufus are searching the basement right now. Rufus knows it so well, he can do it in the dark."

The old woman turned away from the alcove and started back toward the stairs, taking the light of the lantern with her, leaving Horace Boone alone in the black.

CHAPTER 56

I will wake up in my room at the Harper Castle.

It will be warm.

The sun will reflect off the harbor.

I will get dressed and walk outside into the cool morning.

I will walk to the Ocracoke Coffee Company.

I will write this scene tomorrow over breakfast.

And if that pretty cashier is there, I will talk to her.

Tell her I'm a writer.

Ask her on a date, because I've never done that before and after to-night what is there to fear?

Horace dropped the hacksaw and tightened the shoulder straps on his backpack.

He sat leaning against the stone wall.

His entire body quaked and the more he tried to deny it the more he knew how gravely fucked he was. He'd never known this caliber of terror. It coated his insides like melted silver. And what magnified it was the knowledge that he'd come here on his own, dragged himself into the shit.

Down the corridor he thought he heard footsteps in the dirt.

Horace came to his feet.

The footsteps stopped.

Someone exhaled.

He strained to listen.

The darkness gaped with a silence that seemed to hum though he knew that sound was only the blood between his ears.

A light overhead flicked on and off.

So brief was its illumination he'd have missed them had he blinked.

But he didn't.

And in that half-second snapshot of light he glimpsed tunnel walls, dirt floor, ax and shotgun, and, not twenty feet away, the two men who held them—one old, one young—grinning at him.

A voice emerged from the darkness.

"What do you think you're doing, young man?"

Horace could hardly breathe.

"I was following Andrew Thomas."

"Who are you?"

"Horace Boone."

Horace backed slowly into the tunnel as they conversed in darkness.

"I saw Andrew Thomas in a bookstore in Alaska last April." Then fighting tears, "I've been following him because I want to write a book about him. I swear that's all. I have a notebook in my backpack that'll prove it." His voice broke at the end.

"You came here on foot?"

"I left my car in the trees near your mailbox. I just want to write a book about—"

"And you're here alone?"

"Yessir. I'm so sorry. I know I shouldn't've—"

"Well, Luther, what do you think? Should we give him a head start?"

"Fuck no."

A flashlight suddenly burned in Horace's eyes.

He saw the twenty-eight-inch barrel pass through the light-beam, *shook shook*, and he dove to the floor as the light went out.

There was an orange blossom.

Earsplitting *boom*.

He smelled gunpowder as the spray of buckshot hit the stone behind him.

And Horace was back on his feet, running blind into the dark.

CHAPTER 57

It was in the late afternoon when the shaft of light passed through the stone and lit the oval patch of rock in our dungeon.

I watched Beth stagger to her feet.

The manacles and a sixteen-inch length of chain still hung from her left wrist. She'd spent several hours to no avail trying to squeeze her hand free.

Beth stood in bare feet, in her filthy yellow teddy, gazing down at Violet and me.

We'd all huddled in darkness last night, listening to the shotgun blasts, wondering what had happened to that young man.

"Come here," I whispered.

She knelt, our faces close in the musty twilight.

"Beth, just get out of this place. That's your first priority. Get somewhere safe before you try to do anything."

She nodded, moved over to the twenty-something blond, whose once smart black suit now adorned her like rags.

"Violet," she whispered, touching her face, running her fingers across the top of her dirty matted hair, "you're going to have your baby."

Violet's eyes welled.

"Be safe, Beth."

And Beth stood, stepped from the alcove into the tunnel. As she glanced back at us, barely visible in the temporary stream of sunlight, I wondered if I was laying eyes on her for the last time.

Beth started into the corridor.

After three steps the darkness was total. She could hear hammering somewhere in the black distance. She dragged her right hand along the wall as a guide. Shards of laughter reverberated through the darkness, the dirt cool beneath her feet. She thought of her children. Drove them from her mind, thinking, *Just get outside, under the blue sky, and go from there.*

She walked into three dead ends before she saw the light.

It came from a doorway twenty feet ahead.

The chain dangling from her wrist knocked into the stone wall.

Spurning the impotence in her knees, she crept forward until the voices became perfectly clear.

Rufus carefully let go of the oak strip he'd been pressing into the back of the chair for the last five minutes. The strip would serve as a sleeve for the heavy copper wire that ran up the backside of the four-by-four. Now that the wood glue had hardened, Rufus stepped back and admired his chair. It was crude, yes, but in a terrifyingly utilitarian fashion.

It would be so beautifully lethal.

Maxine sat in a corner reading *At Home in Mitford.*

Luther was crouched over a sheet of copper.

"Pop, what'd you do with the hacksaw? I have one more cut to make, and I can't find it."

"Haven't seen it."

"Mom, you haven't touched it?"

Maxine peered over the top of her book.

"Do I look like I have any use for—"

"Oh, no."

"What?" Rufus said.

Luther stood up.

"You don't think our visitor took it?"

"No."

"Well, do you see it here? I didn't take it. You didn't take it. Mom sure as hell didn't take it."

"Watch that language, boy."

"The *fucker*," Luther glanced at his mother, "didn't walk off."

"Beautiful, were they all chained up when you fed them this morning?"

"Gee, Sweet-Sweet, I don't remember. I wasn't really paying attention. What kinda question is that? Of course they were."

"We better go check on them, son."

Rufus and Luther were halfway through the doorway when they heard the *dingdong*.

The doorbell had been recently wired to a speaker near the stairs and they stared at it in amazement as it dingdonged again.

Beth froze, watching the Kite family emerge into the corridor. She did not move for fear the chain would clink against the stone or they would hear her footsteps. She wondered if the darkness was sufficient to hide her, should one of them happen to glance back in her direction.

The young man, the old man, and the old woman walked up the corridor away from her, guided by the light of a lantern.

The young man carried a shotgun.

The *dingdong* echoed again through the darkness.

In the orange illumination of the lanternlight, Beth saw them turn and disappear. She thought they had swung around into another passageway until the sound of their footsteps reached her.

They're climbing stairs.

And knowing she'd found the way out, she crept after them.

CHAPTER 58

Rufus alone answered the door with a bright toothless smile that never faltered, even when he saw the badge. Two men stood facing him on the stoop, the sun in their eyes, just moments from sliding behind the house on its way into becoming a puddle of light in the Pamlico Sound.

The one with the badge was a big bear of a man in a JCPenney suit that should've been donated to the Salvation Army years ago. His hair was frosting, mustache just as dark and thick as a stallion's mane. The curly-haired man standing behind the cop looked half his age—mid-twenties, lean and tall, wearing jeans and a pinstripe button-down, with the eyes of a dog who'd been kicked.

The cop closed his wallet, dropped it back into his pocket, said, "Mr. Kite, my name's Barry Mullins. I'm a sergeant with Criminal Investigations Division in Davidson, North Carolina. Could I come in for a moment?"

"Absolutely."

Rufus opened the door wide and stepped back.

Sgt. Mullins whispered to his companion, "Max, please, just go and wait in the car. It would be—"

Max walked into the house.

Sgt. Mullins frowned and followed.

Rufus closed the door, the three men now standing in the dim foyer, the house perfectly quiet.

"Get you gentlemen a glass of iced tea?" Rufus offered.

Sgt. Mullins shook his head.

"Your wife at home, sir?"

"She's out running an errand."

Sgt. Mullins motioned to the long living room.

"Let's have a seat in there, Mr. Kite."

On her way to the stairs Beth stopped and looked inside the room where the Kites had been hammering and jawing and sawing. Tools littered the floor. A bare light bulb burned her eyes, humming directly above what all the ruckus must've been about—a rude chair in the final stage of construction, with copper plating along its armrests and front legs, numerous leather restraints, and thick copper wire coiled in the dirt beside it. The thing had an undeniable presence. As the architecture of a cathedral exudes solemnity and peace, its raw blocky masculine design broadcasted pure malevolence.

Beth shook off the chill and moved on. In the distance she could see where the corridor opened into a larger space. One of the Kites had left a kerosene lantern hanging in a corner to spread its worthless light upon the dirt and stone near the foot of the stairs.

She emerged from the passageway.

She rubbed her bare arms, bumpy with gooseflesh.

The stairs spilled down out of darkness.

Beth peered up, unable to see where they terminated.

And she wrapped the chain around her wrist to keep it from dragging and began to climb, the steps creaking so noisily that she did not hear the whispered footsteps of the old woman creeping out of the shadows behind her.

Sgt. Mullins eased down onto the same ottoman his detective had occupied six days ago during her first encounter with Rufus and Maxine Kite.

The old man lounged comfortably on the flaxen sofa, running his fingers through his cottony coif.

Max King stood by the cold hearth.

"Mr. Kite," Sgt. Mullins said, leaning forward, forearms resting on his knees. "A week ago, I sent my detective, Violet King, to Ocracoke Island to talk with you and Mrs. Kite about your son, Luther. I understand she came here last Wednesday?"

"Yessir, she did." Rufus smiled. "A lovely little thing, I must say. She met briefly with me and Maxine. Like you said, she wanted to know about our boy, Luther. And I'll tell you what I told her. I haven't seen my s—"

"Sir, I'm aware of what you told her. She called me that night. That's not why I'm here."

Sgt. Mullins motioned to Max.

"This is Max King. Ms. King's husband. He last spoke to Ms. King on Thursday morning. Late Thursday night, Ms. King called my home and spoke briefly with my wife. My wife is the last person we know of to have had contact with Ms. King. No one has seen her or heard from her since."

"Oh Lord."

"Now Vik—Ms. King was supposed to come back here and talk with you and Mrs. Kite late Thursday afternoon. Did she?"

"No sir. We'd agreed to meet with her again after five o'clock, but she never showed. Do you think something's wrong?"

Sgt. Mullins twisted his mustache and glanced up at Max, the young man's jowls fluttering against the saltwater in his eyes.

The bare feet of Beth Lancing stopped on the third step. She was squinting up into the darkness at slits of light that framed a door when she heard something like the muffled *thock* of a knee or hip bone popping.

A leathery hand seized her left ankle and the floor hit her hard in the back, the old woman upon her, face contorted in the lanternlight, black eyes shining through a mass of wild wrinkles that looked hardly human.

Something caught the lanternlight thinly, fleetingly, and Beth heard herself gasp at the cold wet burn that was spreading through her abdomen.

Beth rolled on top of Maxine, grabbing at the old woman's wrists as the soles of Maxine's orthopedic shoes found her stomach. Beth slammed into the corner, knees turning liquid.

Both women scrambled to their feet, panting. Maxine was just out of reach, blocking the stairs. Beth unraveled the chain on her left wrist, noting the warm red trickle down her inner thigh, the boning knife in Maxine's right hand, and the weightlessness filling the space behind her eyes.

When Maxine lunged, the chain caught her in the mouth. She choked and spit blood, staggered into the wall, and dropped the knife.

Beth spun Maxine around and punched her so hard it broke her hand and the old woman's jaw at once.

Swiping up the knife, she left Maxine unconscious in the dirt and tore up the stairs toward the slits of light.

CHAPTER 59

As Sgt. Mullins came to his feet he said, "Mr. Kite, this is one big old spooky house y'all got here."

Rufus smiled. "It's haunted, you know."

"That right?"

"There's a ghost lives up on the third floor, gooses my wife every time she walks into our son's old room."

Sgt. Mullins grinned.

"I think I'd bolt that room shut, never go back in."

"Nah, our ghosts are all right . . . just a little horny."

"Mr. Kite, thanks for your time."

As the old man stood, his eyes lit up.

"You know, come to think of it, there's someone else you should talk to. Fellow named Scottie Myers. Works at Howard's Pub. Used to be a friend of Luther's. I told Ms. King about him, so he may have seen her after I did."

"We'll look him up."

Rufus walked them toward the front door.

"Will you let me know when you find Ms. King?" the old man asked. "It'll keep me up nights thinking about her."

"Do you have a phone? We tried to call first but couldn't—"

"Sure don't."

"Well, if I remember, I'll write you a note, let you know when we find her. Because we *will* find her."

Rufus patted Max on the shoulder as he opened the door for them.

"Your wife will be in my prayers, young man."

Sgt. Mullins and Max stepped outside and walked down the disintegrating steps into the waving beach grass. When Max heard the door close behind them he said, "Barry, you have to search that house. I have a bad—"

"Wait till we're in the car."

The black Crown Victoria was parked between the two live oaks in the front yard. Its windshield glinted and then went dark as the sun slipped behind the house.

The men climbed into the car and closed the doors.

"Something isn't right in there," Max said. "Get a search warrant, whatever you have to do, turn that place upside down. That old man . . . I don't know."

Sgt. Mullins put the key into the ignition but didn't start the engine.

He stared through the windshield at the great stone House of Kite, ensconced on the banks of the sound.

"Well, I *do* know," he said finally. "Been doing this quite a while. You learn how to read people, how to know if they're hiding something. If they're nervous. Body language says a lot. Fidgeting. If the eye contact is too intense or nonexistent."

"Barry, look—"

Sgt. Mullins held up a finger.

"That old man," he said, "doesn't have a thing in this world to hide."

"It's your suspect's father for—"

"Means nothing. I looked into his soul, Max. He's telling the truth."

Sgt. Mullins clicked in his seatbelt and cranked the engine.

"Let's go find Mr. Scottie Myers," he said, shifting the car into REVERSE.

Max scowled.

Sgt. Mullins grinned.

"Trust me, Max. I'm right. It's a gift."

Sgt. Mullins turned the car around and they headed back along the dirt road that wound through the thicket of live oaks. Reaching down, he turned on the radio, found an oldies station, drumming his hands now on the steering wheel.

As Max reached to buckle his seatbelt he happened to glance in the side mirror.

"Stop the car, Barry!"

"What?"

"Look!"

Sgt. Mullins stepped on the brake, and both men looked back through the window.

Beyond the tunnel of live oaks, they could see the stoop of the stone house, the front door flung wide open, a woman in torn yellow lingerie falling down the steps, picking herself up again, and running after them, the blood on her left leg visible even from fifty yards away.

Sgt. Mullins said, "Holy God."

He turned back to shift the car into PARK.

The windshield shattered.

His right arm exploded.

Sgt. Mullins stomped the gas and as the car accelerated, the man with the shotgun stepped out of the way and fired point-blank through the window at Sgt. Mullins's head.

The detective collapsed into Max's lap, his foot slipped off the gas pedal, and the Crown Victoria rolled a ways down the dirt road before veering into the thicket. After ten feet, its front bumper collided gently with the trunk of a live oak and the car was at rest, idling quietly.

Max's left shoulder had caught three pellets of buckshot, but he felt nothing as he strained to lift the big detective off his legs.

He heaved Sgt. Mullins back into the driver seat and glanced through the rear passenger window. A man with long black hair was thirty yards away and closing, moving deliberately through the thicket toward the car. He saw Max looking, smiled, and pumped his shotgun.

They killed Vi.

He swept Sgt. Mullins's coat back as the footsteps of the assailant waxed audible over the purr of the engine.

Unbuttoning the latchet, he pulled the Glock from its cowhide holster.

Vi had begged him several times to come shoot with her at the range. He never had and knew nothing of how to use a firearm except for what he'd seen in movies and on television.

After searching for a safety that wasn't there, Max finally aimed through the rear passenger window as the pale-faced man closed in.

Max squeezed the trigger and glass exploded as the .45 bucked in his hand.

The man continued toward him, unscathed.

Max opened the door and scrambled out of the car as the shotgun boomed, glass raining down on him. He crawled to the back of the car, poked his head above the trunk in time to see the shotgun jerk and fire come roaring out the barrel.

Max ducked down, sitting with his back against the tire.

Sweat sheeted down his forehead into his eyes, but it smelled rusty, and when he wiped it away the back of his hand was blood-smeared. He touched his head, felt where the pellets of buckshot had scalped three marble-size trenches down to the bone, the steel November afternoon like ice on his skull.

He looked under the car, unable to see the legs of the man who was trying to kill him.

Max peered over the trunk again.

No one there.

He stood.

Glock quivering in his hand.

Three bloodstreaks down his face like warpaint.

Blinked, and there was the barrel of the shotgun, peeking over the other side of the trunk, and Max felt the ground beneath him and he was staring through the twisted limbs of those haunted trees at flinders of a fading sky the color of his wife's name and he tried to say it, tried to call out to her.

A black moon appeared and descended toward him, filling his violet sky with the reek of scorched metal and death.

CHAPTER 60

Beth bolted barefoot through the beach grass as the third shotgun report erupted from the thicket of live oaks. Glancing over her shoulder, she saw the old man leaning against the rusted pickup truck, hand pressed into his side where she'd cut him with the boning knife.

The adrenaline waned, her own stab wound beginning to throb like the worst cramp she'd ever felt, as though something were trying to burrow out of her stomach.

Another shotgun blast echoed across the water.

She plunged into the thicket north of the house, running like hell, not looking back, tearing through the cooling darkness of the live oaks, the sun at her back, not long for the world.

Beth crossed a patch of sandspurs.

She screamed and fell, dug three organic spikes out of her right foot, and ran on, dead leaves clinging to the blood on her left leg.

After two minutes she collapsed, lying in leaves in the swarming cold.

She rolled onto her back, stared up at the fading sky.

She closed her eyes.

Excruciating now to inhale.

She pushed her palm into the wound, felt blood seep between her fingers . . .

When her eyes opened she could see a solitary planet in the cobalt.

Her breath steamed.

Leaves crunching somewhere in the distance.

She wondered if the man with long black hair would kill her in the woods or take her back to that awful house . . .

Beth woke colder than she'd ever been, the sky starblown, woods gone quiet, her bleeding stopped. She sat up, staggered to her feet, and limped along through the thicket.

After an hour she broke from the trees into a field of marsh grass, her feet sinking every step in the cold mud. She tramped on, so delirious with exhaustion that she hardly noticed when her eviscerated foot touched the pavement of Highway 12.

Beth stepped bewildered into the middle of the road. To the north it ran into darkness as far as she could see. Southward, it extended toward what could only be the nighttime glow of civilization.

The moon was rising.

Sea shining.

She stumbled along toward the village.

Rufus's wound was long but shallow. He sat in a chair in the kitchen while, in lieu of stitches, Maxine used a strip of duct tape to close the three-inch slice to the right of his bellybutton.

The left side of her jaw was swollen, but the pain was sufferable. There was little she could do about it anyway. They didn't have much time. People would be coming soon, looking for the men their son had murdered.

While Maxine packed suitcases, Rufus took a lantern down into the basement.

The good news was that the project was nearly finished. He had only to install the power supply and wire it to the chair. He would work all night if he had to.

Flicking on the overhead light bulb, he rolled the generator from the passageway into the death chamber.

Rufus hoped Luther would return soon so they could put the finishing touches on their beautiful chair together.

At midnight Beth came to a dirt road. It branched off to the soundside of Highway 12, crossed a hundred yards of marsh, and terminated on a piece of dry land, upon which sat a modest saltbox, its porchlight beckoning.

The name on the nearby mailbox read Tatum.

She could see the warm glow of the Ocracoke Light in the distance, a comforting presence above the dark trees. The village was less than a half mile down the highway, but everything was sure to be closed at this hour. Besides, the sole of her foot was shredded. She doubted she could stand the pain of walking much farther.

Her wound started to bleed again as she trudged down the dirt road. The closer she got to the house the more light-headed she became and the deeper the cold bored into her. She wondered how she'd lasted this long, felt a brief tinge of pride.

Live oaks massed behind the saltbox, blocking a view of the sound. But eastward the dunes were just low enough to offer a glimpse of the sea—shiny black in the strong moonlight.

She neared the house. An old sailboat foundered in weeds on the edge of the marsh, like something washed up after a hurricane, stripped of sails, its hull cracked.

A Dodge Ram gleamed in the yellow porchlight, parked parallel to the garage, "BOATLUV" on the license plate, a fishing rod holder mounted to the front bumper, the rods standing erect in their PVC pipes.

Beth climbed five brick steps to the front door.

Moths loitered above her head, bouncing off the porchlight, over and over like maniacs.

Nausea hit her, but there was nothing in her stomach.

Through slits in the blinds, she saw the shadow of a man lying on a couch, blue light flickering on the walls around him.

Beth opened the screen door and knocked.

The man did not move.

She banged on the door, saw him sit up suddenly and rub his eyes.

He staggered to his feet.

She heard his footsteps coming.

The front door opened and a white-bearded man gazed down at her through glassy eyes. He cinched his robe and she smelled gin when he said, "Do you have any idea what time . . ."

He rubbed his eyes again, blinked several times, and squinted at her, Beth crying now, the warmth of his home flowing out onto the porch, reminding her what safety felt like. The man saw the blood pooling at her feet, traced it to the hole in her stained and ragged lingerie.

She heard audience laughter on the television.

Cold blood trailed down her leg.

"Help me," she whispered.

Her knees quit and she fell forward.

He caught her, lifted her off her feet, and carried her inside.

CHAPTER 61

Rufus pushed the Generac Wheelhouse into a corner of the death chamber, fired up the soldering gun, and proceeded to fuse the no. 4 copper wire to the copper plating on the chair's front legs, the room filling with the sweet sappy odor of the melted alloy.

When the soldering was done, he took the hacksaw he'd found in a corridor near the alcove, and cut two four-foot lengths of no. 4 copper wire from the dwindling coil. With a hammer, he beat out the ends of the wire until they were flattened enough to fit into the two legs of the generator's 220 volt outlet.

Behind the toolbox he found Maxine's contribution to the project—a homemade skullcap. She'd taken a North Carolina Tarheels baseball cap, cut up one of her thin leather belts, and sewn the pieces into the sides so the buckle could be tightened under the condemned's chin.

Maxine had drilled a hole through a square-inch of copper plating and put a brass screw through it. She'd then superglued a square-inch piece of sponge to the copper plate, removed the button from the top of the baseball cap, and bolted the electrode to the inside so it would rest flush against the condemned's head.

Rufus grabbed one of the four-foot copper wires and hammered its other end so that it had enough surface area to accept a screw. He drilled a hole through it, then took both the wire and the skullcap and sat down in the chair.

Unscrewing the bolt that fastened the electrode to the cap, he slipped the copper wire onto the brass screw, tightened the bolt back into place, and grinned.

He now had his own personal electric chair, and though he had doubts about whether it could actually deliver a lethal jolt, it would certainly be fun to try.

Rufus came to his feet.

His side was hurting again.

He walked upstairs to tell Maxine that everything was ready and see if Luther had come home.

Charlie Tatum was sobering up fast. He set the broken creature down on the soft leather sofa where he'd been drifting in and out of sleep for the last two hours, and called out to his wife down the dark hallway:

"Margaret! Come out here!"

The woman was still unconscious.

Charlie knelt down on the carpet and straightened the lingerie so her nipples didn't show. He lifted her satin chemise to see where all the blood was coming from.

The wound was located just above her hip bone, like a small black mouth, open with surprise, blood oozing from its corner, down the woman's side, and onto the leather sofa.

"What in the world are you yelling about, baby?"

Margaret emerged from the hallway and stood in her flannel nightgown, a woman with heft, her dyed red hair in turmoil, sleeplines down the right side of her face.

"Are you drunk?" she asked, pointing at the empty tumbler and the half-empty bottle of Tanqueray sitting on the driftwood coffee table between the sofa and the television.

"Just put your glasses on, Mag," he said.

Margaret pulled a pair of thick-lensed frames from the patch pocket on her nightgown, slipped them on, and gasped.

"My God. What in the world happened to her?"

"You tell me. She just knocked on the door. When I opened it she said 'help me' and fainted right into my arms."

Margaret moved a step closer across the carpet. She turned on a stained glass lamp sitting on an end table.

"Is that blood?" she asked.

"Yeah. She's got a bad cut right here. And her arms and legs are all torn up."

"I'll call nine-one-one. Or should we just take her to the medical center? I'll drive."

Charlie laid his ear against the woman's heart, her mouth.

"No, she's breathing. Just tell them to send an ambulance."

While Margaret called 911 from the adjacent kitchen, Charlie leaned in close to the woman on his sofa and spoke in a low and calming voice into her ear.

"You're safe now. An ambulance is coming and they're gonna take good care of you." Charlie felt her burning forehead, then held her swollen shattered hand. "Just hang in there, okay? Everything's gonna be fine now. You came to the right house."

Margaret walked in from the kitchen, sat down on the end of the sofa.

"Ambulance is on the way and they're also sending a police

car since I told them she might've been attacked. What do you think happened to her?"

Charlie shook his head.

He stared at the television for a moment, then reached for the remote control and turned it off.

The woman stirred.

Eyes opening.

Wide with fear.

"Remember me?" Charlie asked.

A nod.

"You're safe now. The ambulance is coming."

There was a knock at the front door.

"That was fast," Margaret said, rising from the sofa.

"See, there they are," Charlie whispered. "Lightning quick."

As Margaret reached to open the front door she said, "Wonder why they didn't use the siren or the lights?"

Charlie was staring into the woman's glazed eyes when Margaret opened the door.

He said, "We'll come see you in the hospital tomorrow, maybe bring you some—"

Margaret emitted a strange gurgling sound.

Charlie glanced over his shoulder at his wife.

She turned slowly.

Faced him.

Standing in the open doorway, stunned, face pale as sand, sheets of blood flooding out of the long dark smile under her chin.

"Mag!" Charlie shrieked, coming to his feet, leaping awkwardly over the coffee table as his wife went to her knees and fell prostrate across the carpet.

A man with long black hair stepped into the low-lit living room as the sound of distant sirens grew audible.

Charlie lunged at the intruder who simply held fast to the

ivory-hilted bowie, letting the old sailor impale himself with his own inertia, the carbon blade turning, riving its quiet devastation inside him.

Charlie tumbled backward and fell dying onto his dead wife.

Luther drew the blade between his thumb and forefinger, flung blood onto the walls, and turned his attention to the leather sofa.

Beth was gone and the sirens were approaching.

CHAPTER 62

The inside of the wicker clothes hamper smelled of fish guts and mildew. Beth had burrowed down into the laundry, covering herself in underwear and panties and damp jeans and a blanket that stank of gasoline.

The old man was no longer keening and above the moan of sirens she could hear hallway doors opening and closing.

Once she had managed to put the lid on the hamper from inside, her only view of the master bedroom was through a gap in the wicker. But there was little to see. A blue night-light by the doorway provided the sole illumination.

Footsteps stopped behind the door.

Doorknob turning.

Sirens closing in.

Stay alive one more minute and you get to live, see your children again. He can't stay once the police are here.

The bedroom door swung open.

"Elizabeth."

A voice without a shard of emotion.

Through the wicker she could see his legs in the electric blue glow of the night-light.

"We don't have much time. Come on."

The flashing lights of the ambulance passed through the bedroom's only window, bursts of vermilion streaking across the walls. She could hear the rocks crunching under its tires as it sped down the dirt road toward the saltbox.

"I'm just gonna cut your throat and leave. You'll be dead in a minute tops. I think that's very reasonable."

Beth watched him walk past the hamper, kneel down, and glance under the bed. He rose, moved toward the adjoining bathroom, disappeared inside.

Her heart banging.

Sirens blistering the frozen November night outside.

Reaching out of the clothes, hands on the wicker lid, she heard him rip the shower curtain from its rings.

Go now. Climb out. Go.

A cabinet under the sink opened and closed.

She started to lift the lid when his footsteps reentered the bedroom.

Walk past. Please just go. Leave. Run away. They'll catch you.

The ambulance parked in front of the house. She could hear its engine, doors opening, slamming.

The man sighed and rushed past the hamper to the doorway.

Oh yes thank You God thank—

He stopped abruptly in the threshold.

Paramedics pounding on the front door.

"Almost," he said. "Almost."

And he spun around and moved toward the hamper, Beth peering up through the stench of strangers' laundry as the lid disappeared.

The man with long black hair gazed down at her and smiled, flashing lights rouging his pale and bloodless face.

The voices of the paramedics reached them, yelling for someone to unlock the front door.

What Beth heard next was the sound the blade made, moving in and out of her—footsteps in squishy mud.

He did the work with the casual efficiency he used to clean fish, then put the lid back on and ran out of the bedroom.

Beth heard a window break across the hall. He was escaping through the backyard.

Her heart sputtered, trying to beat, failing, the pain tempered by the expanding vacuum the life left as it rushed warmly and fast out of her throat.

It occurred to her that she couldn't breathe, but she was gone before it mattered.

CHAPTER 63

My head was clearing, the bleary shapes clamoring back into focus.

Still disoriented from a bash on the head that had knocked me unconscious, I found myself immobilized in an uncomfortably straight chair in a low-lit stone room that smelled of solder and copper and freshly-hewn oak.

Violet had been thrown in a corner onto a pile of sawdust, hands bound with duct tape, another strip across her mouth, tears streaming down her face as she watched me through horrified eyes.

The Kites operated in a tizzy of movement all around me—Maxine cinching the leather ankle restraints, Luther tightening the chest strap, Rufus pressing my head against the tall chairback. He pulled a leather strap flush against my forehead, ran it through the buckle, and said, "Best be pulling these straps tight as can be, 'cause he's gonna jerk like the dickens."

As all six leather restraints were buckled and viciously tightened, I noticed the copper wire running from the chair into a generator.

"What are you gonna do to me?" I asked, my throat tight with dehydration and fear.

"Boy, we're gonna run electricity through your body until you are dead," Maxine said, coming forward in a daisy print housedress, her jaw swollen, bright black eyes shining.

"Why?"

The old woman knelt at my feet, and with a pair of rusty scissors began cutting away my fleece pants below the knee, the backs of my legs pressed against the cold plates of copper. Then she trimmed the sleeves of my shirt below the elbows so my bare forearms made contact with the electrodes on the armrests.

"Why are you doing this?" I failed to hide the tremor in my voice.

"Because we can, my boy, because we can." Maxine chuckled.

In the corner opposite Violet, Rufus poured a big bag of seasalt into a basin of water while Luther vigorously stirred the saline solution with a wooden spoon.

"Luther," I said. "Luther, you look at me and tell me why—"

"Where's that razor, Sweet-Sweet?" Maxine asked.

Rufus pulled a razor from the pocket of his tattered leather jacket and handed it to his wife. She walked behind the chair and I felt the blade scraping across my skull as she shaved a ragged circle on the crown of my head.

Logic told me to shut the fuck up, that nothing I said would make any difference.

But I wasn't operating on logic now.

I saw Maxine reach behind the generator and lift a Carolina Tarheels baseball cap, jury-rigged with a chinstrap and a long copper wire curving out of the top.

"Please listen," I said as she walked over to the basin and

dipped the underside of the hat in the saltwater, letting the sponge affixed to the inside saturate. "Look, I've done terrible things. I understand how a person comes to be that way, but you don't have to do this. Let's find a way to—"

Rivulets of lukewarm water ran down my face, salting my lips as she fitted the skullcap onto my head. She fastened the chin-strap, moved out of the way as Luther and Rufus approached bearing dripping sponges.

"Luther, I apologize. I feel terrible about what happened. You have to believe that. I'm so sorry I left you—"

"To freeze and bleed to death in the desert. I'm sure you are *now*. But aren't you curious?"

"About what?"

"How I escaped."

"Oh, well yes—"

"It was the damnedest thing, Andrew. One of the Maddings' ranch hands showed up on a snowmobile about an hour after you left. Young man saved my life. Took my place on the porch. If it wasn't for him, I guess you'd be doing a lot better right now."

They began to rub my legs and forearms with a peculiar solemnity, sousing with saltwater wherever my skin touched the copper plating.

Don't you dare beg these monsters for your life. It's what they get off on.

"Maxine, please look at me."

She looked at me.

"What if it were Luther sitting here? Wouldn't you want someone to show your son a little mercy?" On "mercy" my voice broke. "I'm someone's son, too."

"Not anymore," Luther said.

There was a can of unleaded gasoline sitting next to a circular saw. Rufus picked it up, unscrewed the gas cap on the generator, and topped off the tank.

"Beautiful, would you christen the chair?"

The old woman picked up a bottle of Cook's from behind a stack of unused lumber, stepped toward me, and swung the bottle into the chairback. It broke off at the neck, soaking my lap with warm fizzing spumante.

Maxine said, "And we're operational."

The Kites applauded, hugs all around.

"Remember, son," Rufus said, "we don't have all night. Keep in mind we're not safe here anymore. We need to be on the first ferry of the morning. Now, Andrew, don't you worry about little Violet. She's coming with us. I think my boy has a crush."

Maxine and Rufus stepped back, standing arm-in-arm in a corner as Luther approached the generator.

"No," I said, "please don't do that, Luther, just wait a—"

When he gripped the pull string I raged against the restraints.

To my surprise, Luther waited, watching me with a sort of perverse patience, allowing me to exhaust myself, making sure I knew I wasn't leaving his chair under my own strength.

I quit struggling.

Nothing left.

Hyperventilating dizzy black stars.

I looked at Luther.

Looked at Rufus and Maxine.

At Violet.

She was sitting up now, her eyes closed, lips moving.

Are you praying for my soul?

Luther yanked the pull string and the generator roared to life, flooding the small stone room with the stench of gasoline and a growling lawnmowerlike clatter.

He squeezed his hands into a pair of rubber gloves and spit out the white pit of a Lemonhead, looming before me now, one hand grasping the skullcap wire, the other holding a wire sticking out of the vibrating generator.

All they had to do was touch.

He adjusted his grip, the ends just inches apart.

I haven't made peace with anything.

And the circuit closed, a blue stream of electrons arcing between the wires, sparks flying, the generator sputtering, a sharp coldness spreading from my head through my knees to the ends of my toes, the current glutting me with its boundless ache.

Then came the lightning slide show of last images:

Smoke rising from my arms—my body shaking—the Kites' fixation on my pain—Violet slipping out of the room—my world detonating into pure and blinding white.

CHAPTER 64

The generator shuddered to a halt.

Andrew Thomas sat motionless in the chair, candy-scented smoke rising from his arms and legs, billowing out of the skull-cap.

In the new silence, soft sizzles could be heard emanating from his body.

Luther put an ear to Andrew's heart and listened.

After a moment, Rufus said, "We good?"

Luther grinned.

"If it is beating, I can't hear it and it won't be for long."

Luther started unbuckling one of the wrist restraints, but Rufus said, "Just leave him, son. We don't have time to mess with . . . Where's Violet?"

Vi was running through a pitchblack corridor, her hands and mouth still duct-taped, praying again for the soul of Andrew Thomas.

She stopped and took five deep breaths through her nose.

The generator was silent now and somewhere in the black maze she heard the Kites coming.

And she was running again—straight into a door.

The way out.

She kicked the door open and moved through into a place of awful-smelling darkness.

The old woman's voice echoed down the tunnel.

Vi closed the door with her foot, eyes desperate for even a sliver of light.

All around her burgeoned the fetor of death.

Just keep walking. This is the way out.

She walked headfirst into someone's chest.

The person moved away and she jumped back into someone else.

She shrieked through the tape as the door behind her burst open.

A lantern illuminated the room and what she saw in that fire-lit semidark brought Vi to her knees.

There were perhaps ten of them, hanging by chains from the ceiling, in various stages of decay, their feet just inches off the floor so they appeared to stand of their own volition.

Why have You sent me to hell?

Though she knew the Kites were standing in the threshold behind her, blocking the only way out, Vi couldn't resist the impulse to look at the faces all around her.

Some had been there for a long long time and they'd disintegrated into carrion, rags, and bones.

The boy who'd tried to save them dangled in a mangle of damage in a far corner.

The ones she'd bumbled into were still swinging—two men near where she knelt, their clothes and wounds still fresh, heads drooped down, masked in gloom.

She peered up at their faces—wrecked.

One of the men was large and mustached.

The other was thinner, taller, younger, and something fluttered in Vi's brain.

The duct tape arrested her screams, but she managed to bash her head into the stone wall three times before Luther came over and dragged her away.

She'd seen the dead man's long soft hands, recognized the wristwatch, and she knew the pinstripe button-down, rent by buckshot, because she'd given it to Max for his last birthday.

"That's a bad girl," Luther told her. "Don't you do that. You're precious. He's gone, and you're never going to see him again, so what's the use in crying?"

Luther knelt down and stroked her cheek.

He took a syringe from his pocket and jammed the needle into her arm.

"You make my insides taste like sugar," he said. "I'm gonna love you up so much."

"Guess it's time," Rufus said.

Luther lifted Violet in his arms and the Kites walked together out of the hanging room, through the basement corridors, past the electric chair, and up the creaking stairs.

They emerged from the front door into a Bible black predawn, Violet asleep now, in the arms of Luther, in the arms of the drug.

And the yellow rind of a moon was sinking into the sound, the live oaks wrenched and gleaming, frost murdering the beach grass, as they piled into the ancient pickup truck and fled their crumbling house of stone.

KINNAKEET

CHAPTER 65

When I came around, the odor of my death was everywhere: scorched hair, leather and gas, hot copper, cooked flesh.

I was still strapped to the chair, now in total darkness.

So many shades of pain I couldn't pick the worst.

I strained against the leather.

The left wrist strap must've been partially undone because my arm broke free.

I unbuckled my right wrist, and with both hands ripped off the singed and crumbling restraints.

I staggered to my feet, fell back into the chair, stood up again.

My burns raged as I floundered through the darkness, hobbling along as fast as I could, limbs shaking, one arm outstretched to protect my face, the other tracing the stone wall.

It occurred to me that I was dead, wandering through some outlying region of hell, and still I walked on in the dark for what seemed decades, into dead ends and black rooms, through corridors that turned back into themselves, all the while the pain mounting.

I leaned over and puked.

Then came the sharpest stab of dread I'd ever known.

It whispered, *Welcome to eternity.*

Panic eclipsed the pain, my mind beginning to splinter, when I tripped and fell into a staircase.

My frenzy abating.

Gazing up into darkness.

Still no sign of light.

I crawled up the steps, rotten and doddering beneath me.

My head collided with a wall of wood.

I groped for a doorknob.

The door squeaked open and I tumbled into the foyer of the House of Kite, draped in the sulky gray silence of early morning.

Struggling to my feet, I moved on through the narrow hallway into the kitchen, the dead quietude of the house convincing me they'd fled, taken Violet with them.

I glanced at my forearms in the weak dawn light that spilled through the kitchen window, the undersides blistering and striated with electrical burns. My calves and the crown of my head had been similarly ravaged, all scorched where the electricity had entered and left my body.

There wasn't a phone in the kitchen and a search of the library and living room turned up nothing.

Through the living room's gothic windows I saw a gray Impala parked in the front yard.

Limping back into the kitchen, wreathed in a miasma of spoiled flounder, I found the lopsided ceramic bowl on the breakfast table, filled with keys.

I grabbed them all and, disowning the pain, started for the front door, for Violet.

CHAPTER 66

I moved like a wavering drunk through the bending beach grass, crumpling finally across the hood of the rusting Impala, winded, stonewalling the pain.

The day had dawned cloudy and freezing, pellets of sleet tinkling on the metal, the soot-colored sound writhing in chop beyond the house of stone.

I climbed behind the wheel of the car, started shoving keys into the ignition. The fourth one turned and the engine hiccupped and revived to a stammering idle.

Shifting into DRIVE, I stepped on the accelerator, the back tires slinging weeds and sand as the car surged between the elegiac live oaks and sped down the dirt road into thicket gloom.

Curtains of dying Spanish moss swept across the windshield, the Impala bumping along through puddles, over washboards that threatened to rattle the car apart.

When I reached the pavement of Kill Devil Road, I followed

it east toward the ocean, past slumbering beach houses nestled among live oaks and yaupon.

I stopped at the intersection of Old Beach Road and Highway 12.

My insides quivered with nausea.

Night thawing in the eastern sky.

I knew the Kites were leaving Ocracoke by ferry.

That left me two choices.

They could take either the one departing from Silver Lake Harbor or the ferry that embarked from the north end of the island. The ferries that left Silver Lake for Swan Quarter and Cedar Island ran less frequently and required reservations to ensure passage. The ferry from Ocracoke to Hatteras was free and ran on the hour, beginning at 5:00 A.M.

The dashboard clock showed 4:49.

I scoped Highway 12, vacant at this hour, lights from the Pony Island Motel twinkling nearby.

Hatteras.

I punched the gas, accelerating through the northern outskirts of Ocracoke Village, past Jason's Restaurant, the post office, Café Atlantic, and Howard's Pub.

It was twelve lonely miles to the north end of Ocracoke and the ferry to Hatteras. I had eleven minutes to get there, in a shitty car, on the verge of losing consciousness.

The speedometer passed eighty, the engine screaming as the Ocracoke Light waned in the rearview mirror.

Gray dawn sky, dunes, and marsh blurring by.

The wild dog sea rabid and foaming.

Sleet ticking dryly on the windshield.

Pavement streamed under the car, the road reaching north into the dull-blue nothingness of daybreak.

4:56.

I pushed the engine past eighty-five, the stench of hot metal seeping through the floorboards.

4:57.

For the first time I noticed my clothes—the fleece pants melted, my undershirt pocked with quarter-size, black-rimmed holes where the electricity had eaten the polyester.

4:58.

The world dimmed.

My head went light.

I slumped into the steering wheel, swerved into the other lane, tires dipping over the shoulder.

My vision sharpened.

I swung back into the road.

It ended.

Taillights ahead.

I stomped the brake, tires screeching.

In the immediate distance five cars waited in the boarding lane at one of the docks. As I steered the Impala to the back of the line, a crewman started waving vehicles onto a ferry vessel called the *Kinnakeet*.

First to board was a dilapidated old pickup truck, its puttering engine expelling gouts of smoke into the stone-gray dawn.

CHAPTER 67

The *Kinnakeet* is a long barge, broad enough for four cars to park abreast. From the center deck rises a narrow three-story galley—restrooms on the first level, an observation lounge on the second, and crowned by a small pilothouse. North Carolina and United States flags hang regal from the mast.

The six vehicles on the 5:00 A.M. ferry were directed into two single-file lines—three cars starboard, three portside.

I was parked in the back of my line, the Kites in the front of theirs, separated by the galley so that we couldn't see each other.

As I turned back the ignition, the ferry's engines went to work and the *Kinnakeet* wended slowly between the pylon bundles and away from the Ocracoke docks.

We chugged out into open water. The wind picked up, gusting now, shaking the car, sleet bouncing off the concrete deck, seagulls swarming the vacant stern, crying for a breakfast they would not receive at this hour.

The tip of Ocracoke dwindled into a smudge on the horizon, and suddenly there was nothing but mile upon mile of mercury-colored swells, the eastern sky flushing now with a tincture of purple.

Several passengers abandoned their cars and ascended the steps to the lounge—departing vacationers, workers making the long watery commute from Ocracoke to Hatteras. The gentleman in the Chevy Blazer directly in front of me crawled into the backseat and lay down.

I sat listening to the sleet.

My burns killing me.

There was no movement on my side of the deck.

I opened the door, stepped out into the cold, motes of ice needling my face.

I walked back to the sternside of the galley, crouched by the steps that rose to the lounge and pilothouse. Portside, three cars were parked along the railing—a Honda, a Cadillac, and an old Dodge pickup truck the color of a zinc penny save for its rusting blue doors.

The Kites had left the truck.

I peered around the steps.

They stood at the bow, their backs to me, gazing north across Hatteras Inlet. Rufus, his white hair twisting like albino snakes in the wind, was pointing west at an inconsequential land crumb, dry and visible only for moments at the nadir of low tide.

The Kites and I were the sole passengers on deck.

I made my furtive way to the navy Honda at the rear of the Kites' three-car line and ducked under the back end. Through the side mirror I glimpsed the reflection of its driver, sleeping, his head resting against the window. I crawled between the Honda and the railing amid a brief spate of sleet, finally reaching the next car in line, a Cadillac, its passengers having retired to the lounge.

I leaned against the back bumper to regain my breath. Glancing under the sedan, I saw the three pairs of legs still standing by the canvas-lattice gate at the bow.

I crept on.

My scorched clothing did little to shield me from the piercing cold, and I was shivering violently by the time I arrived at the back of the Kites' truck.

The tailgate was closed, the truck bed covered by a bright blue tarp.

The seagulls had discovered the Kites and besieged the bow of the ferry, their lamentations cut and diminished by the gale. I crawled to the driver side door, peered through the glass. The cab was empty. Violet had to be in the truck bed.

I noticed a pistol and a pump-action shotgun on the floorboard, tried the door, but it was locked.

I sensed movement, looked up.

Rufus walked quickly toward me, just three steps from the passenger door.

I hit the ground, rolled under the truck as he pulled it open.

Staring at the corroded innards of its underbelly, warm motor oil dripping on my throat, I heard Rufus shout, "You want the whole loaf, Beautiful?"

Then the door slammed and I watched his legs propel him back to the bow, a bag of squashed bread dangling at his side.

Get Violet to the Impala before you do anything.

As the gulls regressed into a ravenous frenzy I wriggled out from under the truck. Their squawks and the ferry engines and the moan of the wind masked the grating squeak as I lifted the handle and lowered the tailgate.

Still fettered with duct tape, Violet lay unconscious on the rusty truck bed in a smattering of damp pine needless and splinters of bark—remnants from a load of firewood.

While the Kites fed the seagulls—three bread-bearing hands

thrust into the sky—I climbed into the truck bed, took Violet by the ankles, and pulled her onto the tailgate. Breathless, on the verge of blacking out, I lifted her from the bed and set her gently on the concrete deck beside the railing. She stirred but did not wake. I closed the tailgate and proceeded to drag Violet by the shoulders toward the end of the line.

Exhaustion stopped me beneath the driver side window of the navy Honda. Fighting pain, I stared at the dozing driver, his face still pressed against the window, drool sliding down the glass. I willed his eyes to stay shut.

At the Honda's back bumper I glanced up to the bow, saw the Kites' attention still engaged with the feasting birds.

I slung Violet over my shoulder, struggled to my feet, praying no one in the observation lounge would see us.

A dozen tenuous steps and we'd reached the Impala.

I stowed Violet in the backseat and climbed behind the steering wheel.

Sleet pouring faster than it could melt, ticking madly on the roof.

It stopped.

In the east, bits of early morning indigo showed through, the clouds cracking like ancient paint.

As the sky aged through warming shades of purple into oxblood, a wire of land materialized to the south and east.

Now emerging on the horizon—the silhouette of the Cape Hatteras Lighthouse, at 208 feet the tallest in America, its beam still sweeping over Diamond Shoals, graveyard of the Atlantic.

I ached to drive off this ferry with Violet, get her safe, get myself something for this terrible fucking pain.

Drawing the keys from the ignition, I climbed into the backseat and sawed the longest key through the duct tape binding the young woman's wrists. Then I ripped away the strip across her mouth.

"Violet," I whispered. "Violet, do you hear me?"

She mumbled and shifted onto her side.

"You're safe now," I said. "You're with Andy."

It grew cold inside the car.

As I maneuvered back into the driver seat, key readied to crank the engine and start the flow of heat, I glanced through the windshield, saw Maxine Kite, her eyes cupped and peering through the tinted side windows of the Chevy Blazer just ahead.

She wore an old frayed gabardine coat, so long on her withered frame it fanned out beneath her like a black wedding dress.

I locked each passenger door.

Stepped out onto the deck.

Maxine looked up when my door slammed.

She bolted, disappeared around the galley.

I limped after her.

The coming daystar tingeing the clouds with a soft peach stain.

Gulls screaming.

These Outer Banks turning into the sun's dominion—a cuticle of pink fire peeking over the edge of the sea.

The Kites stood at the bow, awash with sunrise, ruddy-faced, watching me approach with a fusion of shock and amusement.

Except for Luther.

He lunged for me, but Rufus grabbed his arm and jerked him back.

"Not here, son."

Rufus stared at me, shook his head, grinning.

"Christ, Andrew, what are you made of—rubber?"

I stood five feet from the psychopaths.

"I have her," I said.

"I see that."

"What do you say you get in your truck, I get in my car, and we go our separate ways when we reach Hatteras? I think we're even, Luther. I left you for dead; you left me—"

"I don't give a fuck about even."

Eddies of dizziness enveloped me.

Sky spinning.

Faltering, I stumbled backward, caught myself.

"But you sort of admire him, don't you?" Rufus said. "I mean, he took some nasty voltage. We left him charred, no respiration, no . . ." A crewman strode past, lips moving to the music that blared from his headphones. "No pulse. It's a resurrection."

Hatteras was close, its mammoth soundside homes like mythic dollhouses in the distance.

"Look," Rufus said, "you're telling me you'll let us leave this ferry without any commotion? Let us just drive off into the sunrise? No revenge? After all we did to you?"

"I just want to take Violet."

"Well. I suppose you've earned that."

"Pop, come on. What the—"

"Shut your mouth, boy," Maxine hissed.

"Look me in the eye, tell me you won't follow us," Rufus said.

I looked the old man dead in his oil black eyes and told him.

As I started back toward the Impala something occurred to me.

I turned to face them again.

"What happened to Elizabeth Lancing?" I asked.

Luther just smiled.

CHAPTER 68

I sat seething behind the steering wheel, the Hatteras shore looming.

No fucking way I *wasn't* going to follow the Kites off this ferry. I'd finish them right now if it wouldn't endanger the other passengers.

The ferry engines quieted as we neared the island.

My thoughts turned to Beth, but I shut them down. The coming hours would require my full attention. And if I lived beyond them there'd be ample time to grieve.

Violet drew a sharp breath. I glanced back, saw her eyes fluttering. They opened. They died. Went broken and void as though she'd ingested some awful truth.

Turning into the vinyl seat, she wept.

The engines quit altogether.

I climbed into the backseat, let my fingers slide through her hair.

"Violet. We're on a ferry, about to dock on Hatteras."

She looked up at me, said, "How are you alive?"

"I have no idea."

Glass exploded.

We both jumped.

Something crashing through the windshield.

The ferry captain, headfirst, his torso draped backward over the dashboard, spraying the car with a warm burgundy mist.

I wiped blood out of my eyes as gunshots resounded from the observation lounge, three cataclysmic booms carrying the thunderous authority of a shotgun.

Elsewhere on deck there erupted the dry staccato cracks of a lesser firearm.

Screaming.

Another thud caving in the roof of the Impala.

Blood sheeting down the back window.

Someone moaning in the lounge, pleading for help.

The driver of the Chevy Blazer stumbled out of his idling car, suit wrinkled, bewildered.

I called out to him through the busted windshield. He looked at me, then moved dreamlike toward the bow, gazing all around in a sort of stupefied disbelief, as though he'd fallen into a movie.

At the front of the ferry he stopped abruptly, backpedaled, and went to his knees.

Rufus approached him, revolver in hand.

The businessman raising his arms in surrender.

I didn't see him die, just heard the tiny *pop* as I opened the door and dropped down between the railing and the car.

"Stay here," I told Violet.

"What's happening?"

"They're killing everyone on board."

I closed the door and crawled on between the cars and the

railing, glancing back at the Impala, the crewman sprawled across its devastated roof like a giant mortar shell.

Sternside, Maxine emerged from the gun-smoky observation lounge, two of its starboard windows blown out. Swallowed in her black coat like a demon queen, she bore the long pump-action shotgun I'd seen in the cab.

Luther descended from the pilothouse, met her on the second level.

Rufus fishing the pockets of his leather jacket for more bullets.

I froze. Bereft of strength or will. Heaving, I disgorged what little water I'd been given in the last twenty-four hours.

Gonna sit here, let them kill you? Let them have Violet?

As Maxine and Luther walked down the steps together, I sprang to my feet and charged Rufus, the old man looking up when I was ten feet from the bow, still fumbling to reload the .38, bullets spilling on the deck. He closed the breech anyway, pointed the gun between my eyes, and pulled the trigger.

It clicked as I swung at his face, felt his tender bones fracture. He tripped over the man he'd just executed, Maxine and Luther running toward me now from the stern.

I fled to the other side of the galley and took cover between the railing and the Kites' truck, crouching behind the left front wheel.

I opened the revolver.

Rufus had managed to shove two bullets into the cylinder. Had he squeezed the trigger once more I'd be dead or dying.

From portside I could see the carnage up in the observation lounge. Two silhouettes leaning against each other, the glass behind them splintered and shimmering red in the early sun. Wind gusted and the window collapsed, glass raining on the deck.

Closing the breech, I peeked over the hood of the old Dodge.

Maxine and Luther were helping Rufus to his feet.

I aligned Luther in the sight, pulled the trigger twice.

Luther looked in my direction, his raven hair windblown and twining about his bone-white face, the gunshot echoes fading fast across the water.

He fell.

His parents knelt around him, Maxine lifting his shirt.

I could hear Luther talking.

Then his mother roared, struggled to her feet with the shotgun, and started for the truck, eyes soulless, raging, Rufus trailing after her.

I scrambled toward the stern, passing the navy Honda again, a single bullet through the window, the driver shot through the cheek while he slept.

I heard the shotgun cocking, glanced back between the railing and the cars, saw Maxine leveling the barrel on me.

I rolled behind the Honda.

The twelve-gauge boomed, pellets shattering the windshield, chinking on the metal. As the old woman pumped the shotgun again I made for the sternside steps and climbed to the rear entrance of the observation lounge.

The door stood open.

Row of seats in the middle, more along the windows.

Dead couple on the left.

Still sitting upright.

Shotgun blasts to the face.

Obliteration beyond all reckoning.

Another facedown on the floor, heavy sluglike smear where they'd tried to crawl.

The pink sun brilliant through the fissured glass.

Quiet now save for a few idling engines and the sound the bow made ripping through water, the ferry moving with its own deteriorating momentum.

I peered down through the glassless windows, saw the Kites rounding the stern. In five seconds they'd be climbing the stairs.

Rufus dropped bullets on the deck.

I rushed toward the front of the lounge.

The Kites' footfalls on the steps now.

As I reached to open the door it swung back.

Luther faced me, smiling and unscathed, his Windex breath warm on my nose.

"You're a lousy shot, Andrew," he said as his mother entered wheezing through the back of the lounge.

I tried to punch him in the throat.

He caught my fist and I was tumbling down the steps.

I lay dazed on the concrete deck, my head throbbing, left arm sprained or broken.

The Kites came down the stairs.

Luther grabbed me under my armpits, dragged me to my feet.

They surrounded me at the starboard bow, backed me up against the railing.

The wind cold and blasting.

Everyone squinting in the sunlight.

Maxine aiming the shotgun at my stomach.

Rufus at her side, one arm around her shoulder, the other holding his jaw.

Their son stepped toward me.

"What'd you think, Andrew? No hard feelings? We all just go our separate ways?"

"Wasn't necessary to kill everyone on—"

"Couldn't have you borrowing someone's cell phone, having the police waiting for us at the dock. You killed these people, Andrew. No one would've died if you'd let us go. Now we've got a little swim ahead of us, so . . . ."

I noticed Orson's bowie knife in his left hand, thinking, *So that's how I end.*

"What about Violet?"

"She's amazing," he said. "I look at her and think maybe she'll make me different."

It happened so fast.

Engine revving.

Screech of tires.

Heads turning.

Luther and I dove out of the way as the Chevy Blazer clipped Rufus and Maxine and slammed them into the railing, Violet gunning the engine, the tires pressing the crushing weight of the Blazer directly into Sweet-Sweet and Beautiful.

She shifted the vehicle into PARK, pinning the Kites solidly against the railing.

Stepping out, she lifted the shotgun from the deck.

Luther back on his feet.

Running.

She shouldered the twelve-gauge.

He leapt over the portside railing as the shotgun bucked and boomed.

We dashed over.

Violet pumped the shotgun, trained it on the water.

"Where is he?" she asked.

"I don't see him."

The ferry was still drifting, the spot where he'd gone in falling farther and farther behind.

We ran back to the stern, leaned over the railing.

"You hit him, right?" I said, scanning the churned water in the ferry's wake.

"I'm not sure."

The light gleaming off the chop made it difficult to see, but we stood watching, the water reflective and glimmering, a smashed liquid mirror catching all the colors of sunrise.

"Andrew," she said finally.

"What, you see him?"

"I hear sirens."

CHAPTER 69

I hurt everywhere as I followed Violet to the bow, the *Kinnakeet* foundering seventy-five yards off the soundside shore of Hatteras, bottomed out on a sandbar.

The sky filled fast with daylight, the sun half-risen from the sea.

Sirens wailing in the distance.

We approached the Blazer.

Violet stopped at the bumper, Rufus pinned at the waist, head resting on the hood, Maxine glassy-eyed and fading, struggling through sodden inhalations.

I reached into the Blazer and killed the ignition.

Violet let the steaming barrel of the twelve-gauge graze Rufus's mouth.

Her eyes were glacial.

"I'm not going to ask if you know what you took from me."

Her finger fidgeted with the trigger.

"All I want to do is cause you pain."

"Do it," he croaked.

The shotgun clicked.

Violet looked down at her trigger finger, incredulous, as though the digit had acted apart from her will.

"You took *everything* from me."

She pressed the barrel into his face, pointed across the deck—a floating battlefield.

We could see three dead from where we stood, the crewman, the captain, and the passenger Rufus had executed.

"Why did you—"

"Because we could," Maxine hissed, unable to produce anything louder than a whisper. She expelled a long breath, eyes enameling with death.

Her chin fell forward onto the grille.

Eyes rolling back in her head.

"Beautiful," Rufus rasped, trying to turn his head. "Beautiful!"

I told him she was gone.

"Don't you say that to me. You don't . . ."

The old man closed his eyes and whimpered. His left hand was free. He reached over, felt his wife's paling face, stroked her disheveled white mane.

"My joy," he murmured, eyes red-rimmed and leaking, voice strained, deflating with suffocation.

His last breath came like a sad sigh.

A half mile up the sound, blue lights flickered near the docks.

Violet looked so tired, so much older than a week ago, her clothes a shamble of ripped and soiled fabric.

"Violet." The detective gazed up at me, pushed her dirty yellow hair from her green eyes, the sunrise lending false warmth to her pretty broken face. "I have to go."

She dropped the shotgun, sat down on the deck, buried her head in her arms.

"You gonna be all right?" I asked.

"Yeah."

"They'll take care of you."

"Just wait a second."

"I can't."

Leaning down, I kissed her forehead.

"Take care of your baby."

And I headed for the starboard railing. It was a four-foot drop to the water. I straddled it, glanced back at Violet—the tiny blond sitting at the bow, staring off toward the distant commotion on the docks, an eerie silence settling over the ferry, all quiet save the Stars and Stripes flapping from the mast.

I looked down into the dark water.

I jumped in.

The pain was exquisite.

I came up gasping, freezing saltwater stinging my burns.

Cormorants had congregated on a nearby sandbar, squawking, divebombing fish in the shallows. My howls scattered them into the waking sky.

The pain mellowed as I swam shoreward, my left arm aching with every stroke.

The south end of Hatteras lay before me, uninhabited, all marsh and beaches.

Halfway to shore I crossed a shoal, rose up shivering out of the water, standing knee-deep in the cold sea.

Something splashed behind me.

I turned, faced the *Kinnakeet*.

Violet resurfaced, legs thrashing, arms flailing, moving toward me with a gawky stroke that somehow kept her afloat.

At last she climbed up onto the shoal with me.

"What are you doing?" I asked through chattering teeth.

She was shivering so hard it took her a moment to find the words.

"They killed my husband."

She was wet and she was crying.

Her breath smoking in the cold.

"What are you talking—"

"I saw him, Andrew! Max was hanging in this terrible room!"

She looked into my eyes with something akin to desperation, as though she were praying I would tell her a beautiful lie.

I wrapped my arms around her, our bodies trembling in the bitter dawn.

"I have nothing to go back to," she said.

"You have family and friends and—"

"None of that works without him."

I cupped her face in my hands.

"Tell me what you want to do, Violet."

"I don't know, but everything's changed. I can't go home."

She pulled away and glided off the shoal, beginning the last forty yards to Hatteras.

I followed her.

The sun lifting free of the sea, in full radiant bloom.

My head grew light.

My limbs cumbersome.

The world dim.

I slipped under, fought my way back to the surface, thinking, *Next time just stay down.*

Violet had reached the shore where she stood crying in the beach grass.

It finally registered.

She'd been made a widow, witnessed things that, outside of war, few people ever see.

Monsters had set her adrift in a lonely desert.

But I'd been there.

And I'd found a way out.

I could show her.

EPILOGUE

Nine Months Later

I would like to unlock the door,
turn the rusty key
and hold each fallen one in my arms
but I cannot, I cannot.
I can only sit here on earth
at my place at the table.
—ANNE SEXTON, "LOCKED DOORS"

Violet awoke.

She rubbed her eyes.

It was morning.

Max was cooing.

At the kitchen table in a threadbare flannel robe, Andrew sat hunched over a pile of pages, pencil in hand, scribbling corrections on his manuscript. He'd built a small fire in the hearth that had yet to drive the night cold from her corner of the cabin.

The place smelled of strong coffee.

"Morning," she said.

Andrew looked up through a snarl of shaggy hair.

"Morning."

She crawled to the end of the bed, reached down into the crib, and picked up her son. As she lifted her undershirt, his little wet lips opened and glommed onto her brown nipple. Leaning back against the smooth timbers, she watched him nurse.

The infant gazing at his mother through shiny orbs.

Andrew got up from the table, started toward her.

"What's wrong?" he asked.

Violet shook her head.

"It's all right. These are good tears."

The pond was dark as black tea, steeped in tree roots, clear to the bottom, and rimmed by black spruce—a glade of water in the forest. Even in mid-August the pool carried a cold bite except at noon, in the middle, where sunlight reached all the way to the soft and silty floor. There, the sunbeams made a shaft of luminous green, warm as bathwater.

There, Andrew surfaced. He treaded naked, basking in the direct Yukon sun, contemplating how his autobiography should end, wondering if perhaps it should conclude here, in this pond in this valley at the foot of the mountains.

Everything had been chronicled: the desert, Orson, the Outer Banks, the Kites, the *Kinnakeet*. All that remained was to bow and step behind the curtain.

Andrew waded the last few feet to shore and climbed up onto the bank. He pulled his hair into a ponytail, wrapped himself in a towel, and flopped down on a sunwarmed blanket. Violet handed him his pair of sunglasses and he slid them on and lay flat on his back and closed his eyes to the sun.

"How was it?" she asked.

"Amazing."

"Think I'll take a dip." Violet set her son on Andrew's chest. "Don't look at my pooch, Andy," she warned though her belly had nearly contracted back to its pre-baby girth. Violet had given birth to Max just three weeks ago after a long labor at Whitehorse General Hospital. Andrew had not left her side.

Now he stared at the bundled and sleeping infant while Violet stripped.

"All right, I'm going in," she said.

"It's warm out in the middle."

"No peeking."

She stepped down from the mossy bank and eased into the water, her short hair kindling in the sunlight—champagne-colored and traced with strawberry.

Max woke, emitted a tender microscopic cry.

Andrew shushed him.

The baby yawned, his eyes flittering open, taking in the familiar bearded face.

"God, it feels so good in here!" Violet yelled, laughing from the middle of the pool.

Andrew knew the ending to his book:

Vi's panic attacks are fewer and farther between, though I occasionally wake up in the night, hear her crying into her pillow. Sometimes she calls for me to come down from the loft and sit with her. Sometimes she wants to cry it out alone. We rarely speak of the Outer Banks. The scars on my calves and forearms are fading. We have no future plans. She needs very much to live in the present. As do I.

What a strange and beautiful summer with Vi in these woods.

I haven't known peace like this before.

The sky had begun to pale toward evening when they started back for the cabin—a quarter-mile hike through the woods on a moose run.

Andrew stayed out to split firewood.

Violet went indoors.

She laid her son down in the crib and sat at the kitchen table with a pen and paper.

Not knowing what to say, she spent most of her words describing Max.

She imagined Ebert and Evelyn in the North Carolina countryside, reading this letter about their grandson. It would be dusk and they'd sit out on the big wraparound porch of their white farmhouse, the pleasant stench of manure present in the mist.

She could smell her father's pipe, see the long view from the porch—rolling pasture, barns, the soft blue-green horizon of lush deciduous trees that would not survive one Yukon winter. For a moment, Violet felt as homesick for those eastern woods as she did for her parents.

I miss your trees, she wrote.

Andrew made dinner while she rocked Max to sleep, the cabin filling with the incense of tomatoes and garlic and boiling pasta.

They dined on the back porch, their sunburned faces lit by a solitary candle, its flame frozen on this windless night.

Though it was after ten, light dawdled in the sky.

This far north in late summer, true darkness doesn't come until after midnight.

There had been a passing shower some time ago and the smell of the wet spruce was sharp and clean. Firs crowded the porch, their lowest branches draping within reach.

Andrew set down his fork and took a sip of the excellent Chilean wine.

A branch snapped nearby. They turned to the woods and listened.

After a moment of silence, Andrew said, "I finished the epilogue while you were in the shower."

Violet stared at her plate.

"Vi?"

When she finally looked at him across the rickety card table, he noticed her hands were shaking.

Andrew had converted the loft into a bedroom, managing to fit a mattress where his writing desk had been.

It was very late and dark and quiet.

Moonlight came through the windows and bleached the floorboards.

Violet had calmed down.

They lay awake, Max between them, the infant snoring delicately.

"Is it hard for you?" Violet whispered.

"What?"

"You know. Lying here with me . . . doing nothing."

Andrew smiled.

"Go to sleep."

He almost said go to sleep, angel.

Her head rested in the crook of his arm.

She rubbed her cheek against his.

"What are you doing?"

"Max never had a beard. I like yours. I like how it smells."

"You gonna keep me up all night?"

"I just might."

10/14/03

Haines Junction, Yukon

Spent last night at the Raven Hotel. Pricey. Look for something more reasonable this evening. Breakfast at Bill's diner. Coffee. Two delicious bearclaws. C$11.56. AT came to the village again in that old CJ-5. (he went to the library) I drove out to his cabin. 5.9 miles down Bore-

alis Road. A one-laner. Rough. Beautiful weather. Cold.
Saw his driveway but didn't turn in. Too nervous. (don't
be such a chickenshit) Think I'll return on foot tonight
and approach through woods under the cover of

The intercom broke in: "At this time, we would like to begin
boarding Flight 6346 with nonstop service to Whitehorse,
Yukon."

The tattered purple notebook closed.

On its cover, "H. BOONE" had been neatly printed in black
Magic Marker.

The passenger of seat 14C slipped the notebook into a leather
satchel, slung it over his shoulder, and strolled toward the gate.

His hair is blond and short now, but if you look closely, the
roots are still black.

INDEX OF GREEK WORDS

REFERENCES to the words *atē* and *dikē* and to *daimōn, Erinys,* and *hybris* are so frequent in the notes that I have listed only the more significant entries in which they appear.